# Dead Man's Doll

## *Sugarwood Mysteries Book 2*

## *Diane Bator*


Print ISBNs
BWL Print 9780228623731
LSI Print 9780228623748
Amazon Print 9780228623755

# Dedication

*To my kids – as always! Love you!*
*To Marcel, thank you for believing in me*
*and doing all the cooking.*
*To Karen Grose, thank you for the*
*continuing support and encouragement.*
*To Linda MacGregor and Barb Gilmour, my*
*two biggest fans. Love you both to pieces.*
*Thank you for always asking when the next*
*book is coming out!*

# Chapter One

### Thursday, November 24

Sugarwood, Ontario, half an hour from Lake Huron, was known for two things: maple syrup and the Christmas tree lighting festival. While the festival always suffered a variety of creative challenges, it never failed to impress the semi-enthusiastic crowd. This year, fluffy snowflakes fell over the town making Sugarwood look like a Christmas card photo. They'd help make the event even more magical. As long as we didn't end up finding a body on a bench like we did during the town's Halloween bash.

"Do you think we have enough decorations for tomorrow?" Merilee Rutherford asked, making me jump. My partner, both in Stitch'n'Time and crime solving, chuckled. She'd circled November twenty-fifth with a fat, red marker weeks ago.

Where other Ontario towns held their Santa Claus parades and tree lightings a week or two earlier, Sugarwood preferred to do the whole shebang one month before Christmas. No matter which day of the week the twenty-fifth fell on. Call it one of the quirks that gave us charm and created a nightmare for those who worked out of town.

"I think Santa would feel right at home in our workshop. All that's missing are the milk and cookies." I grinned, gazing around the store at the large shiny balls hanging from the ceiling.

Strands of garland draped over the top of every cupboard filled with threads and every cabinet stacked with fabric. A plastic, four-foot tall, green tree that once belonged to my dad glistened in the front window. We'd spent a couple of hours wrapping assorted sizes of empty boxes to pile underneath, then added needlepoint kits, fabric swatches, and sewing kits to show off our inventory and attract customers.

"Good idea," she said. "We can put them out for the sewing circle next Wednesday."

Drake, my Golden Retriever-slash-Husky with massive puppy paws, raised his head as though he expected cookies to magically appear.

"How about the Wednesday before Christmas?" I asked.

"Okay," she grumbled. "I'm going to run to the bakery to grab lunch, lattes, and cookies."

"Santa will have to bring me a whole new wardrobe at this rate." I tucked a thumb inside the waistband of my pants which were getting snug and it wasn't even December. I had half a mind to tell her to hold the latte. No way was I giving up cookies a month before Christmas. In the end, I kept my mouth shut.

Once she left the store, Drake returned his full attention to the heat vent and took a nap while I strung one last string of lights around the inside of the front window. I swayed to the soft Christmas music we'd discovered on YouTube that morning almost forgetting a couple times that I was on a stepladder.

Winter was off to a snowy start, I'd taken to crossing my fingers whenever I thought about the tree lighting tomorrow. Usually we got this much snow in January and February, not so much in November. I hoped the ceremony and carol sing would go off without a hitch. I could deal with spilled hot chocolate, but not another body.

I shuddered as the gloom brightened with an abrupt swirl of blue and red lights from a passing police car. Since there was no way anyone could speed on Main Street given the current slick conditions, I had to assume the police were on their way to an accident.

Drake stretched, doing a downward dog before he ambled toward the door.

"Do you need to go out?" I asked, holding the top of the three-step ladder as I descended.

Rather than paw at the glass, he sat and yawned.

"Good to know it's not an emergency. I'll take you out when Merilee gets back."

Less than a minute later, she bustled through the front door carrying a cardboard tray and a paper bag. Her head and shoulders were coated with feathery snowflakes. Drake blocked her path with a string of drool seeping from one corner of his mouth.

"The weather's getting worse," she said. "This snow would be perfect for the tree lighting tomorrow," she said, stomping snow off her high-heeled boots. "The bakery's deserted, so Hilda threw in a free handful of cookies."

I chuckled. "Ahh. He smelled cookies. What a surprise."

Closing the front door behind her, I stared out the frosty glass at the snow. The meteorologist had promised—the man even pinky swore on air!—the snow would hold off until later tonight. I should've known better than to believe a tall, handsome man who mispronounced precipitation on a daily basis. Differently every time, too. While I itched to go down to the Toronto studio to teach him how to say it right, Merilee figured it was part of his charm. She figured he pronounced it wrong because he wanted to be the sportscaster. People never blamed the sportscaster when their team lost, but woe to the meteorologist who got the forecast wrong.

"Looks like you'll be walking home in puffy flakes of snow." Merilee leaned over my shoulder as a cab pulled up in front of Stitch'n'Time.

"Drake will be happy. He can eat as many snowflakes as he wants." I glanced toward the counter where my eighty pound dog sat licking his massive paws. "Rex is supposed to be out of town today. I hope he and Andrew changed their plans to stay in the office. Or make it back to town safely."

Merilee handed me a latte as I watched the cab driver emerge. "Figures it would snow like crazy the one day this week I have to pick Tony up from work. It'll take a few minutes to warm up the truck. I can give you and Drake a ride home. It won't be fun walking home in a blizzard."

"It's not exactly a blizzard, I can still see the real estate office across the street," I told her. "Walking will be more fun than loading Drake into your truck. Riding in cars isn't his idea of fun. Last time we took him to the vet, he howled all the way there and all the way home."

"I would, too. Good thing he loves the truck. He wanted to stick his head out the window last time, but kept hitting his nose on the glass.”

“You’re right. It’s the vet he doesn’t like.”

She chuckled. “You think? Last time he was there he lost part of his manhood.”

The cab driver opened the trunk to remove a walker as an elderly lady pushed open the back door. Judy Wells, our friend Charity’s mom and a vocal part of our Wednesday afternoon sewing circle, emerged. She’d finally resorted to taking cabs since she could no longer drive nor walk as well as she used to.

Guilt seized me when she leaned on the walker and shuffled out of the way of the cab door. “I should go clear the sidewalk.”

Merilee caught me by the upper arm. “You’re not well enough to be shoveling snow. I’ll clear a path while you unpack our lunch.”

“I feel fine,” I insisted.

“You have cancer, remember? You’re tired and have bags under your eyes big enough to fit my entire wardrobe—and that’s saying something. You’re also still green, although it’s a much nicer shade today. More of a soft avocado.” She patted my shoulder. “You hold down the fort. I’ll shovel the snow.”

Breast cancer. The words still clawed their way into my soul and ate my Christmas spirit away in nibbles whenever they came up. Over the past couple of weeks, I'd blinked back more tears than Hoover Dam held water and stitched most of the stocking for Drake in one hour increments just to keep my hands busy while Rex was away at work. I will still awaiting more test results, but the doctor had already referred me to an oncologist. Just in case.

While Merilee went to get the shovel, I turned to see how far Judy had progressed. She used kind of a lift-and-lean method to inch her way toward the dimly lit curio-slash-alternative treatment shop two doors over where Miss Lavinia created salves and potions for her patients who suffered from a wide variety of ailments. Some she used on miniature replicas of her clients. Voodoo dolls to the rest of us.

Miss Lavinia wasn't a certified physician, more like a witch. The whole town saw the voodoo dolls she'd placed in her front window on Halloween. Most people thought they were cute. I knew better. I'd discovered her massive collection around Halloween and still had nightmares.

I was happy my father's doll and mine were safe in embroidery thread boxes in my closet at home. Somehow my father's doll had ended up in an old box of decorations at Halloween. Miss Lavinia returned mine when I saw it in her window, but she'd kept Rex's likeness to give him further top secret treatments. Some days that bothered me more than normal on days where my husband drove me crazy. The ones where I wanted to beg her to loan me his doll.

"Wish me luck." Merilee brushed past me still bundled in her designer winter parka with a bright yellow shovel in one hand.

I was surprised when Drake nudged my hand with his nose. "You must be desperate if you want out now. It's cold, your least favourite thing."

Cold and snowy meant I'd turn the fireplace on once we got home and spend the evening working on the Christmas stocking I'd started this fall. It also meant Drake would curl up in front of said fireplace for the evening and sleep.

When my phone pinged, both Drake and I jumped, turning toward the counter. I took one last glance at Judy trudging through the snow before I checked the text message, crossing my fingers it was from Rex who was more than likely working late tonight.

Or had a dinner meeting.

Or was stuck out of town after a meeting with a client.

Tonight's message was, *"Meetings in Toronto. Be home tomorrow. Don't wait up."*

"What a surprise," I told Drake. "Looks like it's just you and me again. What should we have for dinner tonight?"

To my chagrin, he was already gnawing on a lovely skein of red, green, and white yarn with silver thread woven through it. I grabbed the rest before he could polish it off. Cleaning up after him was never dull. The snow in our backyard was covered in bits of red and green fabric the birds loved. I pictured quilted nests decorating our yard come spring.

Merilee thumped the snow off her shiny boots as she came back inside. Three-inch heels, ice, and snow didn't go well together no matter what fashion designers said. "The wind's picking up. You're not walking home. You'll blow away and drag Drake with you."

"Okay. Thanks. I'm sure he'd agree. Did Judy get into Miss Lavinia's?"

"Yeah, I cleared the path for her, which actually made her flash one of those little smiles we rarely see." She put the shovel away and took off her coat. "She hates the snow because it makes her arthritis worse. That's why she's seeing Miss Lavinia."

"I can sympathize." It made me feel worse for many reasons.

She met my gaze then said, "Let me guess. Rex is out of town tonight, isn't he?"

"In the city. He'll be home tomorrow."

"Then you and I are calling for takeout. We'll get dinner and a bottle of wine before I drop you and Drake off then pick up my sexy hubby."

It was sweet how, after all these years, Merilee and Tony still fawned over each other. When they were over at our house for dinner, I hoped Rex would pick up on the little things Tony did for his wife. No such luck. He seemed more concerned with getting them to sell their fifty acres of prime real estate.

"You're too good to me," I told her.

"Don't take it personally. I can't run this shop on my own. Why don't you take tomorrow morning off and greet Rex at the door in lingerie?"

My face burned. "I'm not sure he deserves lingerie after the way he's been acting lately. Lunch would be nice though."

Speaking of lunch, we dug into ours. Now that we'd taken all the decorations from the storage room, we could put away the table and chairs the sewing circle had used yesterday along with a couple Christmassy table cloths at the liquidation store outside of town when Merilee and I took a shopping trip. Two red and two green. Patterned ones would've made us all crazy if someone dropped a needle.

It was ten to four when Merilee turned away from the window. "Let's lock up. The snow's scaring everyone away."

I called the Thai place for two separate orders. When she pulled out her credit card, I batted her hand away. "It's on me. Tony will be happy to have his favourite tonight, too."

While Drake filled up on dog food later that afternoon, I reached for the jar of green supplement powder from Miss Lavinia. The canister was almost empty. I'd have to drop by to order more since it would supposedly boost my immune system and help keep up my strength. With Christmas coming, I needed all the help I could get.

Our house seemed quieter than usual that night. I ate Shrimp Pad Thai on fine china by candlelight with a glass of wine and my evening dose of green sludge to wash it all down. No updates from Rex or the kids, who were making holiday plans around new significant others I hadn't met yet. With a deep sigh, I settled to watch a movie while I cross-stitched Drake's stocking.

My furry friend spent a couple more hours in front of the fireplace before he curled up next to me. He placed his head on my lap and closed his eyes. The warmth of his body against mine made me grow drowsy enough to give up on the movie and go to bed.

Tomorrow was the tree lighting and I wanted to be well rested. Just in case.

# **Chapter Two**

### Friday, November 25

Dawn broke with shards of yellow-orange light dancing through the snow-covered tree branches outside the bedroom window and onto my face. I was so tired last night I'd forgotten to close the curtains. Rather than leave my cocoon, I pulled the blankets over my head and groaned, "Ugh! I don't want to get up."

Drake seemed just as unconvinced. Until I dozed off again, then he nosed beneath the blankets to give me several head butts to the abdomen.

"All right. Breakfast it is." I threw my covers over him.

He wriggled out and licked my face before nudging me toward the edge of the bed.

"You've got worse morning breath than I do. I need coffee, then a shower. After that, I'll figure out breakfast. Daddy will be home later today. That'll make you happy."

Yawning, I shuffled to the closet to pull out my fluffy pink bathrobe with the hood and slippers. I didn't care if I did look like a pink bunny, I was warm and cozy. I caught a glimpse of my face in the mirrored closet door. Today, I appeared less avocado green and more mossy.

After discovering a lump on my breast, Miss Lavinia gave me a barrage of herbal treatments that gave me an eerie glow. It didn't look healthy. The green sludge was supposed to help detoxify my forty-something-year-old body. The balm I applied directly to the lump contained essential oils, which smelled like chamomile tea. It also made me feel better. Even if people insisted it was all in my head.

Drake led the way down the stairs with his nails clicking on the hardwood.

The house seemed unusually cold, even for this time of year. Had the furnace gone out again? Hopefully, Rex could fix it, or hire someone before he left for his next trip. In spite of his promise to be around more, and his long chat with Andrew Laney to change positions in the company, his work took him away on business a lot more. Every time I tried to talk to him, he'd change topics to work, his obnoxious co-workers, and the lousy restaurant food he had to endure. While I tried to sympathize, these days that wasn't as easy as it used to be.

Since Merilee was in charge of the store today, I planned to suggest lunch at a local restaurant where Rex and I could catch up. It might be easier to discuss my treatment plans after I fed him.

Depending on what time he got home.

Drake paused at the bottom of the stairs and whimpered again.

"Keep moving, scaredy cat. Go do your thing while I whip up a delicious pate for your breakfast." I yawned once more. "What's your preference? You can have chicken, sweet potato, or beef."

A loud groan came from the couch. Drake turned and ran toward me nearly knocking me backward.

"What was that?" I asked as climbed over him. "Some guard dog you are."

A loud buzz caught my attention. I froze. Rex's phone.

The Christmas tree lay on the floor amid the remains of the glittering glass ornaments, knots of garland, and blinking lights. My husband lay sprawled on the couch with a bottle of scotch standing next to one of his shoes. I must've been really tired to not hear Drake, or Rex, considering all the destruction.

Déjà vu hit me like a tidal wave. Hadn't I woke up to a similar scene not so long ago?

"What on earth…?" I asked aloud.

When Drake whimpered once more, I glanced back in time to see him pee on the floor. He hadn't had an accident since we had a prowler in the backyard a couple of weeks ago. He slunk toward the patio door and covered his nose with both paws.

When my husband moaned, I tossed a glare in his direction and told him, "This is not what I'd wanted to wake up to this morning."

Rex's tailored suit was rumpled and his tie undone. His socks were gone, probably deep in Drake's intestinal tract. His usually sculpted hair stood on end. A twinge of pity tugged at me. The guy was exhausted and still had a week-long business trip ahead. He also smelled like he'd spent the night at the bottom of a barrel, or at least a bottle. Rather than come straight home after a white-knuckle drive from the city last night, he must've gone to the bar for a stiff drink. The thought helped me feel sorry for him.

"Why do you keep doing this to yourself?" I asked as I took the pale gray blanket off the back of the loveseat and unfolded it. That was when I noticed bruises around his left eye and a thin gash at the top of his left cheek. He must've smacked his face on the coffee table when he passed out on the couch.

My focus became riveted on a single spot on his dress shirt. A two centimeter red dot that screamed out in the dim light. Wine? It had to be. Although wine would've soaked into the fabric looking more like watercolour paint. This red dot was thick and dark with no fermented, yeasty smell. The closer I got, the more Rex smelled like a wet dog.

I turned my head and came nose to nose with Drake who licked my face. Nudging him away, I leaned closer to Rex for a better sniff.

"What do you think you're doing?" my husband mumbled.

When I shrieked and dropped the blanket to the floor, Drake barked and bolted across the room.

"Stop that racket!" Rex sat up clutching his head as he yelled, "Drake. Lie down."

The dog got in a couple more sharp barks before I ordered him to sit. Instantly, he stopped and sat at my feet.

Rex snorted. "He doesn't even listen to me anymore."

"Because you're never home. When you are here, you yell instead of taking him for walks or playing with him," I pointed out. "I thought you were staying in the city."

"Andrew had a family emergency. We followed a snow plow and got into town for a late dinner with a client," he said.

Near the fallen Christmas tree lay the empty bottle of wine I'd left more than half full last night. "What happened to your face?"

"I walked into a door."

"Doors have knockers, not knuckles."

Rex eased to his feet, stiff from sleeping on the couch, then shrugged off his jacket and tossed it over the arm of the couch. "You're overreacting."

I stared at the red spot. "You've got something on your shirt. Let me see if I can get it out while you take a shower."

"My whole world's caving in and you're worried about a stain on my shirt?"

His whole world? What had I missed? I was facing cancer. I could worry about the stain if I wanted to.

Rex unbuttoned his shirt and peeled it off. He dropped it on the couch as he headed for the stairs. Drake followed until Rex stepped in the puddle at the bottom. He growled a string of obscenities as he headed up the stairs, which made the dog wisely retreat to the patio door.

I counted to five before setting the tree back on its base. After I'd swept the shattered ornaments into the garbage, I went in search of the mop and bucket. Once I heard the shower running, I filled a bucket with hot water and biodegradable cleaner then lugged the mop and bucket into the livingroom.

Drake hadn't moved from the doorway. He stared at the couch with his gaze darting around the room while I cleaned the floor.

"It's okay, honey," I told him. "Things'll be back to normal soon."

Whatever that was. I doubted things would ever be normal again. Not as long as Rex worked for Laney Developments.

Dumping the water from the bucket into the powder room toilet, I retrieved Rex's dress shirt to take a closer look at the spot. I also found a couple of small specks of what could be blood on his suit jacket, likely from that gash on his head.

"Maybe he just had a nosebleed or something."

I draped them both over my arm to take to the laundry room and two feet away before a folded piece of paper fell from one of the pockets. Scooping the paper between two fingers, I'd barely walked into the laundry room when Drake gave a sharp bark.

"Oh, sure. Now you want out." I placed the clothing on the washing machine and tucked the paper in the pocket of my robe. "You're going in the backyard, pal. Daddy's upset enough. We can go for a walk later."

When I opened the patio door, Drake sat near my feet. I sputtered as I dragged him outside then turned around and paused. What was I was doing before he barked? Honestly. Lately, I was able to forget what I was doing while I was doing it.

Breakfast. I stirred the last of the green powder into my orange juice then plugged my nose before tossing back the concoction. Horrid, but if it helped, it would be worth it.

I stuck a couple slices of bread into the toaster and decided to soak Rex's shirt after work. He wouldn't need it until Monday and I had other things to do.

Drake scratched at the patio door alerting me to the abrupt end of his tolerance of the cold. The second I opened it, he headed straight for the fireplace to huddle in front of the cold hearth. Snow melted in his wake. The very thought of fire warmed him, that or he was dropping a not so subtle hint.

"You need to clean him when you let him in," Rex snapped from the staircase.

With my face burning, I pulled out the mop again. "He runs too fast."

My husband grumbled as he sauntered into the kitchen buttoning the sleeve of his fresh dress shirt. "You don't try hard enough. Where's the coffee?"

I counted to ten before I swung the mop at his head or said something I'd regret. "Miss Lavinia says it's bad for the pH balance in my body. Too many toxins and stuff."

He raised his eyebrows. "And stuff? Sounds like a real pro. Is she the 'naturopath' you're seeing? She'll turn you into a toad before she ever cures you."

"Are you calling Miss Lavinia a witch?"

"If the broom fits, honey."

The few remaining strands of my good mood gone, I muttered on my way up the stairs to have a shower and texted Merilee to say I'd be at the shop soon. I'd grab a bagel with cream cheese and a coffee on the way. I hadn't made coffee at home in two weeks and this was the first time he'd noticed.

We'd be busy today due to the tree lighting tonight. Mostly because Merilee and I always bought extra decorations the previous year when they went on sale. The tree lighting was also the kickoff to Christmas shopping season.

If I took Drake with me, he wouldn't eat the clothing Rex had left on the bedroom floor. Not that it wouldn't serve Rex right, but it was bad for Drake. Plus, I was tired of hearing how my husband had to buy new socks and underwear bi-weekly when mine were full of so many holes, not even the dog would touch them.

For today, my dog could sample a yummy swatch or two of quilting fabric while we finished decorating and put up signs for our annual Christmas sale.

By the time I returned to the kitchen, Rex was gone while Drake lounged by the fireplace.

"Wow." I grimaced as I reached for my pink parka. "He didn't even say good-bye or offer us a ride. I don't know what's going on, but I know it has to do with his new job. Come on. We'll grab breakfast on the way to work."

When I tried to fasten his bright blue coat with snowflakes around his torso, he nosed my hand away. Five minutes later, I strapped on the coat, snapped on his coordinating blue leash, and dragged him outside. Right before he peed on the welcome mat.

In spite of trying to detox my body, I desperately needed an extra large coffee. This was one of those mornings where coffee and a doughnut would go a long way to make me feel human. So would a chat with Miss Lavinia. I needed to order more powder, which was a good excuse.

Drake seemed to forget about his own bad mood by the time we reached the end of our street. He slurped fat snowflakes off his nose and danced to catch more in mid-air.

A fresh snowfall always seemed to clean up the town. It covered the dirty ground and hid all the secrets, including the ice that took my foot out from under me. Luckily, I didn't fall. Nothing bruised or twisted, just the humiliation at flailing my arms wildly at traffic. Hopefully, Miss Lavinia would be able to get my green powder ready by the end of the day and Merilee could help find makeup to cover my green skin.

"Bless your heart. You brought tea." I smiled when I spied Merilee.

She snorted, balancing a cardboard tray with two paper cups in one hand with a small paper bag as she unlocked the front door. "Tea's for wimps. This is one hundred percent Columbian coffee from the bakery and a side order of vanilla dip doughnuts with Christmas sprinkles."

The mention of sugar made my smile bigger. Only a teensy part of me acknowledged the pang of guilt about what Miss Lavinia would say. "It's like you read my mind. To what do we owe the pleasure of junk food?"

"I figured you had a rough morning," she said. "That text was pretty abrupt."

"Rough doesn't begin to describe it."

"Did Rex get home early?" she asked handing Drake a doggy treat.

I closed my eyes and sniffed the full-bodied scent of coffee before I filled her in on the events of life in the Clemmings household over the past twelve hours.

"He said *what* about Miss Lavinia?" She handed me a doughnut with red icing and green sprinkles. "Eat up, you definitely need this. You need to stay strong."

"Not before I see Miss Lavinia. She can smell sugar on my breath from fifty feet. I'd better not have any coffee yet either. She'll already know I sniffed it."

"Oh, come on." Merilee chuckled. "She's not that good."

"Last time I went to see her after I had one bite of a cookie, she practically made me spit it out. It makes me feel bad lying to her. She's such a sweet old lady."

Merilee grinned. "Not to mention she makes a mean potion and voodoo dolls. She put the doughnut back in the bag. "I'll keep them safe until you get back. You'd better hurry so the coffee doesn't get cold. You should get her to make a doll of Rex. A couple pins in the right places might straighten him out."

"You're not helping. Besides, she already has one."

"Maybe you can borrow it. You'd better get going," she said with a wave of her hand. "The shop will only be quiet until people come looking for extra decorations. Don't forget the empty embroidery thread boxes."

"Consider me gone." I scratched Drake's ears before I told him to go lie down.

Since he had treats and his own bed near the heat vent, he was happy to oblige. Days like today, he was perfectly happy nibbling cookies in front of the crackling fireplace. Who could blame him?

On my way out, I grabbed the bag filled with little embroidery thread boxes for Miss Lavinia then headed to her shop. Her storefront was two doors up the street from Stitch'n'Time. Narrow with a tall, thin front window and a black door, the shop was a curiosity for tourists. For those of us who lived in Sugarwood, Miss Lavinia outranked most local doctors.

I walked past the former suit and costume rental shop that had closed years ago. Mr. Ossington sat on the bench out front of the shop feeding the pigeons in better weather. Around here, they were better known as seagulls or flying rats. He didn't care, as long as they ate the stale bread he brought. Rain or shine, but not in snow. I guessed he either missed his shop and customers, or simply had nothing better to do. It was odd not seeing him on the bench each day, since he'd moved to the senior's home near the hospital back in early October and the shop stood empty.

No one had shoveled the sidewalk in front of Miss Lavinia's front door that morning. Fat flakes of snow had already filled a couple sets of footprints. Someone must've had an early appointment, which was normal with so many people commuting to Toronto these days.

I swept the low drift out of the doorway with my boot then kicked off as much snow as I could before I tried the latch. When the door swung opened, I entered the shop calling out, "Good morning, Miss Lavinia."

No reply.

The shop was dimly lit, as always. Blackout curtains covered the front windows to deter gawkers and to protect the integrity of her oils. To compensate, she'd strung colorful Christmas bulbs above every display case and table. I wasn't sure how accurate the notion of protecting her oils was, but it did cut down on gawkers. Except at Halloween when she filled her front window with voodoo dolls.

The tourists thought they were adorable. The locals knew better.

Closing the door, I paused. The store seemed stiflingly quiet. As though not a single breath stirred the dust motes that glided through the air. The absence of sound sent a shiver down my back.

"Miss Lavinia? It's Audra. I'm here to get some more green powder."

I shivered both at the silence and the cold. Normally, the heavy curtains kept in the heat. Today, the shop seemed colder inside than out. I glanced back to make sure I'd closed the door and hadn't tracked in snow. Last time, she made me sweep it back out before it could melt on the hardwood floors.

"Mighty cold out there this morning, isn't it?" I asked as my eyes adjusted. "I hear there's a cold snap coming this weekend."

Miss Lavinia usually perched on a stool behind counter near her assorted herbs and powders. Today, she was nowhere in sight.

I gazed past glittering crystals and coloured potion bottles. "I ran out of the green stuff this morning. Not that I like it. It actually tastes like pond scum, even after I mix it in juice, but..."

On the counter, stood a couple of small vials and a bigger bottle as if she'd been mixing something only a second earlier. One vial held red liquid. The other was yellowish and cloudy. Each bore a black label with white writing.

"Miss Lavinia?" I had the overpowering impression something was horribly wrong.

A faint gasp punctuated the silence.

As I moved closer, a pair of flat black shoes and a black stocking-covered leg came into view. Fear surged through me as a rush of heat. "Miss Lavinia. Are you okay?"

A bloody gash split her temple. The pale pallor of her skin frightened me. Her pulse was faint. I whipped the purple velvet cloth off her round appointment table and rolled it to put beneath her head.

That's when I took a quick glance around.

I didn't recognize the man who lay on the floor at first since his face was smooshed against the floorboards. Blood pooled around the blade of an ornate dagger in his back before trickling toward the floor. The dagger was a decorative piece from behind her counter. So much for decorative. It had to be sharp considering someone used it to...

I gagged as I reached into my pocket for my cell phone.

Before I could hit speed dial, I realized the man was Dave Spencer who used to own a butcher shop up the street near the deli. Now he worked in the meat department of the local A&P and lived above Lara's Hair Salon. His ex-wife and her new husband-slash-former boss lived in a custom-built, five-bedroom home on Blue Hill.

All of those thoughts scuttled through my head in the precious seconds it took to pull out my phone, drop it on the floor, then pick it up again to call for help. Once an ambulance and the police were on their way, I focused on looking around the crime scene and making sure Miss Lavinia was still breathing.

Dave lay face down about four feet away. In between them, stood a black chalice filled with liquid and a crude pentagram drawn in chalk on the wood floor. Was it part of some kind of spell gone wrong? She'd explained the dagger's purpose before, but I couldn't remember anything at that point.

With my hands shaking and sirens wailing in the distance, I called Merilee and said, "Miss Lavinia's hurt and Dave the Butcher is dead."

"Dead?" Merilee squawked then lowered her voice. "Are you sure?"

I glanced at the abundance of dark liquid around him. "Pretty sure. Someone stabbed him in the back."

"So why are you calling me? Call the police."

"They're on the way. I needed a little moral support."

Miss Lavinia's lips moved and she

whispered something.

"Gotta go." I hung up then asked, "Are you okay?"

Was she okay? It sure looked like someone tried to kill her as well as Dave. While I didn't want to leave her alone, I had to make sure the door was open for the ambulance and the police.

By the time I returned to Miss Lavinia's side, tears flooded my eyes then spilled over my cheeks. What was it about me and dead people?

# Chapter Three
### Friday, November 25

I managed to evade the young police officer while I answered questions for the paramedics and hovered while they loaded Miss Lavinia into the ambulance. I wasn't eager to make my statement despite the fact I hadn't done anything wrong except stumble across another body.

Once the ambulance left, Dave became the subject of a photo session for forensics. I was fingerprinted then asked to step outside. Suddenly, there was no alternative.

I turned to the officer and asked, "Who are you and where's Officer Grant?"

"Officer Grant's out sick. I can assure you, I know how to take notes," he insisted as he tried repeatedly to get my name and address.

"Yeah, I know. The problem is I can't remember my information and he already knows me." Shock had set in from the sight of the man lying on the floor and concern for Miss Lavinia. "Can we talk somewhere other than in the doorway?"

The fact the young officer was one

handsome devil, despite the angry bruise along his jawline, didn't help matters. Blond hair, pale brown eyes, and a smile that made my stomach flutter. The scent he wore seemed familiar, but I couldn't place it. Just as well, he was about the same age as my son, twenty-two.

Finally, he nodded toward the bench out front. "It's cold out here, so I don't want to keep you any longer than I have to, but—"

"But the shop's a crime scene and you have to ask what I was doing here and determine if I killed Dave and attacked Miss Lavinia," I finished.

"You're right." Dimples burrowed into his tanned cheeks. He must've been on vacation somewhere sunny recently. "I also have to make sure you're okay before you go back to whatever you were doing. Let's start with an easy question. Why were you in Miss Lavinia's shop?"

My cheeks warmed against the wind. "I needed to pick up a refill."

The officer's brown eyes crinkled at the corners as he asked, "A love potion?"

"I have cancer," I whispered.

"I'm sorry to hear that. I've heard she makes some powerful stuff." The officer pulled out a small notebook and a bright yellow pen. "Did you happen to remember your name yet? I need work and home addresses as well."

"Audra. Audra Clemmings. I work two

doors over." What was that smell? Spices? Herbs? Something exotic. "I guess you can only get away with an address like that in a small town, huh?"

"Yes, but the captain still likes things done the old-fashioned way. With building numbers and names and all."

"My shop's right there, Stitch'n'Time. Number 88 Main Street. I live at 37 Springer Road. Do you have a name? I mean, I know you *have* a name, I just mean..." I blew out a white cloud. "I'm going to stop talking now. I'm sure I'm in enough trouble."

"Officer Alister Trent," he said. "And no, you're not in trouble, Mrs. Clemmings. You found two people in distress. Miss Lavinia will appreciate that when she recovers. The other guy, not so much. Did you see anything unusual? Any strange people coming or going, disgruntled customers, that sort of thing."

I shivered. "Any footprints were barely visible when I got here. She must've had a couple of early customers. Since Miss Lavinia lived upstairs, she wouldn't need to go outside. Will she be okay? It looked like someone hit her on the head."

"I'll let the doctor deal with that part. My job is to figure out how she got hurt and *who* killed the man who was with her."

"His name is Dave the Butcher."

He raised one eyebrow. "Excuse me? Is

he in the mob?"

"No, he used to own a butcher shop up the street before…," I trailed off before I said anything he might think was incriminating. "Dave Spencer."

"And how do you know Miss Lavinia?" he asked.

"I've been her patient for years even though my husband thinks she's a witch. He works for Laney Developments. He's convinced she's a fraud who takes people's money and gives them fake medicine." So much for not talking too much.

He made a note in his book, which made me cringe. Mostly because I couldn't read it. "And what do you think?"

What *did* I think? When was the last time anyone actually asked me that besides when we ordered lunch or supplies for the shop?

I took a deep breath and gagged on cold air. "I think she sells us hope."

Officer Trent smiled, but only with his mouth. The rest of his face seemed less convinced. Even his dimples. "I'll buy that. Look, why don't you head back to your shop and get warm? I'll stop by if I have more questions, okay?"

"Okay." I blinked back more tears.

Merilee met me at the entrance of Stitch'n'Time with my lukewarm coffee, my doughnut, and my dog. The second I closed the door, she launched a barrage of questions in my direction. "Is Miss Lavinia okay? Who died? Who's the cop? Is he married?"

Drake pranced around my feet in concern.

Nudging away the doughnut, I walked past her in a daze then slumped onto a stool. I ached to run home to snuggle on the couch with Drake and a carton of Haagen-Dazs, but the thought of Officer Trent showing up gave me a stomach-ache.

"Coffee? I added sugar for the shock. What happened?" Merilee handed me a cup.

I cleared my throat as I blinked away tears. "I went to get my green powder, but Miss Lavinia was on the floor with all the powders, herbs, and stuff. There was a gash on her head and a pentagram and a cup on the floor. Dave the Butcher had that decorative dagger in his back. His skin was blue. It looked so awful, yet fake at the same time. Like the makeup the kids used to make at Halloween."

"Ew. Those things still creep me out." Merilee shuddered. Her two boys were usually the ringleaders in creating zombie makeup. Her oldest was a movie makeup artist in Toronto.

I shivered. "Who'd want to hurt Miss Lavinia or kill Dave?"

"Disgruntled customers, most likely. Do either of them have family here?"

"No idea," I told her as I took off my parka. "I really didn't know Dave and all Miss Lavinia and I ever talked about was herbs and powders."

"All I know is her parents used to own the house Charity lives in now."

"Sad how little we know about our neighbors, even in such a small town." I swiped a finger in the doughnut icing.

When the door opened, a tall figure dusted with snow walked inside. Officer Trent took off his hat and nodded. "Ladies."

Merilee straightened her sweater and swept her pale blonde hair over one ear. "Well, hello there. What can we do for you, Officer?"

Drake backed away from the officer growling.

"Relax, buddy. He's here for me, not you." I grabbed his collar and patted his head.

Officer Trent flashed a dimpled smile. "I'm investigating the incident that took place in Lavinia Brevil's shop. I need to ask Mrs. Clemmings a few more questions."

Merilee gathered her purse and coat. "I'll go to do the banking. Do you want anything, Officer...?"

"Trent. Alister Trent."

She shot me a loaded glance. Like there was something she really wanted to tell me, but not in front of the officer. Drake's growl grew louder.

"Merilee, can you take him with you?" I
asked. "Please? He's been acting weird
since Rex came home. That, and he's been
eating too many socks lately."

"You know that's no good for his
digestion, right?" the officer asked.

"Thanks for the heads up." Merilee
reached for Drake's leash and a couple of
dog poo bags. She didn't seem as eager to
leave as she was a minute earlier. She
snapped the leash on Drake's collar and
practically had to drag him to the door.
Once he was past Officer Trent, he took off
at a run. My mouth fell open as she
stumbled down the sidewalk after him.

Trying to hide my smile, I turned to the
officer and asked, "What can I help you
with?"

He met my gaze. "Actually, I don't have
any burning questions. I just wanted an
excuse to get warm and check out your
shop."

"I didn't think you were into embroidery."
I caught a whiff of that smell again. The
officer must've touched something in Miss
Lavinia's shop Drake didn't like. Was that
why Drake was grouchy?

"My mom and grandma are," he said. "I
thought I might find something for them for
Christmas gifts."

Chilled, I hugged my parka around me
while I showed him the new kits we'd
brought in for the holidays. "Do they like

flowers? Seascapes, maybe?"

"My grandma loved the sea. I mean, she still does, she just can't get there anymore."

"I'm glad she's still able to do needlepoint though."

Officer Trent reached for one of my favourite seascapes. "How long have you known Miss Lavinia?"

"Since Merilee and I opened the shop," I said. "I went to her for a skin rash. Then I saw her when I had pneumonia, and now for my…" I fought back a fresh batch of tears, suddenly unable to say the word.

He shifted in his wide-legged stance. "Like you said, she gives people hope."

"What kinds of things does your mom like?"

"Excuse me?" His head snapped back.

"To embroider." Had he made up the whole gift story as an ice breaker, or was he merely distracted? The guy was young. This could be his first murder investigation.

While Officer Trent studied a couple of embroidery kits, I took the opportunity to catch my breath and grab a tissue to wipe my eyes. When he gave a nod and left the shop without buying anything, I blew out a heavy breath. Rex would never believe me when I told him about my day. He'd roll his eyes and ask what I did this time.

Merilee returned with Drake who headed straight to his bed. She doubled over near the counter gasping for breath. "What's wrong with that dog? You need to take him home or to the vet before he explodes."

"The sock-eating is one thing, but he wouldn't go near Rex earlier and now he was avoiding Officer Trent." I knelt beside my dog to stroke his back.

"Maybe he knows something's up with Rex," she said. "He's been travelling more. The poor doggy has a sensitive nose. I'll bet he's confused by all the funky smells."

I nodded. "Animals do react to stress around them. We've definitely been stressed."

"Why don't you talk to Rex about going away for a weekend? Tony and I could look after Drake. You guys go to Niagara Falls or Collingwood. Somewhere not here."

"The kids are coming home for the holidays and I have a lot to do. Miss Lavinia said…" I paused, tapping a finger against my lip as tears filled my eyes.

"What did she say?" she asked, her voice gentle.

"That the way to get Rex's attention was with meatloaf." It seemed so silly once I said it aloud that I laughed. "He's been so busy trying to impress Andrew Laney, he's forgotten how to relax."

She hugged me. "Then maybe you should go home and make meatloaf. The police know where to find you and the shop is quiet, although I'm sure we'll have people stopping by all afternoon to find out why the police are hanging around."

"The tree lighting's tonight. I don't want to miss all the excitement." That and I had questions of my own.

"Uh-huh. I know that look," Merilee said. "You want to figure out who did this."

I didn't have to feign surprise. "Don't you? Why did you get that weird look on your face when he told you his name?"

"Who?"

"Officer Trent."

She shrugged. "He reminded me of someone I knew."

"Someone you used to date?"

"No. Is he new in town?"

"We were at a crime scene, it's not like we're on a first name basis, although he mentioned his first name is Alister."

Merilee nudged my arm. "Yet. Once you start digging into his case, you'll get to know each other much better. Just wait until he gets a load of our suspect board."

I deflated. "That's not funny."

She pulled me into a crushing hug. "You've had a long morning, Audra. Go home. I'll look after things while you make meatloaf and remind that man of yours why he married you."

At the mention of home, Drake raced to the door and sat waiting before I could even grab my coat.

# Chapter Four

### Friday, November 25

I finally convinced Merilee that staying at the store for a couple more hours was a much better idea than me being alone. Every time I shut my eyes, I pictured Dave and Miss Lavinia.

She, in turn, finally convinced me at three o'clock to get out before she personally walked me home. Drake and I headed home. After I let him inside, I went up the street to the grocery store to grab groceries. Meatloaf, potatoes, green beans, all the basics. Even an eggnog cheesecake. The thought of making my husband his all-time favourite dinner was enough to put a smile on my face and shove what I'd seen aside. For now. Maybe later we'd go downtown for the tree lighting. Christmas lights always cheered me up. Except when they were smashed all over the floor.

By the time I got home, I was in a great mood. Until I discovered Rex and Drake in mid-showdown in the living room. The Christmas tree lay on its side once more, with the few remaining ornaments strewn across the floor. In front of the fireplace lay a chewed piece of clothing that resembled a pair of Rex's former pants.

At a loss for words, I nearly returned to the grocery store.

"What's gotten into you?" Rex threw a cushion at the dog, which ran to cower behind my legs. "I can't take another piece of chewed up clothing. Last weekend he ripped one of my best dress shirts. While I was wearing it. I'm tired of coming home to chaos caused by an undisciplined dog. Either he goes, or I do."

"Do I get time to decide?" I asked, setting down the grocery bags.

"Audra," my husband growled.

I rolled my eyes as I hung up my parka. "This is the first time he's touched the tree since we put it up and he wouldn't chew your clothes if you didn't leave them lying around. Besides, he's a good watchdog when you're gone."

"Are you saying I cause him to act like this?" Rex narrowed his eyes.

Taking off my boots, I picked up the groceries, afraid to deny or confirm his remark.

Drake sauntered toward the ragged pants and give them a vicious shake. More ornaments shattered before Rex lunged for the patio door and ordered the dog outside. With a snort, Drake took the remains of the pants with him.

While I put away the groceries, I counted to ten. Then twenty. "He's never acted this way before. This morning he was afraid to go near you, now he's tearing those pants apart like they attacked him. Did you spill something nasty on them that he doesn't like the smell of?"

"I can't believe you're blaming me for this." My husband gave a snort, sounding like Drake when he sneezed. He went to the cupboard to pour two fingers of scotch into a glass. Once he'd tossed back the drink, he poured another.

"Rex?" I leaned in the doorway. "We need to talk."

He swallowed the second drink. "I work all week to put food on the table, keep our kids in college, and make sure your little hobby shop doesn't fold. All I want is to come home at the end of the day and relax. I don't need to worry about anything else, especially a sick wife and a schizophrenic dog."

His remark hit like a punch to my solar plexus. Was he serious?

"So what you want is a bachelor apartment with a house keeper and a chef."

Rex flinched as a tense silence fell between us.

"You go right ahead and live that life. I doubt you'll be consumed by guilt when our kids ask why you abandoned their mom during chemo." I started to walk away then paused. "By the way, Drake's not schizophrenic. He just wants your attention like everyone else around here."

I let the dog back inside, tattered pants and all, then paused. The pants matched the jacket with the blood stains. I coaxed Drake to hand them over, giving him a handful of treats as a reward. While Rex poured another glass of scotch, I took the pants into the laundry room. Not only were there splatters of red on the legs, but they had an oddly familiar smell I couldn't place.

All thoughts of meatloaf went out the window. I tossed the pants into the drawer with his shirt and jacket then closed the laundry room door. Rather than head to the kitchen, I made my way up the stairs.

"Where are you going?" Rex asked.

"To take a hot bath and think," I replied without looking back.

After a bubble bath, a good cry, and a nap to restore my sanity, I heard voices downstairs. I crept to the top of the stairs still half-asleep, afraid the police had arrived with more questions before I'd even told tell Rex about Dave's death. Instead, a short, bald man handed Rex a large paper bag before he closed the door.

The pathetic, naked tree now stood in a corner and Drake was nowhere in sight. We needed new ornaments.

"I wasn't sure if you'd come back down,"

Rex said as he glanced up. "I got a peace offering just in case."

Wary, I joined him in the living room, keeping my distance. "Where's Drake?"

Rex sat on the couch while he pulled containers and paper plates from the bag. "Eating leftover chicken. I hope you're hungry. I ordered your favorites."

"I thought you were leaving."

"I'm not gonna lie," he said. "I thought about it. Then I realized all the things I'd miss. You, the kids, the dog... You were right, Audra, I'd feel like crap. There's no way I can get out of going to Chicago, but I'll take time off over the holidays. Once I get home, we'll talk to the doctor about options. I'll even see Miss Lavinia with you."

My stomach churned. Was that odd scent my imagination? I was sicker than I thought. I sat on the nearby chair. "It's been such a crazy day I never even told you."

"Told me what?"

"Miss Lavinia was attacked this morning," I said. "I found her when I went to pick up a new batch of green powder. Dave Spencer was on the floor with a dagger in his back."

Rex paled. His chopsticks clattered to the floor. "Dave's dead? Are you sure?"

Dave's dead. The words suddenly sunk in and I closed my eyes. "Very."

"And you found them together?"

"In Miss Lavinia's shop."

He got up to pace the livingroom. "Who's

investigating? What do the police think happened?"

"Officer Trent. He says she was probably..."

"Trent?" He frowned. "Why do I know that name?"

I shrugged. "Beats me. Merilee did too. How well did you know Dave?"

Rex raised his right eyebrow. "Why? Are you investigating?"

Crossing my fingers behind my back, I told him, "I hadn't given it much thought."

"Sure, you didn't." He smirked. "All I know is Dave had that great butcher shop near the deli then suddenly he sold it and went to work at the grocery store. I heard a rumour the health department shut him down."

"Huh." I sat on the couch and stared into the fire. "I thought it was because of the divorce."

Rex flopped into the arm chair. "Dave got a divorce?"

"And lost everything he owned."

He paled. "I had no idea."

We were almost done dinner when Rex glanced at his watch. "Hey, isn't the tree lighting tonight? Usually, you and Merilee have the store open late."

"After finding Dave and Miss Lavinia, I'm..." I paused thinking of all the rumours already spreading without me. "Maybe I'll go watch. I can take Drake with me so you can rest."

Rex shook his head. "I owe you a night out. This isn't exactly what I had in mind, but it'll do for now. Right?"

After insisting Drake and I wanted more of his time and attention, I couldn't turn down his offer. "That sounds great."

While Rex and I bundled up complete with scarves and mittens against the cold, Drake pranced around in excitement making it hard to put on his festive coat. It had been a long time since Rex and I both took him for a walk. I was worried I'd have to clean up another puddle.

Outside, Rex started toward the garage to pull out the car then reconsidered. "Are you okay if we walk? I could use the exercise and Drake's always up for a good walk."

"Sure," I told him, although I would've preferred the warmth of the car to ward off the shivers I wasn't able to shake off.

"Come on," he said, draping his arm across my shoulders. "If you're good, I'll buy you a hot chocolate at the bakery. Maybe even a cookie."

Considering it was the best offer he'd made me in a long time, I didn't argue. We took our usual path through the park. I slowed my pace as we reached Miss Lavinia's shop.

"Have you heard how she's doing?" Rex asked.

I shook my head. "Not yet. I hope that officer's there. I want to ask if they've found her next of kin yet."

He stopped and held up a hand. "Can we not talk about death, bodies, or next of kin for one night?"

"Of course." That didn't mean I couldn't keep my ears open.

By the time we arrived at the fifty-foot, Colorado Blue Spruce hung with plastic ornaments and unlit Christmas lights, Rex was the one shivering. "Do we have time to get hot chocolate before they hit the switch?"

I glanced up at the clock on the brick front of town hall. "We have ten minutes."

"Perfect. Then let's get a snack before the show starts."

When I spotted Charity, I held back. "Why don't you go? I'll wait here with Drake and save our place."

He smirked. "Like it matters where we stand. You'll be able to see those lights from space once that thing's lit."

"Hey, if it isn't my favourite customers," Charity gushed as she headed toward us and patted Drake's head. "If I knew you were coming, I would've grabbed some treats."

A buxom brunette who never seemed to stop smiling, Charity Wells worked at the deli. In her spare time, she ran a local bed and breakfast with her elderly mom Judy.

"Nice to see you, Charity," Rex said. "I'm doing a hot chocolate run. You want one?"

She flashed a smile. "I'd love one, thanks."

"What about your mom?"

Charity shook her head. "She's at home. She hates these things."

"I feel her pain," Rex grunted then disappeared into the crowd.

"I'm surprised to see you both here," she said. "How'd you get his highness to loosen up and come out in public?" she asked.

"Believe it or not, this was his idea. I was happy to sit at home in front of the fire tonight, especially after finding Dave and Miss Lavinia."

Charity hugged me. "I heard about that. Are you okay, honey?"

"Shocked more than anything. I don't suppose you've heard how she's doing, have you?" I asked.

"Funny thing about that," she said. "Usually I see the cops in and out for lunch or coffee, but today I didn't see any of them. Must've been because of the snow."

"Yeah. I'm surprised Rex and Andrew got back from Toronto last night."

Her left eyebrow twitched. "That was a fast trip. Rex picked up a coffee carafe with a dozen muffins yesterday morning then I catered lunch for their meeting this afternoon."

Drake tugged against the leash as

Merilee and Tony strolled toward us arm in arm.

"Audra, what are you doing here?" Merilee asked as she pulled me into a hug. "I take it Rex didn't make it home from work yet."

I nodded toward the bakery. "He went to grab hot chocolate and cookies. Coming here was his idea."

"Your husband Rex?" Tony asked. Merilee nudged him.

"About that," Charity said. "What happened this morning?"

Lowering my voice, I told her what I'd discovered at Miss Lavinia's shop then asked, "Do you know Officer Trent?"

"Only that he's obnoxious, drinks his coffee black, and hates mustard."

Merilee laughed. "That's more than we needed to know."

Rex zigzagged through the crowd with a tray of paper cups and a white bag. "Looks like the gang's all here."

"Hey, old man, I haven't seen you in a couple weeks," Tony said just as someone tapped the microphone. "We need to catch up soon."

The mayor of Sugarwood, Billy Benson, made his way to the mic. Billy owned the drycleaners I passed every day. He was followed on stage by a tall, blond man wearing a dark suit and a camel wool trench coat.

His brother, Chuck Benson, was a former professional hockey player with one of the most familiar faces in Sugarwood. His image was on more billboards and benches than anyone else's in town. A local realtor, he appeared at every public event he could.

"Oh, brother," Charity groaned. "How does he get to help with the tree lighting?"

Merilee held up her hand and rubbed her fingers together. "Nepotism and money."

"Not even Andrew Laney's that narcissistic," Tony said.

"What's that supposed to mean?" Rex asked.

I handed my husband the end of the leash. "Can you take Drake?"

Merilee shot me a grin as I tried to head off an argument between our husbands. The last thing we wanted was to be stuck in the middle.

"Good evening, everyone," the mayor spoke into the mic right before the sound system gave an ear splitting screech.

While he droned on about the holiday season being a time of love, peace, and good will, my attention flickered around the crowd. Anyone of these people could've attacked Dave and Miss Lavinia. At least half were Miss Lavinia's clients. Did someone have an appointment after Dave and couldn't wait?

"Can you believe that man?" Charity whispered.

Chuck Benson stepped up to the mic amid thunderous applause. He held his arms in the air like he'd won the Stanley Cup. "Greetings, citizens of Sugarwood. I'm honoured to have the opportunity to light the Christmas tree this year. It's been a banner year for Benson Realty and I'm happy to pass on the wealth to the place I call home. Right after we brighten the night, I'm presenting a cheque to the local food bank for fifty-thousand dollars."

A deafening cheer went up through the crowd.

"Okay, Sugarwood, time to do the countdown!" he shouted. "Ten. Nine. Eight."

The crowd joined him from there until they hit one and…

For the first time in twenty-five years, nothing happened.

Billy held out his hands and looked around helplessly.

Chuck burst into laughter. "I can assure you whoever strung these lights doesn't work for me. Sorry, folks, bear with us for just a minute while my brother the mayor works his magic. Keep in mind next year is an election year. Just saying."

A murmur swept through the crowd like an ocean wave.

"I wonder where his wife is," Charity said.

"Whose wife?"

"Chuck's. I haven't seen her lately."

I shrugged. "I don't even know who she

is."

Before she could fill me in, the countdown began again with renewed vigor. This time, the lights blazed.

"Isn't it beautiful, folks?" Chuck asked. "That right there is fifty-thousand lights on a fifty-foot Colorado Blue Spruce courtesy of Benson Realty. Merry Christmas, Sugarwood. Complete with a fifty-thousand dollar cheque to the Food Bank."

"Told you they'd be able to see it from space," Rex muttered. "Let's go."

Tony frowned. "What's your hurry? Let's go grab a drink or something."

Rex glanced down at Drake. "We have to get the dog home. See you around."

"I'll text you," I told Merilee.

Sipping our hot chocolates, we wound through the crowd and headed toward the park. Rex hooked his free arm through mine and steered me toward the shrubs and trees decorated with soft, white lights. In the distance, the town tree glowed like the spotlight at the car dealership on the far end of town.

He let Drake off the leash since we were the only ones in the park. For that one hour, things felt like they had in the past. Before we had kids. Before Andrew Laney and Laney Developments took over my husband's time. Even before we were married.

As we strolled home arm in arm, I

considered offering my condolences to Dave Spencer's ex-wife before I popped into the office tomorrow to give Andrew Laney a piece of my mind.

"Do you want more hot chocolate?" Rex asked as he turned on the fireplace. "I saw some little marshmallows in the cupboard earlier."

I would've preferred a glass of wine. "What's going on, Rex?"

He flashed a sheepish grin. "I'm heading out early Monday morning. Andrew and I have a breakfast meeting in Barrie before we head to Pearson and fly to Chicago."

"I'm worn out. Enjoy. I'm going to bed." I got off the couch.

Rex tried to shove Drake out of his way, but the dog refused to budge. "Oh for… Audra…"

"I've had a long day, too, Rex. I'm the one who found Miss Lavinia and Dave and I've had to listen to you fight with Drake ever since I got home. Tomorrow, I'm going to check in on Miss Lavinia and what the police have found."

"Come on, Audra." Rex managed to get Drake out of his path with the promise of a treat. "You were just saying how you can't get my attention then when I give it to you, you get suspicious and go to bed."

He had a point. I slumped onto the couch again and said, "I'll take whipped cream instead of marshmallows, please."

"That's my girl." He ran into the kitchen before I could change my mind.

Reaching for the throw blanket, I draped it over my legs to shake off the chill. If we planned to spend quality time over hot chocolate, I wanted to be comfortable.

Drake, chewing on a dog treat, joined me while Rex created magic in the kitchen.

I patted his head absently. Since Rex was going with Andrew to Chicago Monday morning, he'd need to pack tomorrow while I was at work. I'd have to channel my energies elsewhere.

Like on whoever attacked Miss Lavinia and Dave the Butcher.

# Chapter Five

Saturday, November 26

Rumours swirled into our store all day Saturday with each customer who walked through the door. Some customers said Miss Lavinia had a stroke and died in hospital. Others said her only remaining relative was on their way to take her back to the Louisiana bayou. Still others were convinced she'd staged the whole thing.

Whatever the real story was, I heard about three more variations by the time I arrived at the deli and came face to face with Charity Wells. She could've retired ten years earlier but enjoyed her job far too much.

"Hey, Audra, your skin's looking better today," Charity said. "Where's your sidekick?"

"I dropped Drake off at the groomer on my way to work, mostly to keep him from eating Rex's socks and underwear right out of his suitcase. I'll have to pick him up soon. Good thing Sadie doesn't mind him hanging around while I'm at work."

"What can I get for you?" she asked then

handed me a paper cup and lowered her voice, "Was everything okay last night? Rex didn't seem thrilled to see us. "

With a wince, I placed my order. "Did you know Dave Spencer very well?"

"Uh-oh. I had a feeling you'd be poking around soon." Charity placed two cheese sandwiches on the grill. "I get it. The theories I've heard so far are a little out there."

"Like the one where Miss Lavinia staged the whole thing?" I asked. "Whatever happened, Dave's still dead."

Charity motioned for me to sit at the nearest table. A couple minutes later, she brought over a paper bag. I didn't have to peek inside to know it held the grilled cheese sandwiches, two cups of soup, and about eight packages of crackers.

She sat across from me with a mug of steaming tea and said, "Mom and I bought our meats for the B&B from Dave. It came from local farmers and wasn't loaded with hormones and crap. I don't know who'd want to kill him, but his ex-wife would be at the top of my list. She used to tell everyone how badly Dave treated her."

"Do you know her name?" I pulled a little notebook out of my coat pocket.

She grinned. "Look at you all formal like. I'd almost think you'd done this before. Her name is Joelle Spencer. Well, Benson now. She remarried that hot shot real estate guy seconds after she got the final the divorce papers."

"That was Dave's ex-wife? Wow. Did he have any disgruntled employees?"

"Everyone I know loved him," she said. "Cliff Rose worked at the butcher shop from the day it opened until the end. Dave's daughter Bree was learning how to run the place. My neighbour's son Jesse grew up there working as the delivery boy."

I met her gaze. "That's it?"

"In twenty years, Dave only ever fired one person. Joelle."

My mouth fell open. "He fired his wife?"

"To be fair, he didn't fire her until he caught her in their bed with Chuck."

"That seems fair." I sipped my coffee.

When the door opened, Charity patted my hand. "I'll talk to my mom and see what she knows. I'm sure she'll show up at the sewing group on Wednesday and fill you in. She's had that cold that's been going around."

"That would be great. Thanks, Charity." I stood and picked up the bag of food.

"Oh. Do I report to you or Officer Grant?"

My face burned. "Very funny."

She waved a hand. "I'll tell you first then call Grant. I can't stand that young punk he works with now. I think he's trouble."

"Yeah, we've met. Drake seems to think he smells weird."

"Then you'd better trust that nose. You

can't fool a dog."

Back at Stitch'n'Time, Merilee picked at her sandwich while I told her about my chat with Charity. Finally, she met my gaze across the counter. "I had a thought."

"Let me guess," I spoke around my grilled cheese. "You want to make a suspect board. I need to get stuff done for Christmas."

"No, I think we should check on Miss Lavinia's shop."

I tried to hide my enthusiasm. "Why?"

She held up a silver key. "Because as the temporary landlady of the building while my father's out of town, I need to make sure my property isn't damaged after the attack, nor left in disarray after the police search. I owe it to my tenant."

"And because Miss Lavinia's still in the hospital."

Merilee rolled her eyes. "You thought of doing the same thing, didn't you? Come on. We'll put a note on the door and be back in fifteen minutes. I'm sure Miss Lavinia would appreciate knowing we're checking to make sure nothing's missing and her plants don't die."

"What plants?" I asked. "There's not enough light in there to keep anything alive."

"So we'll check upstairs."

I chuckled. "Isn't it usually me suggesting things like that?"

"Would you rather we break into Rex's office to find clues he's having an affair or something?" she asked.

My mouth dropped open. "Why would you say that?"

"Sorry, I just assumed things were still rocky. Let's go before we get customers."

I flipped the sign and stuck a note on the door. With Drake at the groomer, our food was safe unattended for the first time in ages. We looked both ways as we snuck out the back door of Stitch'n'Time and into the cold.

When Merilee pulled a key out of her pocket, my stomach slithered into a knot. Her dad owned the building. With a renter upstairs and her parents in Florida, she had a legitimate excuse to check on the place. Merilee—or anyone else in her family—could've snuck into the shop unnoticed.

I gave my head a shake. Merilee's family had founded the town and had known Miss Lavinia for years. There was no way she'd harm Miss Lavinia or Dave.

"What are we looking for?" Merilee whispered.

"Miss Lavinia was near the counter. Dave was over there."

When she didn't speak again, I turned. She stood with her flashlight beam aimed at a dark spot on the wood floor. "This is where he died, isn't it?"

Tears sprang to my eyes. I was so

absorbed in finding the mysterious scent, I'd blocked it out. I started to lean against the counter, then stopped myself. "Yeah."

"I'm glad you found them, not Judy or Maddie," Merilee said. "I have no idea how they would've handled the shock."

"I don't know how I have," I muttered.

We prowled around the room for a couple more minutes scanning bottles and jars. Too bad neither of us knew what we were looking for. We both avoided the dark spot.

"Was the dagger you saw the one she kept on a shelf for spells and stuff?" she asked. "The one with the fake rubies?"

"That's the one." I searched her tarot card table trying to find an appointment book. No luck.

Merilee searched the shelves. "Where's the cup she kept with it?"

I shrugged. "It was on the floor near Dave and had something inside. The police might have it as evidence."

"The blood of a vestal virgin?" she suggested.

"Seriously?"

Merilee stood in the middle of the store with her eyes closed. "I need to get out of here. This is creepier than I expected. Her plants will be fine if she has any."

Rather than remind her that this was her idea, I rifled through the books that lay on the counter. A few had bright sticky notes to mark pages. I flipped through a few and discovered information about fatigue, incontinence, and snoring.

When the front door swung open and the lights flicked on, we both froze in place. Officer Tyler Grant stood in the doorway, his nose red and his eyes watery. He sneezed then lurched toward us reaching for the box of tissues on the counter.

"Is there a reason you're skulking around Miss Lavinia's shop?" he asked before he sneezed again.

"We're not skulking," Merilee said. "We're checking on her plants."

"I've been her patient for long enough to know she doesn't have plants."

I put my hands on my hips. "You don't sound well enough to be out of bed."

He nodded. "I came to get some of her cold blend and that eucalyptus bath stuff. I don't know how I forgot…"

Merilee folded her arms across her chest as she gazed at the floor. "It doesn't seem real. It's horrible."

"Do have any suspects?" I asked as I wandered behind Miss Lavinia's counter then gasped. "I forgot about those."

As they came toward me, I tugged out a translucent plastic container loaded with small drawers and placed it on the counter. Officer Grant sucked in a sharp breath which turned into a coughing fit.

"I'll get you some water," Merilee said as

she ran into the back room.

I set the container on the counter, then peered in awe through the plastic walls of the tiny mausoleum. It housed twenty voodoo dolls in individual drawers. "This is cool and creepy all at once."

"Is mine in there?" Officer Grant's voice came out raspy.

I read the tiny labels on each drawer, but didn't see any names. Just dates. "Not in here, but I'm sure she has more somewhere."

Miss Lavinia was some sort of voodoo doll crypt keeper. All four shelves filled with similar containers. She must've had a surge of patients after the cowboy died. Each container had twenty small drawers containing similar voodoo dolls to mine that she gave me at Halloween. Judging by the dates on the drawers, these were dolls for current clients. No sign of all the previous embroidery boxes we'd given her.

"Is that what I think it is?" Merilee held Officer Grant's water glass in one hand.

"Yup. The voodoo dolls she's made of each customer." All except the two that currently resided in the top of my closet. I searched for Rex's miniature look-a-like.

"Where's mine?" she asked.

Officer Grant grabbed the glass of water and chugged it down before he croaked, "And mine. I don't want anyone messing with my juju."

Merilee raised her eyebrows and asked, "Your juju?"

"Do you want your doll to fall into the wrong hands?" he asked. "Who knows whether those things actually work?"

"Are they evidence?" I asked.

Officer Grant grimaced. "Was she beaten with one?"

"No, but they could be why she was attacked, especially if someone was afraid theirs would fall into the wrong hands."

He flared his nostrils before he finally growled, "Give it. Before I search for yours."

I crouched behind the counter and searched until I found a doll that looked like him. "Here. Don't say I've never done anything nice for you."

"You're a peach," he said. "Now get out of here."

Merilee placed her hands on her hips. "Nuh-uh. Not until I get mine and Tony's."

Searching a little more, I found theirs using their birth dates. The likenesses were surprisingly good. "Done. Anything else?"

Officer Grant gazed around the shop. "I suppose it's unethical to take a bottle of cold remedy, wouldn't it?"

"Completely, but only if someone saw you and reported you to the authorities," Merilee said. She walked over to the shelf behind the counter and handed him a bottle with a green label. "Go home. We can't have you spreading more germs. Audra has enough issues as it is."

He nodded as he slipped the doll and the cold remedy into his inside pocket. "So I heard. And I never saw anyone inside the shop. This time. You two need to scram before her next of kin arrives."

The back of my neck prickled as he tucked a twenty-dollar bill beneath the cash register. "Next of kin?"

"Her nephew," Officer Grant said. "His name's Simon and, if you're lucky, he might need a hand. I'm sure you'll find him interesting. I spoke to him on the phone and plan to keep a safe distance from the shop."

"Why's that?" I asked.

"He's one of *them*."

Merilee and I exchanged glances. He was starting to worry me.

"One of who?" She winced.

"A witch doctor."

Yup. Now I was officially worried. Did he have a fever? He'd probably draw his gun if I checked. "A what?"

"A witch doctor," he said. "You don't think Miss Lavinia learned to make all those potions and voodoo dolls by herself, do you? She grew up in Louisiana and trained to be some kind of voodoo priestess or something."

After all the times I gave Rex heck for calling Miss Lavinia an old witch, it turns out he'd been half-right all along. I wasn't in a rush to admit that to his face though.

"Merilee and I came in here to figure out who Miss Lavinia's last client was. Did you find out what was in that chalice that was next to Dave?"

"What chalice? No one found one when they searched the place." He reached for another tissue a heartbeat before he sneezed.

"Are you sure? Someone might've kicked it under the counter or something."

"I saw the photos, Audra," he said. "There was no chalice."

Had I imagined it? I stared at the plastic doll crypts and shuddered. Doll storage bins sounded far less creepy. If I showed him the crime scene photo I took, he might arrest me. "What's with the new guy on the force? Officer Trent."

Officer Grant narrowed his eyes before he asked, "What about him?"

"Why does he think Audra's a suspect?"

"She found the body. We always take a close look at the people who say they found a body, so we can eliminate them." Officer Grant met my gaze. "Don't we, Audra?"

"Yes, sir, we do." I saluted.

"Smart aleck. I have to ask you both to please leave the crime scene. I need to go home and get some sleep."

Merilee headed toward the door. "On our way. Let's go, Audra."

Officer Grant cleared his throat then nodded toward the door. "Yes. Let's go,

Audra.”

“Just need to put this away. I don’t want Officer Trent to think someone’s been disturbing the crime scene.” I returned the plastic bin to its spot on the shelf, tucking the Rex doll into my handbag as I did so.

“What did you just take?” he asked.

I dug Rex back out of my bag. “Just my husband. What’s in your pocket?”

His frown grew deeper. “Get out, or I’ll make sure you get my cold.”

“Don’t you dare or we’ll sic Drake on you,” Merilee snapped.

Officer Grant coughed then escorted us out the front door into the cold. He paused to lock the door behind us. “I’d appreciate if you’d stay out until Miss Lavinia’s nephew arrives. I’d love it even more if you both kept twenty feet away from the building and from Miss Lavinia.”

Merilee eyeballed the distance between her shop and ours and said, “Close enough.”

He sneezed once more then groaned.

“You’d better go home,” I told him. “You’re too sick to be out here. Be sure to stop at the deli on your way. Charity makes amazing cold cure soup.”

As he walked toward the squad car, he held up one hand. I wasn’t sure which finger he stuck into the air though I hazarded a guess.

Merilee dragged me into our shop and

closed the door behind us. "What did you really take?"

"Just Rex. I probably should've left him there, but… You know." I waited until we were behind our own counter and had taken off our coats before I rummaged through my bag for the Rex doll and discovered him at the bottom, his head at an odd angle to his burlap body. For a couple seconds, I debated what to do to it first.

When the cowboy died, I'd discovered Miss Lavinia's cemetery filled with little cardboard boxes of voodoo dolls. That was enough to give me nightmares for years.

"I'm getting boxes for me and Tony. Did you want one for Rex?" She didn't even bat an eye as she reached below the counter.

"That just sounded so wrong, but it's a good idea. It'll save him from more unintentional damage." I straightened the doll's head then placed the doll in the embroidery thread box.

"Huh. There must be wire inside to make them bendable," I mused. "We should've pushed Officer Grant to find out who this Simon is. We don't even know his last name."

She shrugged as she sat next to me. "Let's start with Miss Lavinia's last name, Brevil, and see what we find."

Just like his aunt, Simon Brevil didn't appear on any website, social media or anywhere we looked. We did end up on checking out movie stars more than once. We were also caught up in one of those online articles that promise a remarkable story and ends up featuring an ad for weight loss supplements.

By the end of our work day, we were still left wondering who Miss Lavinia's nephew Simon was. Too bad we didn't know his actual last name. Or why Officer Grant insisted he was one of "them."

# Chapter Six

Saturday November 26 / Sunday,
November 27

By the time Drake and I got home later that afternoon, Rex was still gone. I assumed he'd headed to the office right after I'd left that morning. No matter. I was still trying to figure out not only who Miss Lavinia's nephew Simon was, but who'd want to kill Dave the Butcher. The quiet gave me time to think.

I'd filled three pages in a notebook that had a photo of a quilt on the front cover when the doorbell rang. I jumped. Since Merilee would've texted to say she was on her way, I was wary to open the door. "What are you doing?"

In the pool of porch light, Rex held a bouquet of wilted daisies while he shuffled the snow off his shoes on the door mat. "Hey. Your skin looks better. I mean, you look less like a lime."

"Gee, thanks, I think."

"Is the green stuff helping?" he asked.

I shivered as a fresh gust of wind blew

past me. "I'm not sure if it is or not. Are you coming inside?"

He handed me the flowers. "I should've bought them last. They got cold when I stopped at the grocery store. I picked up pizza for dinner."

"Pizza sounds good." I'd been so absorbed in the suspect list that I hadn't noticed the time. "Why didn't you just come inside?"

"Thanks. I know I've been a real jerk lately. I wasn't sure you'd want me here." When he placed the shoes and his trench coat in the closet, I raised my eyebrows. Had he finally figured out the correlation to Drake eating any belongings he left on the floor?

"Jerk or not, you're still my husband. Where's the pizza?" I asked.

Rex glanced at his hands then groaned, "I must've left it in the car. I didn't want the flowers to freeze. I'll be right back."

"Good choice." I sniffed them, but the December blooms didn't have any scent.

He reached into the closet for a pair of tall, black snowmobile boots then kissed me quick. "I'll be right back."

True to his word, less than a minute later, he returned. With a frozen pizza.

My heart sank. "You didn't say I'd have to cook it."

"You don't. You can sit. Let me toss this bad boy in the oven then you can tell me all about your day."

Concerned, I pressed my palm to his forehead to check for a fever. Something strange was going on. "Did you happen to see my husband while you were out there? Tall guy. Well-dressed. A bit stressed out and self-centered."

"Ha ha. At least you haven't lost your sense of humour." He headed toward the kitchen with Drake and I close behind.

"What's going on?" I leaned against the cupboard.

"You're right. I should at least take care of you before I take off to Chicago. Is that okay?" He glanced up as he pulled out a pizza pan.

I hesitated, not sure I liked going from feeling abandoned to smothered in such a short time. "I'll go find us a movie or something."

He spent the entire cooking time of the frozen pizza hovering near the oven with his phone in one hand. Texting Andrew, I guessed. In the meantime, Drake and I turned on the fireplace, settled into the best seats in the house, and surfed the movie channels for something good to watch. By the time Rex finally appeared with two slices of deluxe pizza on each of two plates, he seemed to have something on his mind.

"Did you hear any more about Miss Lavinia?" he asked. "How's she doing?"

"Merilee and I spoke to Tyler Grant. He

didn't have any information, but he said she was doing better."

"Is that Trent guy is still on the case?" Rex's eyes narrowed. He sat on the armchair since Drake hadn't left room next to me on the couch.

"Probably. Why?"

"Isn't that a conflict of interest or something?"

"What do you mean?"

"Remember I said I knew that name? I finally remembered where from. Alister Trent is the son of former Mayor Roger Trent. The guy who went to see Miss Lavinia about migraines and died a week later because Miss Lavinia told him not to go to the doctor."

I flinched. "Merilee said Roger had a brain tumour. There was nothing Miss Lavinia or the doctors could do except keep him comfortable."

Rex carried his pizza back to the kitchen where he popped the tab on a can of beer. "All I'm saying is Alister Trent has no business conducting this particular investigation. He has an emotional stake in it."

"Dave was the one killed, not Miss Lavinia." Either that or Rex was trying to steer me off his trail. What was I thinking? Rex liked Dave the Butcher. He just wasn't crazy about Miss Lavinia.

"But it happened in Miss Lavinia's store.

My guess is Dave got in the way."

"I'm not buying it."

After dinner, Rex draped his legs over one arm of the chair and closed his eyes. Before my husband even started to snore, Drake settled in and began to drool on the blanket that covered my legs. I curled up with my laptop to do a little digging. There were several on-line articles about Roger Trent as well as an act of vandalism in Miss Lavinia's shop following his death. A younger Alister Trent stood accused of the act, but the charges were tossed out.

While the males dozed, I crept up the stairs to call Merilee. "Do you remember when Mayor Roger Trent died?"

"Oh, yeah. The gigantic tumour," she said. "Miss Lavinia gave him some weird tablets for the headaches, but he died a week later."

"Did you know his son was accused of vandalizing her shop after the funeral?"

"Was that him? I knew there was something about him that bugged me, but I couldn't put my finger on it."

I sat on the bed. "I didn't remember that until Rex mentioned it earlier. Can you believe he came home from work early with flowers and a frozen pizza?"

"Frozen pizza?" She laughed. "I guess it's a start. I doubt Alister was the one who vandalized Miss Lavinia's shop. He and his mom went to Toronto right after the funeral.

There was a big scandal that they left town right after the service before Roger was even buried."

My stomach gurgled, more from suspicion than the pizza. "So why would he come back to work in Sugarwood? Does he still have family here?"

"Roger's sister and her family moved into one of those new homes on Blue Hill. They have that fancy place with the tennis court and the huge swimming pool."

"Do you happen to know her name?"

"No, I just remember her husband had a beef with Dave." Merilee said. "Pardon the pun. I'm tired. Tony and I have been making Christmas cookies since we got home. If I think of it, I'll text you."

I hung up and brought my laptop up to the bed to do a little more research before Drake or Rex woke up. Like me, my husband definitely wasn't the cookie baking kind of guy. We preferred to eat them.

* * *


The doorbell rang early Sunday morning while I set up the coffee maker, sending Drake into a barking frenzy. I pushed him to one side and held his collar, opening the door with one hand.

Officer Trent stood on the front porch. "Could I have a word with you?"

When I stepped back to wave him inside,

Drake barked and strained at his collar so hard I had to grab it with both hands. "We should talk on the porch."

"Good idea," he said.

Shoving Drake into the house, I pulled the door closed behind me. "Sorry about that. He's been acting weird for days. Rex had a smell on his clothes that Drake hates."

"What sort of smell?" He raised his eyebrows.

I didn't want to suspect Rex, but I needed to find out the truth. "His clothes smelled like some new cologne or something when he came home late the other night and there were spots on his shirt." My voice crackled. "I put them in the laundry room."

"Maybe I should take those clothes to examine," he said. "They could be evidence."

"Of what? Rex would never hurt anyone, least of all Miss Lavinia or Dave."

Officer Trent frowned. "He might've seen who did and be the key to solving the case."

"And you think his suit will tell you that?" I asked. "We have no idea if he was there."

He nodded. "True, but this could eliminate him."

It was worth a shot. I hoped Rex was either still asleep or in the shower. "You'd better wait out here."

"Not a problem." He laughed and rubbed

his jaw. The scratch on his jaw didn't seem to be healing well. I almost offered him cream to take down the swelling in case he had an infection.

I eased the door open a crack until I spied Drake near the couch. His steely gaze followed me. The second I reached the laundry room, he bounded toward me. In a panic, I closed the door then shoved Rex's clothes into a bag.

Rex would be angry, but I had to follow my gut instinct. If he had nothing to do with the attack then the police wouldn't find anything. Hunting down Dave's killer was an important community service. No one wanted to think a killer lived in their midst, especially in their own home. Besides, Rex's suit wasn't fit for a scarecrow.

Before I could weigh the pros and cons of turning over the suit, the laundry room door opened. I shrieked fumbling the bag until a sleeve stuck out.

"What are you doing?" Rex stood in the doorway.

"Officer Trent is here and I...um..."

He frowned. "Is that the guy on the front porch Drake's barking at?"

"That's the one."

Rex's nostrils flared as he demanded, "What's in the bag?"

My mouth became a desert. "Nothing special."

"Are you giving him my clothes? Do you

seriously think I killed Dave?"

"No, I—"

Rex's cell phone rang. When he turned to answer, I ducked out of the laundry room and raced to the front door with Drake hot on my heels. I managed to squeeze outside without the dog joining me and shoved the bag at Officer Trent. After that, I doubled over with my hands on my knees, horribly out of breath for such a short dash.

"Take it," I gasped. "There's suit and shirt. Blood. Saliva."

His mouth fell open. "Saliva?"

"Dog. Long story. Go before Rex—"

When the front door opened, Drake flew out of the house. He knocked Officer Trent flat on his back on the sidewalk. Within seconds, he'd torn the paper bag to shreds to gnaw on the clothing inside.

"Oops," Rex said, not looking the least bit sorry.

Officer Trent cursed then froze when Drake snarled. For a long second, cop and ninety pounds of dog stared at each other before the officer snaked his shaking hand toward his gun. Drake let out a low growl.

"Don't you dare!" I lunged between them to grasp Drake's collar. "You need to leave. I can't hold him back for long."

Officer Trent got to his feet with his gaze riveted on the dog. "What should I do?"

Rex stood on the front step with his arms folded across his chest. "Give back my suit.

I need to have it cleaned for work."

"You might want to buy a new one," I told him.

My husband snorted then returned inside slamming the door behind him. I hoped he didn't lock me out.

The officer picked up the bits of pants and said, "I'll take these for evidence. Is there a jacket?"

When Drake growled again, he took a couple steps back.

"I think the jacket's out of the question unless you want bite marks."

"Just take him inside. I'll collect it when he's gone."

When I tried to coax Drake toward the house, he stood his ground. I motioned for the officer to back off. Only once he'd returned to his cruiser did Drake follow my commands, albeit with the jacket clenched between his teeth. The second we got inside, Drake dropped it on the floor before he trotted toward the fireplace. I snatched the jacket, opened the door, and threw it onto the porch.

Rex glowered from the kitchen doorway. "I can't believe you gave him my suit. Do you really think I had a reason to hurt anyone?"

"You were covered in blood spots, smelled like incense, and looked like you were in a fight. What should I think? That jacket belongs on Frankenstein's monster, not in a board meeting. Drake won't sit near you because of some smell the dry cleaner won't be able to get out anyway."

"You were in Miss Lavinia's shop, but he still comes to you."

He was right. Miss Lavinia had anointed me with a few different oils. So why didn't Drake take after me and the clothing I'd worn the same way he took after Rex and Alister Trent? What were they using that I wasn't?

"What've I done?" I sagged onto the sofa with a sigh.

After making a huge breakfast of sausages, waffles, and eggs in an effort to try to make things up to my husband, I sipped one last cup of coffee while flipping through Saturday's paper and skimmed past more coverage of wars, budget cuts, and upcoming holiday sales then I cared to read.

As I turned one page, an item caught my eye. "Miss Lavinia's closing the curio shop."

From where he lay beneath the table, Drake grunted, sounding mildly interested. When I glanced toward him, he dropped his head back onto his paws.

Rex walked toward me drying the dish in his hand. "She was what?"

"Closing the shop." I pointed to the paper. "There's a quarter page ad for a half price sale. Fixtures and everything must go. I imagine that's on hold now. Why wouldn't she say anything?"

"She's old. I guess she finally wants to retire," he said sitting next to me. "Did this paper come out before or after she was attacked?"

My heart raced as I checked the date. "After. It's Saturday's paper. She wouldn't have had a chance to cancel the ad. Either someone knew she was selling the shop and wasn't happy about it, or they wanted to speed up the process."

Rex whistled. "That's harsh. Then why kill Dave?"

"Good question. How *did* you get blood on your clothes?" I asked.

He met my gaze. "You think I killed him? I stopped to see Miss Lavinia after work Tuesday to ask why you were turning green. The powder she gave you is a mix of seaweeds and vitamins. It's harmless. She had no idea why you're turning green and thought maybe…"

"That I'm making it up?"

Rex grimaced. "That it's more of a mental manifestation than a physical one."

"You think turning green is all in my head? How can you say that when you can see the colour of my skin?"

He held up his hands. "I got you a refill. It's in the cupboard near the coffee, since I figured you'd find it there. I also got a listed of ingredients."

The sheet of paper that fell out of his suit

pocket. I'd forgotten all about it in the pocket of my robe. "Then where'd the blood come from?"

"When I was leaving, someone opened the door which smacked me in the face. I didn't see who it was. I was too embarrassed to stay." Rex paused. "I do remember this weird smell."

"What kind of smell?"

"Kind of sweet and musty. I'd know it if I smelled it."

I waited for him to add that it smelled like an oil he used. He didn't. "Miss Lavinia's shop is full of oils. If we can get inside, we can find the smell and figure out who bought it."

Rex smiled. "Look at you. You're becoming a grown up Nancy Drew."

"Thanks for noticing." I sipped my coffee while trying not to smile. "I've been this way for years. I simply get nosier with age."

"Do you still suspect me?" he asked meeting my gaze.

My good mood fell off the cliff. "I can't rule you out. Not after I found you passed out on the couch looking like you'd been in a bar brawl."

"I was, actually," Rex said. "After I left Miss Lavinia's, I went to the bar. Some guy made a comment about my face and I got mad. More like embarrassed, but I took my frustrations out on him. We each got in one punch before the bartender threw us out. All the cops will find is my blood and a bit of beer."

"And dog drool," I added. "Lots and lots of dog drool. I'd hate to be in that poor lab guy's shoes."

Drake sauntered over and placed his head in my lap. He gazed up at me with wide eyes as if to apologize. When Rex reached to pat his head, he inched out of his reach.

"Looks like you two still aren't friends yet."

"Nope," Rex said. "I guess I have some making up to do. On all counts. So what do you want to do today?"

I had a couple of ideas. One of which Rex wouldn't like at all.

# Chapter Seven

### Sunday, November 27

My first thought was to sneak back into Miss Lavinia's shop and sniff every last one of her oils with the hope I could figure out the mysterious scent that drove Drake crazy. I called Merilee to borrow her and the key, but she and Tony were out of town at their son's place in Toronto.

Plan B was to figure out where Joelle Spencer-Benson lived. Google was little help. Until I thought to look for her new husband's name. It seemed odd that the new wife of such a high profile man in town didn't appear alongside him at every events and gala.

Chuck Benson was one of the top realtors in Southern Ontario and the current mayor's brother. The image of his face was plastered on the three bus stops in Sugarwood as well as on two billboards out in the middle of someone's field along the highway. I doubted the big Spanish mansion on Blue Hill would be hard to find.

"Hey, Rex," I called out, "do you want to

go for a walk?"

"I'll pass." He came out of the kitchen wiping his hands on a towel. "I need to pack. I thought I could whip up a nice roast for dinner. That'll give you leftovers for part of the week."

Did he know something I didn't? I decided to cut him slack after giving his clothes to the police. "Do I need to pick anything up?"

"I've got it covered. You and Drake enjoy your walk."

After layering on a parka, boots, mittens, and a hat, I fumbled with the leash before we headed out into the street. Drake peed on the front lawn then turned back to the house. With a grunt, I half-dragged him toward the sidewalk before we headed toward the park we normally strolled through on a Sunday morning. Instead of going to the park, however, I steered him uphill toward the mansions on Blue Hill, named for the abundance of blueberries every summer.

Thanks to Laney Developments the blueberries were gone, but the name stuck.

Rex and I used to wander through the development when these homes were little more then holes in the ground and dream about what sort of mansion we'd live in if we ever had the money. Those dreams went up in smoke when the kids became teenagers then went to college. I still enjoyed strolling Blue Hill now and then to see what was new. Mostly without Rex.

I didn't remember Joelle from the butcher shop. Probably because I rarely set foot inside. Rex insisted he knew cuts of meat far better than I did.

The Benson's Spanish villa stood near the top of Blue Hill. A Mediterranean-style castle overlooking the peasant realm below. I shook off the thought. Chuck had imported the fancy boulders that lined the driveway from up north because they glittered with pyrite. Fool's gold. There was speculation they were real gold from the mines near Kirkland Lake, but Chuck insisted he'd tested each rock. He made sure everyone knew they were worth less than the gas it would take to steal them.

Drake and I strolled through the open front gates and along the winding driveway lined with glittering boulders and ten-foot tall cedars that shivered in the breeze. My dog stopped to sniff every large rock on our side of the drive. Either several curious people and their dogs came to check out the rocks, or Chuck had dogs of his own.

As I neared the house, I caught a glimpse of a woman in a pink parka similar to mine directing a couple young men hanging Christmas lights and greenery. She looked younger than me. Chuck's daughter perhaps?

"Hello," I called out.

The woman turned and peered at me over dark sunglasses. While the day was bright and sunny, her pink-framed sunglasses seemed out of the ordinary in Sugarwood on a November afternoon. "Can I help you?"

"I hope so. I'm looking for Joelle Benson," I wheezed as Drake pranced around me, straining at the leash to get to her.

She narrowed her eyes. "If you're a reporter, I'm not giving interviews," she said sternly. "Dave and I were married. We got divorced. Now he's dead. End of story."

I'd expected Joelle to look much older. Closer to my age. "I'm not a reporter."

"No? I thought I saw you on television. You look familiar."

"You might've seen me in the butcher shop." I shrugged.

"That's not it." She hesitated then her face lit up. "I know. You own the craft store. Audra, right? My mother-in-law's part of the sewing circle. She told me all about how you solved that cowboy's murder."

When she held out a hand to Drake, he backed away whimpering. Not a good sign. What had I gotten myself into?

"Which one's your mother-in-law?" I asked.

"Maddie Benson. She makes incredible quilts."

"She sure does." Not to mention

incredibly meddlesome. But who was I to talk?

Joelle seemed to relax. "It was kind of you and your partner to take the ladies in after the church rudely evicted them. Maddie's always going on about how generous you've been with the group. You have good taste in coats, too."

I held out an arm. "Pink makes me happy."

"Same here." She flashed a smile. "The church elders had told the sewing circle they planned to do renovations to the community hall, which is why they had to move. Once you let them move into your shop, all plans for renovations stopped."

My jaw tightened reflexively. "Really?"

Her eyes widened as though she'd said something wrong. "You're here to ask about Dave, aren't you? All I can say is that he was a good butcher but a lousy husband. I have no idea why someone would…you know. Telling the kids their father's dead was the worst thing I've ever done."

I wanted to ask, "besides have an affair?" but thought better of it.

"Actually, I've been planning to stop by the store," she said. "I wanted to ask if you sell gift certificates. Maddie doesn't need anything, but I know she loves your fabrics. She'll be happy to stock up."

"We sure do. Come by this week. Just not Wednesday afternoons. That's when the group meets. Although, they've been asking if we can add another day when they can come in to work on their holiday projects. They enjoy being able to get together."

The acrid stench of murder seemed forgotten as we chatted about kids, Christmas, and crafts. It was interesting to learn Joelle was an avid painter. I'd started to fill her in on the great craft kits we were expecting that week just as Drake decided to water a nearby cedar.

"That's my cue to get moving," I said.

Joelle reached out to shake my hand. Suddenly, she pulled it back and hugged me instead. "I'm so happy you stopped by to chat. I'll come by the shop this week. I'd love to take a look at your stock."

As Drake led me down the road toward the front gate, my nose itched. I rubbed it with the back of my glove and realized Joelle wore the same scent as Rex and Officer Trent. No wonder Drake was restless. I needed to find Miss Lavinia's notes and see who else in town used the same blend of oils.

Too bad Merilee was out of town today.

We were home when someone called out and a hand waved over a fence along the walkway. Judge Harry Lyons was just tall enough he could peer over top of the six foot boards.

"Out for a stroll, are you?" he asked.

"Meet me around front."

By the time Drake and I climbed the front steps of the judge's porch, he held a steaming mug in each hand. While he wore a toque and parka, his hands were bare. "How about some hot apple cider to take off the chill?"

"That sounds lovely."

Drake gave a bark then sniffed out the freshly filled water bowl near the bistro table. He curled up beneath one of the black bistro chairs protected by the roof from the snow.

"I guess he's done walking for now." I sat on the chair above him before I cradled my cup in both hands. "What are you up to today?"

Harry sipped his drink then met my gaze. "I spoke to Rex earlier. Since he's heading to Chicago on Monday, he asked me to keep an eye on you next week."

"Because he won't be here to do it."

"No, because you found Dave the Butcher's body," he said. "He seems to think you'll do something silly like investigate, which I brushed off until I saw you walking toward Dave's ex-wife's house."

I bowed my head. "Oh."

"Should I assume you spoke to Doc already?" he asked.

Doctor Neil Griffith was our local coroner and the judge's next door neighbour. While most small towns didn't actually have a coroner in residence and sent cases to Toronto or other larger cities, Sugarwood was blessed with a retired medical examiner that helped the police from time to time. A murder case would definitely qualify.

"Not yet."

He raised his bushy eyebrows. "Are you okay? You look a little green."

"That's not funny." I hugged my mug of cider and inhaled the sweet apple scent.

"Good thing it's winter or you'd be camouflaged on the lawn." Harry patted my arm. "Rex told me about the diagnosis and the green stuff. I'm sure Doc could give you good advice. All I can tell you is to watch your back and stay out of jail."

The last time I investigated a murder, I ended up in Harry's courtroom wearing my pajamas. "I promise I'll try to stay out of trouble. Did you know Miss Lavinia was planning to sell everything off?"

"Not until I saw it in the paper," he said. "It doesn't make any sense. I just saw her Thursday morning and she didn't say a word about it."

"I don't suppose you've heard anything about her family, have you?"

He raised his eyebrows. "Now you're fishing. All I know is the doctors are making sure she has no brain trauma and the police have called her next of kin. They're keeping a close eye on her shop until her nephew arrives. I did hear they caught a couple trespassers in the shop already."

My face burned. "Imagine that. What do you know about Simon Brevil?"

"Until you told me his name, nothing. You really have been busy."

I smirked. "Not really. Tyler Grant told us when he caught…I mean when we stopped by to check on her shop."

"Uh-huh. And what were you two good Samaritans looking for?"

I glanced around to make sure Rex was nowhere in sight. "Is this off the record?"

Harry sighed as he met my gaze. "When it comes to you, Audra, there is no record."

"The other day we were checking out the crime scene. Since then, I've noticed several people in town use the same blend of oils from Miss Lavinia's shop. It might not mean anything, but the smell riles Drake up enough that he shredded one of Rex's suits."

"The one you gave the police?" he asked.

I deflated with a long breath. "Rex told you that, too? Is nothing sacred?"

"Just don't tell him I told you," he said. "I don't want him to think I'm picking sides."

"Of course not. Was it you who suggested he make dinner and buy me flowers?"

Harry looked impressed as he raised his

cup. "Nice touch. You deserve both."

I savoured my cider before I asked, "How well did you know Dave Spencer?"

"Well enough that he'd save me some choice cuts of meat each weekend," he told me. "I was sad to hear he had to sell the store and recused myself from any involvement in his divorce proceedings. There was no way I could remain impartial."

"Why's that? Because of Joelle's affair?"

He gave a slight nod. "I was the one who told Dave that I'd seen Joelle and Chuck together in Barrie. Then he went home early from work one day and caught them in action. Thankfully, he reined in his temper and took video for his lawyer. Not that it mattered. Joelle got everything. Including the kids."

"Then he ended up in a little apartment over Lara's Hair Salon and working at the grocery store," I finished.

"Yeah. Part of me feels responsible for that. I wish I could've done more to help."

A shrill whistle pierced the air. Drake sat up beneath my chair nearly knocking me over.

Rex stood on our front porch next door. "So much for going for a walk."

"We just…," I started then waved a hand. "Thanks for the cider, Harry."

Harry grabbed my arm. "Be careful, Audra. We don't know exactly what happened in Miss Lavinia's shop or why.

You could be in danger if you keep poking around." He paused. "You have my number. Keep me in the loop, will you?"

I gave him a hug. "I will. Thanks."

As Drake and I strolled up the sidewalk, Rex tapped his foot on the porch. "I was going to head over to the park to catch up to you but heard voices. Were you at Harry's the whole time?"

"No, he flagged us down on our way home."

"Uh-huh." Rex opened the front door.

"Did you finish packing?" I asked, ignoring his scowl as I unsnapped Drake's leash.

"All but my best suit. The one the dog ate and the police now have."

Guilty, I fought back with sarcasm. "Guess you'll have to find a new one. I'll bet it would impress clients to find out you picked up a new suit on a trip to Chicago."

Rex hung his coat in the closet then strolled toward the couch. A second later, the television came on and the sounds of whistles and sports announcers filled the air. Sunday football was alive and well in our living room.

Rather than watch men in tight pants and thick shoulder pads, although I was a fan of both, I sat near my husband and picked up my needlepoint to work on Drake's stocking. The entire time, thoughts of murder and mayhem danced in my head.

So did two burning questions.

Why did Miss Lavinia plan to sell her shop?

And who would want to hurt her and Dave?

It wasn't like the two of them had anything in common.

Did they?

# Chapter Eight

Monday, November 28

Monday morning, Rex was up and gone by five o'clock. I crawled out of bed long enough to shuffle to the front door for a quick goodbye in time to see Andrew Laney pick him up in a black stretch limo. At least they were hitting the road in style.

Drake and I went back to bed then got up a couple of hours later.

After breakfast and a shower, I searched for the car keys. I looked forward to having the option of driving to work for a change. Ten minutes later, I gave up and texted Rex to ask where he'd left the keys.

*"Sorry, honey. They're in my coat pocket. Guess I took them out of habit. Have a great day."*

Have a great day? Who was he kidding? Cursing with each step I took, I was halfway to Stitch'n'Time by the time I got a text from Merilee.

*"You on your way?"* she asked.

*"There in 5,"* I replied.

By the time I reached the store, Merilee

gnawed on one thumb nail while she paced between the counter and the front door. Her anxiety made Drake whine. The second I let him off the leash, he headed straight for his bed near the heat vent.

"What's going on?"

She paused long enough to say, "There's a man in Miss Lavinia's store. A big man."

"Who is he?"

"No idea. It might be Simon, but I didn't want to go ask."

I started to take off my coat then reconsidered. If it was Simon, one of us should meet him. "Why didn't you talk to him? You are Miss Lavinia's landlady. It's not out of line for you to keep an eye on her store and belongings."

"You don't understand. He's not the kind of guy you walk up to and say hi," she said.

"Why not?" When she struggled to answer, I rolled my eyes. "Never mind. I'll go. Be back in a minute."

"If you're not back in five, I'm calling the police."

Grumbling about the crummy start to my day, I walked the few feet to Miss Lavinia's shop then stopped. What if Merilee's sense about this guy were on point? Normally, I would've walked inside without a second thought, but her nephew might not want to be friendly with the locals. Since someone had attacked Miss Lavinia in her own shop, all the rules had changed. I hesitated at the door and held my breath.

"I've got this," I said aloud.

Summoning a wee bit of courage, I raised my hand to knock. I'd barely touched it when the door swung open. My jaw dropped. Merilee was right. The man inside Miss Lavinia's shop wasn't the kind of person I'd normally walk straight up. More like the kind I'd take a few big steps back from.

He was easily twice my size with dark mahogany skin and a cheery red sweater with a snowman on the front. A quarter-inch thick gold chain hung around his neck attached to a red pendant the size of a toonie and a small gold earring pierced his right ear. He flashed a huge smile as he reached out to grab the front of my coat before he hauled me inside like a trophy marlin. "What'cha standin' out der for, *cher*? It warmer insi'."

Part of me wanted to run, but my feet had turned into ice blocks that no longer touched the ground.

"Seems y'all are afrai' of dis place," he said. "I ain't dat scary, *cher*."

Once he set me down, I took a couple test breaths to make sure I hadn't died from fright before I introduced myself. "I'm Audra. I own the craft store a couple doors over."

"Ah. I taut I'd meet 'cha soon." He reached out a hand the size of my head. "Simon Brevil. I hear you's a wannabe detective an' you find me poor Auntie Lavinia."

"Yes, I did." I focused on not hyperventilating. "She's a good friend. I didn't realize you were…"

Simon's eyes widened. He stared at me for a long few seconds before he burst into loud laughter that rattled the small bottles on the shelves. "Sorry for scaring you. The police seemed to think I was a good ole bayou boy, so I was playing it up. Truth is, I'm a gentleman and went to college. Financial planner by day and witch doctor by the light of the moon. I also dabble in poetry nobody but my cat likes."

I stared. "That was all a show? You had me going."

His rich voice and deep laugh made me feel silly for thinking the worst. "I'm big, I'm Black, and I come from Louisiana. I jus' do what dem police think I should, *cher*." He waved a hand. "I'm actually a pretty nice guy, Miss Audra. Don't worry, I'll come clean the next time they come around. I have to admit it was fun when they thought I was going to put a curse on them. You should've seen the look on your face though. Don't tell me you were scared."

"I'd be lying if I said a little," I told him. "You won't change their minds even if you do come clean. Miss Lavinia probably keeps voodoo dolls of the entire police force. Actually, makes one for every person she treats."

He raised both inch-thick eyebrows. "You don't say. Where does she store them?"

"How long have you been in here?" I asked.

Simon sighed. "Between finding the place, grabbing coffee, then getting her key from the police, I've been here long enough to walk across the room and change my mind."

"Change your mind about what?" I asked, following him to the bare little table in the corner where Miss Lavinia did treatments and tarot readings. The one I'd whipped the cloth off to cushion her head and hadn't noticed all the items I'd knocked to the floor. Since the tablecloth was missing, I assumed it was in the evidence locker at the police station. Either he or Merilee must've picked up the tarot cards that stood on the bare table now.

"About whether I want to be here or run home like a rabid squirrel," he said as he sat. "So far, you're the first thing about this snowy town that makes me want to stay. Well, the second if you count the shop. Does my auntie have a good thing going here?"

I sat across from him. "I'd say so. Some people around here trust her more than the local medical doctors. How is she doing, by the way?"

"She seems well enough. I spoke to her

yesterday when I arrived in Toronto. She said her doctor is letting her out of the hospital today and I'm supposed to pick her up the second she calls." He paused. "If I can find the hospital."

Smiling, I took off my gloves. "Oh good. If you landed yesterday, how come you just got here this morning? The airport's only an hour away."

Simon studied me before reaching to turn on the lamp. "I needed warmer clothing. You don't find many mittens in New Orleans. Heavens, *cher*, you're green."

"I'm taking a mix of seaweed and vitamins." I hesitated. "I have breast cancer."

"Are you using the Castor oil packs?"

"I am."

He pointed a finger at me when he asked, "And seeing your doctor?"

"Yes."

"Good call, *cher*, nothing like hitting it from all angles." He examined my hand. "That particular shade of green should wear off in a few days. It's some kind of reaction your body is having to whatever you're taking."

I swallowed hard. "Is that normal?"

The silence that filled the shop was deafening. My breath came in shallow, horrified gusts as my mind raced.

"No, but it's a great conversation starter."

Simon's laugh started as a throaty chuckle before increasing to a full-out roar. "Why are you listening to me, *cher*? I'm a financial planner."

"But you said you were a witch doctor."

"Only by the light of the full moon," he reminded me. "Now, about those dolls."

"Behind the counter. I saw them there after…" I closed my eyes. "Merilee and I were hoping to find out who her last patient was. Instead, we found dozens of little dolls in plastic drawers before the police kicked us out."

He shuddered. "You didn't find any chicken feet or alligator teeth, did you? Little cloth pouches of smelly stuff?"

"Just the dolls."

Simon nodded. "It might be a good idea to keep the store closed while I do an inventory. I don't want to take it over only to find there's a curse. Black magic's no fun to deal with. They make curses that are hard to break."

"Don't all witch doctors use black magic?"

"Not me or my auntie." He grinned. "We use the good stuff, love, peace, and healing vibes."

I chuckled. "While planning for a secure future."

Another hearty laugh escaped him as he pointed a thick finger at me. "That, too."

"I wasn't sure what to expect, but you're

nothing at all like Miss Lavinia."

He shrugged while he toyed with the tarot cards on the table. "We're more alike than you think. Her life's been much harder than mine though. She didn't become a practitioner because she wanted to. My auntie wanted to be a teacher, but her papa taught her everything he knew from the time she was a little crawdad and wouldn't let her make any mistakes or he'd beat her."

"That sounds harsh." I cringed.

"*Oui,* it was, *cher.* She hides nasty scars that wonderful lady. Don't ever tell her I told you." Simon glanced around the shop. "I don't suppose you know anyone who could help me out around here. I may need help to sort everything out and clean this place before she's back on her feet."

I had to agree. Looking around, I'd never noticed the layer of gray dust on the shelves before.

"Of course. Between Merilee and I, we're good at organizing." We were also good at poking our noses into other people's business, but I wasn't about to mention that. Last I saw Merilee she was pacing a groove in the floor. "Our craft shop is just a couple doors over and I should get back to work. I'll give you my number. Let me know when your aunt gets home. I'll stop by to see her when she's up for company."

Simon gave a nod of his head. "That I

will do, Miss Audra. Until then, I suppose I'll settle in and start cleaning."

As I left the curio shop, I got one of those weird tingles on the back of my neck. The ones that make you feel like someone's watching you even when no one's in sight. I shivered and had barely stuck my nose in the doorway of Stitch'n'Time before Merilee hammered me with questions.

"Was that Simon?" she asked. "How's Miss Lavinia and when does she come home? Is he taking over her store?"

I held up a hand. "I'm going to get coffee. Would you like one?"

"There are two sitting on the counter," she said. "I stopped at the deli when I saw him go into the shop. I didn't want to seem nosy and wasn't eager to meet him."

"You?" I feigned surprise.

She growled, "Spill it. What's he like and what's he doing here?"

I shucked off my coat and hung it up before I replied, "His name is Simon Brevil and he's Miss Lavinia's nephew from Louisiana. He's a financial planner by day and a witch doctor by the light of the moon."

"You're making that up."

"His words, not mine." I reached for my coffee. "He said Miss Lavinia should be home later today. He's just waiting for her to call before he heads to the hospital. In the meantime, he was tidying up and checking out her shop."

"Why haven't we ever seen him around town before?" she asked.

I shrugged as I took a sip. "Maybe she warned him the locals would look at him funny and scuttle off like cockroaches."

Her face reddened as she toyed with the lid of her coffee cup. "It was more the fact he filled the entire doorframe and scared the daylights out of me. The guy's huge and more than a little scary."

"It sounds like he scared the police, too," I told her. "They're afraid he'll put a curse on them."

Merilee grinned. "We could use that in our favour. Can he make voodoo dolls? I'm hoping we can offer a Christmas voodoo doll making class. Miss Lavinia didn't seem to think that was a clever idea, but Simon might."

"The guy just flew in from Louisiana," I reminded her. "Let him take off his coat before you start planning his entire itinerary."

"I suppose," she grumbled.

A steady stream of customers kept us hopping. Ten minutes before we planned to lock up for the day, I strolled toward the window to see how much snow had accumulated. At about the same time, Simon climbed into a cab in front of the bench out front.

My mind swirled with ideas. "It looks like Simon's going to pick up his auntie. Do you still have that key?"

"The one for the curio shop? Of course I do. My dad would kill me if I…" Merilee met my gaze before she said, "Oh! Let me get my coat."

"I'll be right back." I promised Drake then knelt in front of him to scratch his head. "If you're good, I'll give you a treat when we get back. Deal?"

He groaned and shifted before going back to sleep. He'd be ready for a run through the park by the time we went home.

The interior of the curio shop was still dim. Simon hadn't taken down the heavy fabric that covered the front window.

"Where do you want to start looking?" Merilee turned on a flashlight.

I held one hand to my churning stomach as I walked past a red curtain. Another storage area I didn't have the nerve to explore yet. "We need to find her records. There's no way she could've sold potions and powders to so many people without having sales, patient records, and more dolls. We won't have time to search, but if we figure out where they are, that might help."

She backed away from the counter and shone her beam into a corner in the back of the shop. The light illuminated a set of file cabinets. "Bingo. Wow, she's totally old school. No sign of a computer anywhere. Do you think she'll sell the shop and go back to Louisiana?"

"I'd be happier if she stayed. Did I tell you Rex came by the other day?"

"Rex was here?" she asked. "I thought he called her a witch doctor."

I went on to tell her about my husband's run-in with the front door of Miss Lavinia's shop when someone opened it, then added, "I don't think he told me the whole story. I found his doll, which means he's a patient. Either way, we need to find out what he's using before Drake loses his mind and eats his weight in quilting fabric."

Merilee frowned. "Did Rex say you could snoop through his file?"

"What could possibly be in it that I don't know about?" I gazed around the back room while Merilee opened one drawer. "Once we find out what Rex is using, we can search the files to see who else—"

"Are you nuts?" She closed the drawer then reached for another one. "That would take all night. She'll be home long before we get through the As."

Walking across the dark store, approached the shelves full of oils and leaned close to read the labels in the dim light. That scent on Rex's clothes was vaguely familiar, yet I just couldn't place it. Spicy and musty rolled into one. I thought I'd smelled something similar on Officer Trent, but I might've imagined it.

"I had a hunch I should check on my

crime scene," someone spoke from the front door. "I thought Simon locked up when he left."

Merilee shone her flashlight straight into Officer Trent's face. He held a paper bag in one hand and a gun in the other. "I have a key. My family owns the building."

I cleared my throat. "I don't think that's quite what he meant."

She knitted her brows together in bewilderment then sucked in a sharp breath. "Oh."

"It's okay," I told him. "We'll go. We just came in to check on things for Miss Lavinia. She asked us to water the plants."

Officer Trent glanced around the shop. "How? She was unconscious when you saw her and I don't see any plants."

Merilee and I exchanged glances before I gave a low whistle. "She must've hit her head harder than we thought. You should check in on her. Just to be on the safe side."

He holstered his weapon. "I'll be keeping an eye on you. Get out."

"Of course, officer." Merilee held her hands in the air and walked out the front door.

"What are you doing?" Officer Trent's face reddened.

I grinned then copied her. With my hands up, I walked past him into the falling snow leaving him cursing us both inside.

Officer Trent stormed past us and stalked to his car.

Merilee and I stood on the sidewalk with our arms raised to the sky. We exchanged glances before she called after him, "Should I lock up?"

When he got in to start his car, he held up one hand with a finger extended. We burst into surprised laughter as we lowered our arms.

"I wish I had a picture of that. Tony's never going to believe me." Merilee cackled as she reached into her pocket for her keys.

"I don't think I'll tell Rex about this little adventure."

She draped her arm across my shoulders. "It's not like we did anything wrong. I saw Rex's file."

My eyes grew wide. "What did it say? What did Miss Lavinia give him that makes Drake go crazy?"

She stumbled then huffed sending a white cloud in my direction. "No idea. I didn't get that far. I found the folder on the counter, but I didn't open it."

I closed my eyes and sighed. "Well, at least I know he lied to me about seeing Miss Lavinia. I wonder what else he's hiding."

We entered Stitch'n'Time just as Drake did a downward dog stretch and yawned.

Merilee paused to look around. "No shredded fabric. No piles of chewed thread.

Good boy, Drake."

He wagged his tail at the praise.

"What a good boy." I gave him a dog treat. "Should we go home?"

Drake barked a reply I hoped meant yes.

After he ran up and down the park twice, I coaxed him inside the house with the promise of a warm fire and dinner. I sat on the couch with a glass of eggnog—no rum since there was none in the house—and started to make a list of things we needed for the holidays. With both kids coming home two days before Christmas, I refused to be unprepared. I'd need to stock up.

Once I had a set of car keys.

"I'll bet the other set is in the desk drawer at his office." It wouldn't be the first time. Last time someone got hold of them and broke into our house. The thought still sent a wave of goosebumps up my arms. I needed to focus.

Turkey was a given. Maybe a ham. Definitely mashed potatoes. Cranberry sauce and gravy made the list as well. Ooh, and stuffing, of course.

My thoughts flowed from gravy and mashed potatoes to Miss Lavinia and Dave. The butcher shop had shut down during peak barbeque season. Was someone peeved about not getting a good cut of meat for the grill? It seemed odd for someone to follow Dave to her shop to kill him. Odder still they'd use Miss Lavinia's ceremonial dagger to do the deed. The connection eluded me.

A shiver ran down my back prompting me to get up to turn on the fireplace, glad I didn't have to chop wood. I stared into the dancing flames while I tried to recreate the crime in my mind. No matter how I tried to set the stage, nothing made sense. How could the killer sneak up behind Dave, stab him in the back, then strike Miss Lavinia over the head? Were there two killers? Again, not possible. Each victim would've seen at least one attacker.

My shopping list had become a crime scene doodle.

Flipping to the next page of my notepad, I refocused and started fresh. Turkey. Ham. Potatoes. More eggnog. Gravy. Cranberry sauce.

Where was the chalice and what was inside of it? I was positive I saw one that held some kind of liquid, yet Doc insisted it wasn't in the crime scene photos.

The red stain on Rex's shirt seeped back into my thoughts. I doubted it was cranberry sauce. Red wine was a more likely culprit since he was at a dinner meeting. Before I realized it, I'd added stain remover, wine, and a dress shirt to my list.

"Come on, Audra, focus." I turned the page to start fresh. This time I managed to stick to food and gift items. Most things could wait until the week before Christmas, except for the gifts and baking ingredients. All I needed was to recruit Rex to help with the shopping.

Drake padded toward the patio door.

"Good idea. Let's go for a walk," I set aside the notebook and headed to the front door. A break was in order for both of us.

He hesitated casting a wistful glance to the backyard. If he went out back, he could come back in a minute later to plop in front of the fireplace.

"Come on, boy." I held up the leash. A walk would give me time to think and burn off pent up energy.

My dog groaned, but let me clip the leash to his collar. Good sport that he was, he waited until we got to the street before he stopped and refused to move.

I gazed up at the shivering stars in the velvet sky muttering words I didn't want the neighbours to hear me say out loud. They had a certain opinion of me and raunchy wasn't it. Nosy, maybe.

"Can we please go once around the block?" I pleaded. "I need to think without wasting a dozen sheets of paper."

Drake whined before carrying on at a trot. His walk quickly became my run. Thankfully, the sidewalks had already been salted or I would've broken an ankle or worse. I became so focused on staying on my feet that I forgot about trying to think.

"You're late. Where were you?" a man's voice rang out.

Someone answered, but I couldn't make out what they said. Nor did I have any idea where the voices came from. Since the night was cold, sounds could carry for blocks.

Drake trotted past Judge Harry's house then rounded the corner  by Doc's. Lights were one in both homes, but we had no time for social calls. At the end of the block, he made another sharp left. To my dismay, he sped up.

"What is with you? Slow down." I puffed, gritting my teeth as I shortened his leash.

He jerked forward, pulling so hard I flailed my arms to keep my balance. We were halfway home. If he planned to walk like this all winter, I'd have to ask Santa for a toboggan.

"Don't lie to me," the man's voice cracked the fragile winter air once more.

Drake stopped to look back at me with his head tilted.

"I don't know where it's coming from either."

Convinced he was in immediate danger, my dog set off at a dead run without me. The leash bounced along the icy sidewalk behind him.

"Some guard dog you are," I grumbled. "Good thing you don't have a key."

I walked at my own pace until I rounded the last corner. Rather than quietly waiting for me on the porch, Drake pawed at the front door as if his life were in danger. His nails scraped at the metal sending an extra shiver over me. I'd never seem him act that way before and it scared me.

"What are you doing?" I asked as I climbed the front steps.

He whined and danced in circles around me.

"Okay, okay, settle down." Unlocking the front door, I let him inside then stared when he ran straight for the patio door. "Are you kidding me?"

Once I let him out, I returned to the comfort of the couch and drank one whole mouthful of eggnog before he barked at the glass.

"Seriously, dog. I'm starting to think you have—"

"Get in the house." The man's voice echoed through our backyard.

Drake obliged.

So did I.

I locked the door behind us and closed the blinds for good measure. "I don't know who that is, but he scares me, too."

We huddled on the couch together with Drake's head on my left leg. I placed a hand on his torso not surprised his heart raced as fast as mine. This was one of those nights were I wished my husband

was home to make us feel a lot…okay, a
wee bit safer. I pulled the throw blanket
over as much of my legs as I could while I
wondered who the man we'd heard was
yelling at.

# Chapter Nine

### Tuesday, November 29

I called Rex the next morning to see how his trip was going. No answer. He was probably in the shower. I left a quick message before Drake and I headed to Stitch'n'Time.

So far it seemed Officer Trent, Rex, and Joelle had all received similar treatments from Miss Lavinia. At least Drake reacted to them all the same way. I needed to figure out what the mixture was, what it was used for, and who else used the same blend. Oh, and how they were connected to Dave the Butcher. The biggest feat would be explaining why I needed access to Miss Lavinia's records.

A sign on the door of Miss Lavinia's shop read, "Back in 15 min." It seemed he intended to run things while she was on the mend. I strode past with the bank receipts in one hand and a coffee tray in the other. As I reached for the door to Stitch'n'Time, I nearly collided with Simon on his way out.

"Miss Audra, I came looking for you," he said, flashing a wide smile. "My auntie would like to chat with you."

I exhaled my relief. "That's great. I have things I need to ask her, too."

"Don't you dare stress her out or she'll put the *gris-gris* on you." He wagged a hot dog sized finger at me.

"I don't know what the *gris-gris* is, but I promise to behave."

Merilee took the coffees from me. "Simon said she's slowly starting to remember things."

Rather than wait politely at my feet for a treat, Drake jumped against my legs and nearly knocked me over. After his antics last night, I had second thoughts about giving him one.

I handed Merilee the food and stuck my hand in my coat pocket for a doggy treat. "I'm going to see Miss Lavinia. You stay with here and be a good dog. No eating the merchandise. Or my lunch."

"He'll behave," she said. "You go. We need more info for our board."

"What board?" Simon asked.

As I shot Merilee a frown, I asked, "How is your auntie by the way?"

"She thinks my name is Ivan and I'm a knife thrower from Istanbul. As much as I want to hear that story, I'm a bit afraid."

"A knife thrower, huh?" Merilee asked. "Maybe I'll have to stop by and ask for details. I love a little juicy gossip."

"Oh, no. I don't want to know." He held up his hands then covered his ears.

I smirked just to torment him. "Well, we do."

"Don't you have a project or a board to work on?" he asked.

"Just sorting fabric," Merilee said. "Now about that knife thrower—"

She and I burst into laughter when he reached for the door knob. Finally, she asked, "Are you okay, Simon? You seem a bit tense."

For a couple seconds, he looked like he'd burst into either a rant or tears then seemed to reconsider. "Nope. All is fine. If you don't mind a cranky, befuddled woman texting you every five minutes about the same darn thing."

"Befuddled?" Merilee asked.

"What? It's a good word," Simon said.

"Not when you use it to describe someone with a head injury." She shrugged. "The last time I heard it was from my eighty-five-year-old grandmother."

"You need to read more." I patted her arm.

Simon cleared his throat. "I tried talking to that police officer, the young one, but he's as befuddled as my auntie. All I wanted was to know more about the man they found in her shop.”

Merilee excused herself and headed into the back room. “Don’t leave until I get back. Just in case we get a customer.”

“His name was Dave Spencer,” I told him, leaning against the counter. “He used to own a butcher shop near the deli across the street until he and his wife divorced. After that, he went to work at the grocery store across town.”

Simon gave a low whistle. “Tough break.”

“I’ll say. I spoke to his wife, but she didn’t have any idea who’d want to kill him either.”

He paused, taking a deep breath before asking, “Did he blame Auntie Lavinia?”

“Blame her for what?” I couldn’t imagine what she had to do with Dave’s divorce.

“That poor man must’ve thought she’d cursed him,” he said.

“If he did, she’s the one who’d be dead, not him.” I clapped my hand over my mouth as soon as the words popped out of my mouth.

Simon nodded. “I had that same thought. There’s no way my auntie would do something like that, and if he’d tried to hurt her, the dagger would be in his chest not... You know.”

“Exactly. We might be looking for two suspects. One who hit your auntie and the other who stabbed Dave the Butcher.”

Simon's eyes grew wide. "Dave the Butcher?"

"It's a local thing."

"Because he owned a butcher shop. I see," he said. "How did the suspects, as you call them, get inside? Do you think one came in the front door and the other in back?"

"If that was the case, they had to have keys. Either way Miss Lavinia and Dave both know—knew—who they were since they each would've seen one intruder."

"It could be." He didn't sound convinced.

Did he know more than he was letting on?

"That's why we set up a suspect board. It helps us think it over a bit more."

Simon raised his eyebrows. "That sounds interesting. Can I help?"

"Do you know any of the locals?" I asked.

"No," he said, shaking his head. "I can ask my auntie. Something may trigger a memory."

"Did I hear someone mention our suspect board?" Merilee returned wiping her hands with a paper towel. "Good. We can add to it when you get back."

Simon led me toward the shop, then ushered me inside. He locked the door behind us, then steered me to the backroom then motioned to the red curtain I'd dismissed as a storage area.

"Go on up, *cher*, she's expecting you."
He pulled it back to reveal a set of stairs.

Definitely not a storage room.

"I had no idea these were here."

He chuckled. "It's not like you've spent much time searching the place." He paused. "Have you?"

I hesitated and averted my gaze before I told him, "I'll try not to stay too long."

"Miss Audra?"

As I climbed the worn wooden stairs, I had no idea what to expect behind the peeling white door at the top. A lone bulb trapped inside a multi-faceted, cut-glass cover lit the landing and gave the hundred-year-old stairwell a slightly derelict look.

Just as I raised my hand to knock, a voice inside rang out, "Come in, Audra."

Spooked, I gasped and turned the antique crystal doorknob with my heart racing. Stepping inside Miss Lavinia's apartment, I gazed around in stunned surprise. In stark contrast to the gloom of the store and stairwell, her apartment was bright and cheery. Colourful Christmas lights hung on every wall and hugged a four-foot artificial pine tree that stood in one corner near the front window sill which was covered by a jungle-like variety of plants.

Miss Lavinia stood in front of me dressed in a brightly coloured, flowery robe. She looked twenty years younger than I'd ever guessed she was. "I'm so glad you're here.

I wanted to speak with you about the other day."

"Same here. I also need to ask about a medication you mixed for Rex."

"Understandable, but confidential." She waved a thin hand toward two cushy-looking armchairs. "Sit with me. I made tea. I want to know what you saw when you found Dave and I. More than likely your questions will be similar to mine."

"Why do you say that?" I asked, shrugging off my parka.

"Because you know what happened after I collapsed but not before." Miss Lavinia hung my coat on a hook near the door then took my arm as she led me to our seats. The way she leaned on me, I realized she was more tired than she appeared, especially when she asked, "Would you mind getting the tea?"

I helped her to sit then poured us each a cup of tea and set in on the round table between the chairs. When I sank into the puffy fabric, I instantly relaxed. Heaven help me, but I could've fallen asleep right then.

She flashed a smile. "They're great chairs, aren't they?"

"Am I that obvious?" My face warmed.

"I've known you for years. I know when you're not taking care of yourself. Did Rex give you the powder he picked up the other day?"

"Yes, he did. Thank you. Did you remember anything more about the attack?"

She seemed to hesitate. "I don't know if I actually remember seeing something, or if it's more of a feeling. Everything is still so hazy."

"That must be scary. Are you okay?"

"I'll be fine," she said. "Just waiting for a couple more test results."

"Was there anyone else in the shop that morning? A friend or another client?"

Miss Lavinia sipped her tea. Her hand shook as she set her cup down. "I'll tell you what I told the police. I got up and had a cup of tea, then went downstairs. Dave asked to come by early since he needed to be at work before six o'clock then leave for Toronto when he finished work that afternoon."

"Did he say why?"

"I don't recall."

"Can I ask what you were treating him for?" I asked.

She hesitated before saying, "I suppose it can only help to get justice. The poor man suffered from sciatic pain for years. I made him an ointment that contained belladonna, which seemed to help. He also had nightmares ever since his wife left. I made him a sleep elixir that he said helped him relax, but I'm not so sure. He went through it at an alarming rate."

I met her gaze over my tea. "Is that unusual?"

"For most people," she said. "I was concerned that Dave seemed more agitated every time I saw him and doubted the elixir and the ointment were the only things he was using. I thought he might be self-medicating. When Simon told me someone stabbed him in the back, I wondered if..."

When her voice trailed off and she released a long, soft breath, I frowned. "If someone had stabbed him in the back both literally and figuratively? Like he owed someone for drugs."

Miss Lavinia leaned closer before she whispered, "If that dagger was meant for me."

Those weren't the words I expected to hear. My mind reeled, spiraling in a dozen different directions all at once. "You do know you and Dave look nothing alike, right?"

"You want to know what makes me think I was the target," she said. She cradled her cup in her hands as though trying to shake off a chill. "I remember someone saying, 'It's about time,' then Dave got this look on his face. Before I got a good look, I heard two pops. There was a sharp pain in my head before things went dark."

"Someone hit you over the head."

"I assumed the intruder shot us both. The bullet grazed my temple. Head wounds are horrible bleeders. Officer Grant thought that's when I collapsed and hit my head."

Woozy at the thought, I closed my eyes. So much for being a brilliant detective. "Oh wow. You could've died."

Miss Lavinia shrugged. "It's a good thing you came in when you did. The doctor says the stroke and the conk on the head did more damage than the bullet, but they caught it quickly."

"You had a stroke?"

She touched her face near the bandage on her temple. "That's why I collapsed."

I sank back into the cushy chair. "Why would someone shoot you both then then stab Dave? It makes no sense."

"Maybe it was a warning."

"About what?" I frowned.

Her face grew even paler. When she sat back, the large chair appeared to swallow her whole. "I wish I knew. If you don't mind, I need to rest now. I'll let you know if I remember anything else."

"Can I ask one more question?" I didn't bother to wait for her response. "Who's Ivan the knife thrower?"

Miss Lavinia burst into laughter. "How on earth did you hear about him?"

"Simon mentioned him."

"Ivan was my first boyfriend," she said, her eyes twinkling. "He came to New Orleans with the circus when I was sixteen. I skipped school for the whole week to spend time with him. Once he left town, we wrote to each other, but I never saw him again. Anything other burning questions?"

"No, I'll let you rest." I wriggled out of the chair then left her apartment.

Since Simon was no longer in the store, I let myself out.

Not only had someone shot Miss Lavinia, but she'd had a stroke. Fingers crossed that wouldn't affect her memory or her work. If Simon decided to take her home to Louisiana, it would be a huge loss for everyone in Sugarwood.

I shuffled toward Stitch'n'Time where Drake met me at the door and danced in a circle like he was expecting me, or treats. Before I could share what I'd learned with Merilee, I took him for a quick walk. My thoughts remained on Miss Lavinia. Once we returned, I joined Merilee at the front counter.

"How's she doing?" she asked softly as though reading my thoughts on my face.

"She's tired. The doctor figured she had a stroke and hit her head after she got shot." I recanted Miss Lavinia's version of events then leaned on the counter then rested my chin on my fist. "Things just don't add up."

Merilee pointed a finger at me. "That's why we need to start another suspect board. Did you ask about Ivan from Istanbul?"

I filled her in on the knife thrower before turning my focus to the suspect board. Known as a murder board in other circles, Merilee and I preferred to focus on the people not the action.

"Last time someone destroyed our board," I reminded her. "I don't feel like taping two thousand little bits of paper together again. Do you?"

"Good point. We could type it in the computer."

"I'm much better at piecing together Bristol board than computer parts."

She sat at the keyboard. "Humour me, will you? We can print off copies and fill in the board later. You talk, I'll type."

"Okay. We know Dave the Butcher was killed at the same time Miss Lavinia was grazed by a bullet then had a stroke before she struck her head."

Merilee glanced up. "Maybe Dave was killed before she came downstairs."

"Except she knew everything that happened up to then."

"Good point." She returned to typing.

I tapped my index finger to my lips. "We need to find out how Dave died. Miss Lavinia said she heard two shots. What if the killer shot Dave and used the dagger to throw off the police? There was a lot of blood. Maybe there was a second wound."

"We also need to find out if he was the intended target."

"What do you mean?"

She hesitated. "Tony and I have known Dave for years. He's the nicest guy you could ever meet and wouldn't hurt a fly. Why would anyone want to kill him?"

"People say that about murder victims all the time. Some turn out to be real scum bags, depending on who you talk to. Particularly ex-wives and children." I paused to consider her idea for a minute. "Do you think Miss Lavinia was the target and Dave was a witness?"

"Then why not make sure she was dead?" Merilee asked. "If someone wanted to kill Dave, there were a dozen better places to do it. Like behind the dumpster near the grocery store or at his apartment since he lived alone."

"You're right, but if they were after Miss Lavinia, why not knock Dave out and stab her?" I asked. "Officer Trent insists Simon's his lead suspect."

Merilee snorted. "Simon wasn't even in Sugarwood until before Miss Lavinia got out of the hospital."

"True, but if she had died—" The room fell so quiet I had to force in a breath. "We have no idea if he's her only living relative."

She narrowed her eyes. "Now you're reaching. We've been in that shop a million times. There's nothing of value there unless she's hiding gold bars in those doll boxes.

Besides, my family owns the building, not Miss Lavinia.”

“Speaking of, what would someone get from killing Dave?” I asked.

“Bupkis. The man was broke. So, until you get a chance to talk to Doc about how, we’re back to why.”

My shoulders sagged as I blew out a frustrated breath. “I could go to the deli and buy him lunch. He loves their pickles.”

Her eyes lit up. “Ooh, so do I. We should get a container to keep here.”

“Focus. We’re on a mission and you stopped taking notes five minutes ago.”

“You made me have a snack attack,” she said. “Now, I need pickles.”

Chuckling, I glanced at my dog. “Okay, but I can’t bring Drake with me. They won’t let him in the building no matter how much Doc likes him.”

“So, leave him here. We can brainstorm while you’re gone.”

“You’re going to brainstorm with my dog?” I asked with a chuckle. “Good luck. Just keep him out of the fabric bin. Our backyard’s starting to look like abstract art.”

Charity wasn’t behind the deli counter when I arrived, which was too bad. I needed all the help I could get. I was also looking forward to a bit of gossip. I ordered Doc’s favourite sandwich, one for me, and a tub of pickles. I’d pick up pickles for Merilee on the way back.

Once I arrived at the morgue, there was no sign of Sarah, Doc's daughter, who'd started working with him after her university graduation. Doctor Neil Griffith sat behind his desk eating an anemic white bread, bologna, and cheese sandwich. He discarded it in the trash when he saw the paper bag in my hand then rubbed his hands together.

"Audra, you're a godsend," he said. "My wife's visiting her brother and I haven't remembered to get groceries because of the bodies piling up."

I glanced at the bag in my hand and was suddenly revolted. "Bodies?"

He stuck out his hand and motioned with his fingers for me to hand over lunch. "Yup. First it was Dave then Molly Lavier appeared in my waiting room this morning."

My stomach churned as I glanced around his office. "You have a waiting room?"

"So to speak. She's keeping cool in a drawer," he said pulling out the pickles.

"Molly Lavier. Why do I know that name?"

He crunched into a dill spear. "Local activist, newspaper reporter, and busy body. I'm sure you've met her, or at least seen her in action."

"How did she die?" I asked.

Doc shrugged. "It appears to be heart failure, but I'll have a better idea once I dig into her after lunch."

I decided to save my sandwich until later.

"Why's your skin green?" he asked. "Have you been taking one of those weird potions from Miss Lavinia?"

Heat seeped into my cheeks as he offered me a pickle. I took one, partly to be polite, but mostly to keep my hands busy. "Yes."

"Stop it. See your doctor." He wagged a mayo-covered finger in my direction.

"I already saw my doctor," I told him. "He wants me to..."

Doc's thick eyebrows rose when I stuffed the pickle in my mouth and didn't continue. After a minute, he got up and strode across the ten-by-ten office to close the door. Once he'd settled comfortably with another pickle, he asked, "What's the prognosis?"

"Excuse me?"

"I'm a doctor, Audra, don't play dumb with me. Does he want you to do chemo and radiation?" When tears swelled in my eyes and I couldn't answer, he asked,

"Has he done a biopsy yet?"

Again, I could only nod. It was the first time I'd heard Doc swear when he wasn't in his backyard getting stuck by rose thorns. He used the rare opportunity to drop an f-bomb.

"You're dealing with cancer, yet you're questioning me about the dead man you found in Miss Lavinia's shop?" Doc stared before he peeled the foil off his sandwich. The longer he chewed and stared, the more I squirmed.

"Dave's death wasn't due to the dagger or the poison on the blade," he finally said. "It was a bullet wound straight to the heart from behind."

"Poison, a dagger, and a bullet?" I wasn't sure which to react to first.

He continued, "Your death, young lady, will be due to sheer negligence. Let the police do their job. You need to stop chasing shadows and look after yourself."

Another wave of humiliation burned my cheeks. "That's what I was trying to do. The only reason I stopped by to get more green powder. That's when I found them."

"Uh-huh. What does Rex have to say about you ignoring medical science in favour of green powder?" He smirked.

I tensed from head to toe. "In the few hours I've seen him this week, he told me to stay away from the witch doctor."

Doc's expression softened. "I see. Is he still on the road with Andrew Laney?"

Picking at an errant cuticle on my right thumb, I sighed. "More than ever. He says he's negotiating with Andrew to sell new homes on the farmland they purchased near the hospital. So far, he's been to more business meetings than ever and things don't seem to be slowing down."

"You don't think he's having an affair, do you?"

Doubt shot through me. He wasn't the first person to ask that lately. My mistrust of my husband felt like a rock in my stomach. "I've accused him of that before and I was wrong. I just need to trust he's doing the right thing."

"And look after yourself."

While Doc licked mustard off his thumb, a thought struck me. Something he said earlier that I'd nearly forgotten after his reprimand. "You said someone shot Dave. What kind of bullet was it?"

"Audra, really?"

"Humour me."

"It was from a handgun," he said. "A Glock G48 Semi-Auto Pistol to be exact."

The little hairs on the back of my neck seemed to stand on end. "Are those legal in Canada?"

"Yes, they are."

"Will the police be able to track down the owner?"

Doc bit into a pickle. "If it's registered or used in another crime, if not it'll be a bit more difficult. Are you saving that other sandwich for later?"

I waved a hand. "Go ahead. I've lost my appetite. You said it could've been the bullet or the poison. What kind of poison did you find?"

"Still waiting on the lab for that one," he replied.

"But you have an idea."

"Nothing I want or can share at the moment." A sharp knock at the door made him flinch. "Ah, my next appointment is here."

I stared wide-eyed. "You schedule bodies?"

He chuckled as he rose from his chair. "This one is among the living and you already know each other."

Officer Grant stood in the hallway. His smile drooped into a scowl when he saw me. "I should've known. Goodbye, Audra."

"I'll let you know how things go, Doc." I grabbed my purse and headed for the door.

Doc took hold of my arm pulling me into a hug as he whispered, "Please be careful."

As I made my way back to the deli to pick up a second lunch for Merilee and I as well as another tub of pickles, I paused in front of the office for the Sugarwood Advertiser. Founded in the 1930s, the newspaper came out every Thursday. If someone here didn't know what was going on, I'd be shocked. Crossing my fingers, I hoped they'd be able to tell me who placed the ad for the sale at Miss Lavinia's shop. Worst case, I'd price out advertising for Stitch'n'Time.

"Hello, how are you today?" a woman wearing cat's eye glasses with bright pink rims asked as she flashed a smile.

"Good, thanks." I debated on whether to be blunt or ask for pricing first.

She eyed me for a split second before she said, "Oh. You own the craft shop. It's Audra, right? I just love all the great projects I've bought there."

Odd how I didn't recognize her. Then she slid off her glasses.

"Mara. The glasses threw me."

"I only use them for reading, working on the computer, and crafts," she said. "Sorry I haven't been in for a while. Life's been busy. Is there something I can help you with?"

Now that we had a connection, I dove in head first. "I saw Miss Lavinia's ad about closing her shop and wondered when she placed it."

Her pink lips parted. "I heard what happened to her. It's so awful. Is she okay? I mean, I know Dave isn't, but I heard someone hit her on the head. I'll be surprised if she remembers anything. You're the one who found them, aren't you? I told my boss they should interview you, but I guess he forgot."

"Yeah, I stopped by to pick something up and…" I paused and waved a hand at a loss for words. "There they were."

Mara rose from her desk and ran around to give me a hug. "Aww, honey, I'm so sorry you had to see such an awful thing. I mean, I know you found the cowboy at Halloween, but he wasn't really a local. Didn't you help solve his murder?"

I cleared my throat. "Yes."

"I'm sorry," she said. "You came in about advertising and here I am going on and on."

Glancing around us, I lowered my voice and asked, "I don't suppose you can tell me when Miss Lavinia placed that ad that ran on Saturday."

Mara winced then returned to her seat. "Oh, I should call her. After what happened, I doubt she's up to selling things off any time soon, is she?"

"She may have to delay that for a week or two."

"Hopefully, before the building sells," she said.

I raised my eyebrows. "Excuse me?"

Mara met my gaze then typed as she talked. "Well, I assume that's why she's moving. There's such a high demand for all those old buildings lately, I can't keep track of who owns them. The way Laney Developments is going, the whole downtown core will be steel and glass condos with boutiques in the next five years. If you ask me, it's going to kill our small town charm. Oh."

When she didn't continue, I tried to peer over the waist-high counter to see her screen. "What is it?"

"I shouldn't say, but with you being a detective and all…" She hesitated, biting her lower lip as though chewing off her bubble gum pink lipstick. "Miss Lavinia didn't place that ad."

The floor seemed to fall away from beneath me as I asked, "Who did?"

"Whoever took the order didn't enter a name and it was a cash purchase."

I frowned. "Then how do you know Miss Lavinia didn't place the order?"

"Because every other order on her account has a scanned copy of the order form with her name and signature." She stood again. "Give me a sec. I'm going to find her file in case someone just didn't enter it properly."

When Mara disappeared around the corner, I leaned on the counter. If someone else had posted an ad to sell her inventory, they must've tried to speed up the entire process. But why kill Dave?

"This is so weird." Mara returned flipping through a file folder.

"What is?"

She slid a piece of paper onto the counter. "The signatures don't match up. Which means someone else placed the order for that ad. I just want to make sure you see what I see before I call the police."

Scanning the handwritten order form, I wasn't sure what she meant until I reached the signature at the bottom.

"Dave Spencer?" I asked, meeting her gaze. "Why would Dave place an ad for a closing out sale at Miss Lavinia's shop?"

"Search me, honey, but it smacks of motive, doesn't it?"

I itched to take it to show Merilee. "Could you make me a copy of this?"

"Absolutely," she said, "as long as you promise not to mention it to the police."

Considering I'd be in more trouble than her, I nodded. "You have my word."

* * *

Merilee and I munched pickles while we tried to figure out why Dave Spencer would put an ad in the newspaper on Miss Lavinia's behalf. I'd managed to regurgitate everything I'd learned from both Doc and the Sugarwood Advertiser that afternoon while Merilee typed. We were still processing the latest information when the door to Stitch'n'Time burst open wide.

Simon closed it with one foot then lumbered across the wood floors carrying a white plastic tote bin two feet long and about a foot deep.

"Thank you for visiting my auntie," he said. "She texted me when you left and scared me as much as these did. At first, I thought they were bits of fabric, but they're not."

Merilee and I exchanged glances. So much for staying out of things. We both knew full well what was inside.

He shuddered as he set the box on the counter. "Voodoo dolls. Dozens of the creepy little things each in their own little cardboard coffins. The sight of 'em makes me want to go back to accounting."

"Oh no," Merilee said, backing away. "Those things give me the heebie-jeebies."

Drake crept into the other room while emitting a low growl. He refused to remain in the same room.

"I know what they are, but what does my auntie use them for?" he asked.

"Each doll represents one of her clients," I told him. "She treats the person initially then does follow-up treatments on the dolls. Mine's at home."

Simon took a large step back and whispered, "What do I do with them?"

Merilee folded her arms across her stomach. "You don't do anything with them without asking Miss Lavinia first. You don't want her putting a hex on you."

"A hex?" I raised my eyebrows.

"The *gris-gris*," he said.

"What if…?"

She clapped her hand over my mouth. "Don't start. She wasn't attacked because she put a hex on someone. Get that thought out of your head."

I chuckled. "It was worth a shot."

"An unsettling thought, thank you very much," Simon headed toward the door. "I'll leave you to it then."

"Leave us to what?" I asked.

"To figure out who those little people are while I clean. That place is dustier than the Sahara."

Merilee frowned. "Why us?"

"Because you know everyone in town and I'm only here until my auntie is well again," he said with a small wave.

We both stared after him until Drake gave a low growl. The hackles on his back rose as he stood in the doorway to the back room.

"I'm with Drake. Those things make me nervous." Merilee busied herself with straightening up the shop. She tried to keep as far away from the bin as possible.

"Should I take them in the other room?"

"Do whatever you want with them," she said. "The farther away the better."

Ever the nosy one, I carried the bin into the back room and set it on the small table. I unsnapped the lid to reveal dozens of small embroidery boxes we'd given Miss Lavinia over the years. I reached in a tentative hand and pulled out one of the boxes.

We'd figured out Miss Lavinia's organizational system out when the cowboy died. The first numbers on the boxes were the dates the people started treatments. The last numbers we preferred not to think about. Luckily, these only bore one number. These were dolls of the living. Too bad they hadn't come with names.

When I opened one of the smaller boxes, I gasped. The doll had red pendent similar to the one Simon wore and a gold fleck on one ear. Did he wear an earring? I tried to picture him. My preoccupation with my diagnosis was causing my observational skills to slip. The doll wore blue jeans and a black shirt. If it had a red sweater, I would've run out the back door.

"Doesn't this look like Simon?" I asked, holding it up.

"Okay, that's creepy. Simon wasn't even in town until days after someone attacked Miss Lavinia." Merilee shuddered.

I chuckled. "Mer, he's her nephew. She's known him his entire life. Maybe she made one because she missed him or was treating him for something."

"Maybe. There's no way I'm asking his medical history. Do you think these things really do work?" she asked softly as she reached for the voodoo doll.

"Do you want to stick a pin in it to see if he gets back pain? I didn't even think to test

Rex's when I brought it home. It's still in my purse."

Drake lifted his head off his paws and gave a concerned whimper.

Merilee patted his head. "You're safe, buddy, she doesn't have a doll of you."

With a sigh, he settled near the heat vent.

"Is it possible to kill someone using a voodoo doll?" Merilee asked.

My stomach lurched. "How would that be possible? There's no way that dagger could've fallen into Dave's back. Some things require an earthly hand."

"Stranger things have happened," she said. "What else did Miss Lavinia say?"

"That Dave got a strange look on his face before someone shot them." I paused. Had he seen a reflection of the killer or recognized their voice? I didn't recall seeing any mirrors or other reflective surfaces in the shop. "Why didn't he do anything?"

"Simon?"

"Dave. They both heard someone come in, but neither of them ran or fought back."

Merilee gazed into the plastic bin. "So either they didn't have a chance, or neither one felt threatened."

"Or they couldn't. Maybe someone tied up their voodoo dolls."

She rolled her eyes. "Now you're reaching."

The problem was we didn't have the dead man's doll. In order to find it, we'd have to dig through a couple thousand small boxes. Could there be a doll of Miss Lavinia out there? I couldn't imagine her making a doll in her image.

"If you find Officer Trent's doll, let me know," Merilee said. "I'd have fun poking it with needles."

"We already gave it to him when he caught us in Miss Lavinia's shop." I grinned. As I put the lid back on the bin, I wondered if the killer could be one of Miss Lavinia's patients. Chances were Merilee and I knew them. Suddenly, I didn't like the direction my thoughts were taking.

Why would Dave place the order for a sale at Miss Lavinia's to sell off her belongings, or had he? Off the top of my head, I made two guesses. Clandestine affair, or blackmail. Neither seemed right.

Then there was that latest body in the morgue. I didn't know much about Molly Lavier, but I had a gut feeling it was time to do more digging.

I tried to call Rex again that evening, but didn't bother to leave a message. The thought of stabbing his doll in the back with a needle gave me pleasure, even if I couldn't bring myself to do it. Instead, I put on a Hallmark movie and settled on the couch to finish Drake's stocking.

# Chapter Ten

### Wednesday November 30

I was about to push open the front door of the deli the next morning when I spied a familiar figure at the counter. Officer Trent stood next to a young woman wearing a purple parka with black trim. She seemed familiar, but I couldn't place her. I waited until they took a seat in the back corner before I stepped into the deli.

The pair didn't exactly seem engrossed in conversation. In fact, it looked more like an interrogation from my vantage point. The cop did all the talking. The girl seemed unimpressed.

"Audra?"

"Huh?" I faced Charity with wide eyes.

She smirked. "What can I get for you?"

I placed the breakfast order for Merilee, Drake, and I before nodding my head toward the young woman in the purple coat. "Who's that with Officer Trent?"

"Dave Spencer's daughter, Bree," she said. "She just got into town."

"Did they announce a date for the funeral

already?" I asked brushing all thoughts of a will reading out of my head. According to rumours, his ex-wife got everything already.

Charity shook her head. "I haven't heard anything. He doesn't have much family except Joelle and the kids, so I doubt they'll do a big service. More like a little gathering at the funeral home. He wasn't exactly religious, you know."

I asked for a glass of water. "I'll wait over here for my food."

"It'll be up in a minute," she said then paused. "Oh. I'll take my time."

Avoiding the cop's gaze, I slid into the booth behind the young woman in time to hear her say, "I didn't hate my father. We just didn't see eye to eye on a lot of things."

"Like what?" Officer Trent asked.

There was a brief silence before she replied, "Why don't you tell me why we're meeting in a coffee shop and not the police station? You obviously think I know more than I do, or had something to do with his murder, so just come out with it."

He cleared his throat. "Out with what?"

"Asking where I was the morning he was killed. What motive I had to kill him. What I had to gain from his death. Isn't that how you normally interrogate someone?" she asked.

"Since you already know all the questions, why don't you answer them?"

She chuckled. "Because even I know you

should be videotaping our conversation and transcribing it. I watch enough cop shows to know whatever I say will be your word against mine."

I grinned. I liked her already.

When someone moved behind me, I bowed my head over my glass of water.

Officer Trent stopped next to me and glared. "Did you hear everything you expected? Next time, just come and sit with us."

My face burned as he stormed out of the deli.

"You know that jerk?" Bree asked behind me.

I turned to face her and was caught off guard. She had Joelle's bright green eyes, but her hair was dirty blonde on top with a rainbow of colours underneath.

"Not really," I admitted. "I just met him a few days ago. I'm Audra."

"The craft store lady." When I flinched in surprise, she added, "That creep my mom's with talks about your building all the time. He wants to buy it and a couple other ones on the block to build condos. Mom mentioned he's having a dispute with Laney Developments and the town over zoning or something."

For once, I kept my mouth shut. Merilee's family owned Miss Lavinia's building as well as the one I rented space in. Mr. Ossington, as far as I knew from when the cowboy died, owned the one in between. Why hadn't Merilee mentioned any offers on the buildings, especially from Laney?

Bree placed a hand on my shoulder. "Is it something I said? You don't look well."

"No, actually, you gave me an idea. Thanks." I headed toward the counter.

Charity handed me a bag. "You look like you're onto something."

I set my half full glass on the counter. "Who owns the building Mr. Ossington had his rental shop in?"

"Next to yours? I thought he did. Why? What did she—?"

"Gotta go. I need to talk to Merilee. I'll fill you in later."

Charity nodded. "Okay. Oh, hey, I put an extra treat in there for, Drake. Bring him by sometime, will ya?"

"Definitely." I left the deli and didn't realize anyone was following me until I reached the lights to cross the street.

A woman in a black and purple parka reached pushed the button. "Who's Drake?"

"My dog."

"Was it something I said?" she asked. "You don't think Chuck had something to do with my dad's death, do you? I mean the guy's a bas…a jerk, but he can't even tie his shoes without my mom's help."

I doubted that was true but had a hunch Bree Spencer might know more than even

Officer Trent guessed. "Why would Chuck want to buy my building?"

Bree shrugged. "Ya got me. All I know is the last time I was on the phone with my mom he was yelling in the background about how he wasn't going to let a low-life butcher ruin a good thing. At first, I thought my dad was causing them problems. Then I realized they'd already taken him for everything he had except one thing."

This time I paid full attention. "What's that?"

"The property he would've inherited if Grandpa died before he did."

My heart did a little two-step in my chest. "Where's your grandpa's property?"

"Right there." Bree pointed directly ahead of us.

The whole reason for Dave's murder and the attack on Miss Lavinia was right in front of me the whole time. Mr. Ossington's building between Stitch'n'Time and Miss Lavinia's shop.

"Jake Ossington is your grandpa? I haven't seen him lately. Is he okay?"

"Dad's death's been hard on him. The lady at the senior's home says he stays in his room. I'm worried about him, which is why I came back to town. We're a lot alike."

As she followed me into Stitch'n'Time, I winced. Mr. Ossington wasn't the only one I was worried about. Chances were once he passed away, the building would be shared equally between Bree and her brothers. None of them needed to be dinner for the scavengers that bought and sold real estate without a second thought to the impact their deals had.

"It's about time," Merilee said waving a hand toward a mangled pile of cloth. "I was trying to pull out the tables and chairs while he decided it was buffet time. Even treats didn't stop him."

"One of Charity's breakfast sandwiches will help." I set the bag on the counter and dug into it.

Merilee glanced at the woman behind me then flashed a customer service smile. "Hi. Sorry about the mess. How can we help you?"

"I'm with her," Bree said.

Merilee raised her eyebrows. "Oh?"

"This is Dave and Joelle's daughter, Bree. I ran into her at the deli," I told Merilee. Once I'd opened a sandwich and handed it to Drake, he carried it to the heat vent.

"Good thing you got your mom's looks," she said.

Bree laughed. "And my dad's big heart. Too bad I didn't realize that sooner."

"Did you know Dave was Mr. Ossington's son?" I asked Merilee.

Her mouth fell open. She closed it quickly as if biting back a swear word or two. "For real? I've known both of them for years and never had a clue."

Toying with her necklace, Bree met my gaze. "Mom told me they were estranged for years. Grandpa couldn't stand the fact his son was a butcher. Dad didn't like that Grandpa left Grandma before I was born. We tried to get them to patch things up, but one was as stubborn as the other. I'm no better. I haven't cut my mom any slack after the way she treated my dad."

Merilee placed a hand on her puffy coat sleeve. "That's what kids are for. To keep us on our toes. Are you staying at your mom's place while you're here?"

"At Charity's B and B. I could stay with my mom, but…" She paused, glancing around the store. "I don't like Chuck. Mom and Dad's divorce was inevitable, but this wasn't how things should've happened. Mom got sucked in by the money and the promises. She shouldn't be with a bully like Chuck Benson. I'd better go. I told her I'd call her after I saw that cop. She'll be glad to hear it was over before it began."

The second Bree left Merilee grabbed my arm. "What did you hear? Spill it."

"There's nothing to tell. Bree refused to talk to him in a coffee shop and demanded to have their conversation videotaped at the station. I'm not sure if that's because she had something to say, or because he made her uneasy."

Merilee reached for her coffee. "My

vote's on the latter."

* * *

My eyes burned from staring at the computer screen for a couple hours after we'd set up the tables. I'd managed to dig as deep as I could into Dave Spencer, Mr. Ossington, Laney Developments, and Chuck Benson before the first of our sewing circle ladies walked in. Nothing that made my hair stand on end.

The sewing circle ladies had barely settled with their projects when the front door opened wide. A tall man in a thick, blue parka stepped inside and kicked the snow off his boots while letting in swirls of snow. All conversation came to an abrupt halt.

Maddie pressed her shoulder against mine as I took the bags out of a pot of tea. "Now this guy doesn't look like one of your usuals. Look at him, he's huge and..." She lowered her voice to add, "Black."

I glanced up and flashed a smile, ignoring her comment. "Oh, hey, Simon."

Every woman in the group seemed to either poke their fingers or drop their needles at the exact same moment. I wasn't sure if it was his size, his colour, or that he was Miss Lavinia's nephew that caught them all off guard.

"Miss Audra." He pulled back the hood of

153

his coat and threw his arms open wide. "I thought I'd check in on the…inventory I brought yesterday, but you have your hands full. Did I mention you have a nice shop? Very warm and inviting."

"You're fine. Ladies, this is Miss Lavinia's nephew Simon Brevil," I announced. "He's staying in Sugarwood for a while to help her out."

Maddie frowned. "You are?"

"Is that okay?" he asked.

"Of course it is," Merilee said then paused. "I meant to ask if you practice the same kind of naturopathy Miss Lavinia does. She has devoted patients who don't deal well with change."

Maddie gave no response except a twitch of her cheek.

"Naturowhatnow?" he asked raising his eyebrows.

I shot him a glare. "He's kidding. She taught him everything he knows."

"All except manners, *cher*." Simon reached over to snag a cookie off the plate.

"Great." Merilee rolled her eyes. "We work next door to a giant witch doctor with no manners. I hope you don't have a bad temper. I don't want to end up as a toad."

He gave such a deep, throaty laugh that everyone at the quilting tables went from furtive gawking to flat out staring. "I assure you, Miss Merilee, what I lack in manners, I make up for with a great sense of humour."

She chuckled. "Well, if you're going to hang out around here, that'll come in handy."

"Excuse me, dear." Carol waved a hand. "I'm still waiting for my tea."

"A life of servitude is not what we signed up for. No wonder the church kicked them out," Merilee muttered as she carried the teapot toward the table to serve them.

"Can I help you with something, Simon?" I asked.

He glanced around the shop. "Now that you mention it, I need fabric for spells my auntie needs to cast. Colour doesn't really matter, just no flowers. Something plain."

"Spells?" Carol forgot her desperation for tea as she strolled toward Simon. Even though she was less than half his size, she gazed up at him with wide brown eyes. "Are you a witch?"

"Witch doctor, *cher*. Who might you be?"

"I'm Carol. I have an appointment with Miss Lavinia every Thursday morning at ten," she said. "I trust you'll be there to look after me tomorrow. She makes sweet tea and gives me voodoo cookies."

I covered my mouth to keep from saying anything I'd regret until after she'd gone back to sit at the table. "Do you have any idea what she's talking about?"

Simon shrugged. "I need to have a chat with my auntie. If her regular patients are coming to the shop whether she's there or not, I could be in for some serious tongue lashings. Just between us, I don't bake."

"Looks like you might have to start." Merilee grinned.

"*Mais!* Speaking of baking, I'll be right back." He made a hasty retreat out the door.

Maddie walked toward the counter. She poured a cup of tea before she met my gaze. "By the way, Audra, I like your husband's new secretary. Easy on the eyes."

"What?" I nearly dropped my cup.

"Let me tell you. This is one secretary I'd be happy to talk to on the phone all day. Voice like buttery suede," she said, batting her eyes.

Why didn't Rex tell me he had a new secretary? Not that I phoned his office often, nor was I the jealous type, but the surprise threw me for a loop. One more curveball like that and I wouldn't hesitate to let Drake chow down on the rest of Rex's suits. Maybe I'd stick a couple needles in his voodoo doll after all.

Jenny Sampson tossed a wadded ball of paper towel at Maddie. "Oh stop. He's barely old enough to vote."

"Rex?" I asked.

Maddie returned to her needlepoint. "His new secretary. Armando."

His new secretary was a man?

Jenny huffed. "That has to be a fake

name. I'll bet his parents called him Arnold or something equally as nasty when he was born, and he hated it."

"My husband's name is Arnold," Carol said. "It's a fine name."

Judy Wells chimed in, "Yes, but Armando is so much sexier."

When I met Merilee's gaze, she struggled to not burst into laughter. "It's better than some names, I guess."

The door opened once more. Simon stepped inside with a round green tin. "Oh good, you're still here. I thought I might be too late. My auntie felt good this morning, so she made cookies for y'all."

Maddie's eyes grew wide as Simon held out the container. "Those look like Miss Lavinia's voodoo cookies."

All six women practically lunged from their seats and nearly got into a fist fight over who got the tin first.

"Those must be some cookies," Merilee mused as we moved out of the way.

"You betcha, sister," Carol said.

Simon shrugged. "I suppose. They're chocolate chip. Nothing special."

Once everyone had grabbed at least two cookies, they either nibbled on one or squirreled both away into their bags and returned to their crafts. Their chatter turned to talk of snow and Christmas while I cleared the empty tin off the counter.

"Those must be darn good cookies." I

replaced the lid then handed the empty green container to Simon.

He held up his hands. "All I know is she told me to take the blue tin straight here. I never got to taste one."

Merilee frowned pointed to the green container in his hands. "Um, Simon? That's not a blue tin."

His smile faded. "Oh dear."

"It's okay. I'm sure the cookies all taste the same." I tried to console him.

When Simon's phone buzzed, he checked the screen. "Oh no. I have made a horrible mistake, Miss Audra. Those cookies…"

"What about them? What's wrong?" I asked.

"You should keep an eye on the ladies in case of…uh…any unusual activity."

Merilee leaned toward us. "What kind of unusual activity?"

"Trust me. You'll know." He reached for the door and winced before he left.

"That boy worries me," she said. "I hope the cookies aren't tainted with salmonella. We only have one bathroom."

It wasn't long before we noticed a shift. At first, there was a lull in the energy level. Then Maddie began singing show tunes. Apparently, Cats was her favourite musical. Jenny tried to sing along, but didn't know the words, or any words for that matter. She seemed at a loss when it came to clear thinking.

"Audra," Carol called before she slapped a hand on the table. "Why are there spiders crawling all over the table?"

"It's November, honey, there are no spiders," Merilee said.

She smacked the tabletop like she was playing Whack-a-Mole. "Oh, yes there are. I see at least three more."

"What on earth's going on?" I asked.

Merilee chuckled. "I think those cookies are edibles. Simon brought cookies laced with cannabis, not chocolate chips."

A brief shot of horror swept through me until Judy began to chuckle. Her deep belly laugh resounded through the store and soon had us all in stitches. Even Carol seemed to forget all about the imaginary spiders.

"This can't be good." I tried to straighten up but couldn't stop laughing.

Merilee nudged me "Too bad we missed out. They'd help you relax."

"Yeah, but we know where to get them. No wonder Simon booked it out of here so fast." I paused. "I wonder where the green tin was supposed to go."

"No idea," she said, "but those vultures snapped them those cookies up like they knew what was in them."

I chuckled. "They did, didn't they? We'd better make sure no one's driving home. We don't want to be responsible for any accidents."

Her eyes grew wide. "That's right. They're under the influence on our watch. We have to be designated drivers."

"Not exactly the kind of home delivery service we had in mind, is it?" I asked. "When word gets out about this, we might get a surge in the size of the sewing circle."

Merilee pressed her lips together as her shoulders shook. She tried not to laugh but couldn't contain it. "Tony's not going to believe this one."

"At least Tony will just laugh."

"Yeah, and then ask why I didn't bring him a cookie," she said. "Don't worry, Audra, Rex'll laugh, too. Just on the inside. Until you ask him about his secretary with a buttery voice."

I brushed that thought out of my head as we helped the sewing circle bundle up their crafts and get ready to go home. We made sure to kill any imaginary spiders along the way to the door. After we'd sent the majority off in cabs or with spouses, we were down to two women who'd driven downtown that day. Jenny and Maddie.

Jenny lived farthest away, so we took both cars to drop her off. Once she was home safe, Merilee hoped into Maddie's car with us. Maddie lived six blocks from the store, so we dropped her off before walking back to fetch Drake. We laughed about our latest adventure all the way back to

Stitch'n'Time—until we saw the front door open wide.

"What now?" I asked as we broke into a careful run on the ice.

"Please tell me we didn't forget anyone inside," Merilee said.

"Just Drake," I puffed, vowing to cut back on cookies. After Christmas.

Apparently, leaving the dog unattended in the store wasn't one of our better ideas. Drake growled with his teeth bared and saliva dripping to the floor. His full focus was on an intruder while voodoo dolls lay scattered all over.

"Get this thing away from me!" Officer Trent struggled to pull himself on top of the counter without taking his gaze off the angry dog.

"What are you doing in here?" I grabbed Drake's collar and smoothed his hackles.

"I'm glad you're here. That beast wanted to kill me," he said, lowering his feet to the floor then straightening his coat.

Merilee closed the door. "Wishful thinking. At most, he would've shredded your pant legs. What are you doing in here?"

He stammered to catch his breath. "The door was locked, and the lights were out, but I saw someone inside. It turned out to be your dog."

"If the door was locked, how'd you get inside?" I asked.

"Did I say locked? I meant it was closed, not locked."

Merilee sputtered. "There's no way."

I reached into my pocket for my keys one hundred percent sure I'd locked the door when we left. I'd even peeked back at Drake through the mail slot.

"Thanks for checking. We'll make sure it's locked next time we leave," I assured him.

"But I'm positive we…" Merilee waved toward the door.

As he walked past me on his way out, Drake took one last lunge at his ankle. I caught a whiff of the same scent Rex wore lately that drove my dog crazy. That was the biggest reason Drake pinned him to the counter. I was impressed he hadn't sampled a pant leg.

Once Officer Trent was gone, Merilee strolled around the shop. "Do you think someone told him about the cookies?"

"If he did, he's too late. Simon and the sewing circle took all the evidence. He can't prove we ever had them."

"That doesn't make me feel any better," she said.

Snapping Drake's leash onto his collar, I wrapped it around my hand while I looked around. "They sure did a number on the voodoo dolls. It doesn't look like Drake ate any though. He just scattered them all over."

Merilee took the leash while I scooped the dolls back into the bin. For some odd reason, three were piled near the garbage can. Each one smelled the same as Rex's suit. I stuck them into a plastic bag to show Miss Lavinia later then dragged the bin into the backroom.

Once I'd made sure the rear exit was locked, I shut the door to the back room. "They can hang out in there tonight. We'll deal with them tomorrow."

"Why did you put those dolls in a bag?" she asked.

"They have the same smell as Rex's suit. I want to ask Miss Lavinia about them tomorrow."

"Tony's here." She draped an arm across my shoulders. "Come on. We'll give you guys a ride home. It's been a weird day."

Drake barked and backed away from her.

I patted his back. "Thanks, but the boss says we'll walk. He could use the exercise and I need time to think."

"Okay. Call me if you need anything," she said.

"Thanks. I will." We both made sure the door was locked.

Drake tugged me to the left, away from Tony's big black truck. On our way home, we strolled through the park which stretched away from Main Street and wrapped around to the far end of Springer

Street where we lived. The night was cold, but the feathery flakes of snow and white draped trees helped me forget the strangeness of the day. My dog meandered from one ornate metal bench to the next. It seemed the dogs in Sugarwood were busy lately. They'd left fresh marks everywhere.

I didn't mind our lack of progress. Thoughts of the women's reaction to the cookies made me grin, but there were several other things on my mind. Like why someone wanted to kill Dave the Butcher. Why they'd spare Miss Lavinia, only grazing her head and not making sure she was dead. Whether Dave's death was planned, or if he'd simply been in the way. And if Rex and I should consider moving.

It would sure help if someone had witnessed everything and could remember the details. The fact someone had shot, poisoned, and stabbed Dave bothered me. Why use all three methods when one was effective? And why leave Miss Lavinia alive?

"Hello, Miss Audra," a deep voice said.

I'd been so distracted I hadn't heard footsteps coming toward me. "Hey, Simon. What brings you out here?"

He was sufficiently bundled in his thick parka, knitted black hat, snowmobile gloves to his elbows, and heavy boots that rose to his knees. He shrugged. "The same as you, *cher*. Thinking."

Drake interrupting his wandering to sniff Simon's hand and bark hello.

"I'll bet. How's your auntie?"

"Feisty," he said. "At first, she was livid I brought the wrong cookies. A few minutes later, she couldn't stop laughing over what those women must've done to your shop. It made her feel so much better she wants to make roast chicken and all the trimmings."

"That's a good sign."

Simon gave a nod then kicked at a ball of snow. "Yeah, but I don't want her to push herself too hard. I picked up a cooked chicken and mashed potatoes at the deli. Why would someone do this to her, Audra? Most everyone says she's the nicest lady they know and would never harm a soul."

"Maybe that's why they spared her," I suggested.

"Perhaps, but no one has anything bad to say about that Dave guy either." He paused then asked, "Did your doctor friend find out how he died?"

Something made me tell him only half the truth. "He was stabbed in the back with your auntie's ceremonial dagger."

The top edges of Simon's dark eyebrows disappeared beneath his hat. "That seems a bit telling. What sort of person would want to stab a man in the back? Using her dagger makes it seem unplanned, right?"

Drake tugged at the leash so hard I nearly fell headlong into a snowbank.

"Geez! What was that for?" I regained my balance by grabbing Simon's arm.

"He saw something behind those trees," he said.

"A rabbit?"

"Larger. More like a big dog or a person."

Looking around, I asked, "Man or woman?"

"Who can tell the difference when y'all wear so many layers, *cher*?"

I burst out laughing. "Good point."

He seemed to hesitate before removing a familiar box from his coat pocket. The ones Miss Lavinia used to store…

"Oh, no." I held a hand up as I took a step back.

Simon steered me to one side of the path beneath a streetlight and opened the lid. A voodoo doll adorned with a blue shirt was lying on its face inside. The same blue Dave wore at the grocery store. A thick needle stuck out of its back. Something dark stained the doll's shirt.

I released my breath in a white gust that crystalized in the air between us. "Where did you find that?"

"It found me," he said. "It fell out when I opened the cupboard behind the counter. This is the dead man's doll, isn't it?"

"Yes." I took the box in my free hand to get a closer look.

This time, Simon took a step away from me. Then another. "I would appreciate if you could dispose of that."

"Simon, we need to show it to the police."

"I tried," he said. "Officer Trent said I needed more practice to be like my auntie."

I groaned, "A real cop. I don't trust that Trent guy. You're better off talking to Officer Grant, except that he has a cold and he's more miserable than normal. I suppose I can send him a picture of it."

"Then I shall leave that for you to deal with. That thing is bad *juju*." Simon backed down the sidewalk. He turned and ran as fast as he could in heavy boots.

I blew out a heavy sigh. "Drake, how do we keep ending up in the middle of these things? Okay, me mostly."

My dog snorted before he turned toward home. Safe and warm inside the house ten minutes later, I sent photos of both the box and the voodoo doll to Officer Grant before I slid it into a plastic bag and sealed it. I also mentioned Bree Spencer was back in town.

He promised to stop by Stitch'n'Time in the morning to pick up the doll.

I promised to stay home that night and not get into any trouble.

Considering the snowstorm that blew in while I made dinner, I had no choice but to keep my word. For now.

# Chapter Eleven

### Thursday, December 1

I rolled out of bed Thursday morning and reached for my bathrobe to let Drake outside. When I fumbled the robe, then dropped it on the ground, a piece of folded paper fell on the floor. The list of ingredients for the green powder Rex got from Miss Lavinia. I'd wait to read it until I had my morning coffee. At present, our biological needs were more urgent.

"Come on, boy." I led Drake down the stairs and slid open the patio door. While he rolled around and pranced in an inch of fresh snow, I glanced at the coffeemaker on my way to the powder room.

Doc was right. I need to take care of myself. Starting right now. I washed my hands then plugged in the kettle to make a cup of green tea. Frankly, I didn't like it any better than the icky powder, but a promise was a promise.

Drake lasted five whole minutes before scratching at the glass.

Letting him inside, I rubbed snow off his

fur while the kettle came to a boil. I made my tea and a glass of green stuff before I sat in front of the television to catch the morning news. I also wanted to see if my husband had texted back yet. When I sat, the folded paper in my pocket crunched.

"Okay, what's in this stuff?" I asked aloud even though the dog was already asleep in front of the dark fireplace. "Spirulina, turmeric, alfalfa grass, dulse, probiotics… Yikes. I should've read this after I drank it."

There was an indentation on the page that wasn't part of the list of ingredients. "What's that?"

I'd seen a trick on a detective show where someone used a pencil and shaded over the area to read the indent better. It was worth a try. The bigger trick was finding a pencil. Miraculously, I found one in the kitchen junk drawer.

After a little light shading, the words "Nov 25 8:30am" appeared. The day and approximate time Miss Lavinia and Dave were attacked. There was more, but I could only make out an E, a D, or a C. With a sigh, I gave up and chugged the green stuff then checked my phone.

Still nothing from Rex. I was on the verge of calling the police but didn't know what to say. Had something happened to him and Andrew or had he left me?

While I dressed and got Drake ready to go, I thought about those dolls Simon had brought. There had to be a way to organize them. Maybe I'd take a closer look once we got to the store.

Everything seemed normal until we were about a block from Stitch'n'Time. Suddenly, Drake started whimpering and prancing next to me. I shortened his leash but he continued to act strange.

Merilee frowned when she saw us. "What's wrong with him?"

"Beats me. He was fine until we got here." I held tight to the leash as he pulled me across the sidewalk. He only paused when he reached the door and sniffed all along the side of the door up to the handle.

"I don't like this," Merilee said. "Don't touch the door, I'm calling the police."

Since the door was slightly ajar, Drake nudged it open then began to growl. My heart raced even though we didn't go any farther. Half our inventory lay scattered on the floor. Craft kits, quilting fabrics, and rotating displays of needles and scissors were in complete disarray. The cash register appeared untouched, but the bin of voodoo dolls was dumped over, and the back door stood ajar.

"Hi. Yes," Merilee spoke into her phone. "My name is Merilee Rutherford. We've had a break-in at the Stitch'n'Time store in Sugarwood. Our address is 88 Main Street."

After that, I tuned her out. Finding Officer

Trent in our store last night was one thing. This made my head spin and my stomach ache.

"You okay?" Merilee asked as she hugged me.

The fact Drake didn't have his hackles up or his teeth bared assured me whoever broke in was long gone. I tugged Drake away from the door and left it open. My chin quivered as I whispered, "Why would someone do this?"

"No idea," she said. "The police want us to wait outside so we don't touch anything."

"Maybe I should bring Drake home so he doesn't get in the way."

Merilee agreed. "I suspect we'll lose enough stock because of the break in. We don't need Drake getting sick, too."

The morning sun peered out through the clouds as if to take off the chill from the invasion. I crouched next to Drake and hugged him. "Good boy. You deserve a whole steak for this one."

Drake slurped my face just as a voice called out to our right as Simon rushed toward us wearing his parka.

His hat was pulled low, but fear blanketed his face. "Oh, thank goodness you're both here. I need help."

"Not now, Simon," Merilee said. "We won't be much help today."

He stopped in front of us and seemed at a loss for words. Finally, he took a deep breath before he blurted out, "My auntie's store was tossed."

"What do you mean tossed?" she asked.

"Someone broke into the store," he said. "It looks like they were looking for something. They threw things on the floor and scattered papers."

I pointed toward our door. "They did the same to our store. Things are scattered everywhere. It's a mess. I have to take Drake home. I'll be back soon."

"That's awful." The second Simon placed a hand on my arm, Drake's lip curled, and a low growl escaped him. He released me and winced.

"Drake, it's okay." I patted his head. "Simon's scared, too."

Simon flashed a small smile. "I suggest we take him to stay with my auntie. She could use the company while I sort things out."

Merilee nodded. "It's a lot closer than you walking home and back."

"Okay. The police will be here soon, so I don't want to go far. Are we okay walking through the store? There's probably glass all over."

Simon glanced at his boots. "I didn't notice. Should I check?"

"Go through the back alley," Merilee said. "Just hurry. The police are on their way, and I need you back here as soon as possible."

Drake took the lead toward the corner as if he'd understood every word.

Simon grinned. "He's a smart dog."

"Sometimes too smart." I chuckled.

"I've never been this way before," he said. "I've put the garbage back here, but I don't stay out long."

The back door to Stitch'n'Time stood ajar. There were gouges in the wood around the lock. Both Simon and I peered inside. As much as I wanted to close it, I didn't dare touch anything until the police arrived. "Is your shop as big a mess as ours?"

"Yes." He hesitated as we reached the back entrance. "You may want to hold your nose when we go inside. The scoundrels smashed bottles of oils and made a large mess. I just hope my auntie hasn't gone downstairs to see for herself."

As Simon nudged the door open with his elbow, I gagged. A heady combination of scents hit us like a solid wall. My eyes watered. After a minute, Simon waved for Drake and me to enter ahead of him.

Drake sniffed, then sneezed before he moved into the building. He seemed to follow his nose, careful to step over chunks of fabric and reams of paper. Thankfully, there was no glass on the floor between us and the staircase. Once we reached the red curtain, he stopped to sniff the fabric. His hackles rose, but he didn't bark or growl.

"You were up there last night, right?" I asked.

Simon's wide brown eyes welled with tears as he pulled the curtain aside. "I should wait out front until the police arrive. Please don't tell my auntie about this. Not yet."

"Knowing her, I won't have to," I assured him.

By the time Drake and I reached the top of the stairs, the door opened.

"I hoped you two would return," Miss Lavinia said. "I made a lovely quiche, but Simon doesn't have an appetite. Drake, I picked up some yummy cookies for you yesterday. Hilda says they're your favourite."

Just like she knew we were coming.

"I can't stay. Would you mind watching Drake for a while?" I asked. When her head tilted, I added, "Someone broke into the craft shop."

She gazed past me. "I thought I heard someone downstairs last night. Simon won't let me check it out, but I can smell the oils. I doubt he did something stupid to make that much of a mess."

"The police are on their way," I assured her. "Hopefully, they'll figure out who did this, so we can get things cleaned up. I'm just glad you and Simon are okay."

"Yes, I never should've let him go down there last night, but he insisted," she said.

"He told me he didn't see anyone but came back with a cut on his forehead and a bruised eye."

I hadn't even noticed. "I'll talk to him."

She knelt in front of Drake and reached out a hand. "I'm glad you came to visit. I could use the company today."

As if he understood every word, he placed his paw on her hand.

I chuckled. "At least you're both in good hands. I'll be back later."

"Take your time," she said, keeping one hand on Drake. "We're going to have breakfast and maybe a nap."

Simon hadn't moved from the bottom of the stairs. When he took off his toque, I could see a cut across his forehead and a dark bruise at the side of his eye.

"What happened to you?" I asked.

He pulled the hat back on. "What do you mean?"

"Don't bother. Your auntie spilled the beans. Who did you see  last night?"

Simon closed his eyes and sighed as someone rapped on the front door frame. "I'll tell you later. The police are here."

"You'd better tell them what you saw. It might help all of us." I headed toward the back door.

"Stop right there," Officer Trent called from the front door. "Let me see your hands."

I groaned, "It's Audra Clemmings. I'm

going back to the craft shop. I just left my dog upstairs with Miss Lavinia and I'm trying not to contaminate the crime scene."

For a second or two, I expected him to tell us to come out with our hands up.

"Okay," he said. "Go out the back way, but you'd better be out front in the next five minutes, or I'll issue an arrest warrant."

Simon nodded. "We shall be right there."

Just as I was turning away, something familiar caught my eye. Near the table where Miss Lavinia did her readings lay the missing chalice. It lay empty on its side next to a deck of scattered tarot cards.

"Simon," I whispered, "the chalice is back. Near the table."

He followed my gaze and raised his eyebrows. "Now don't that beat all, *cher*."

* * *

For the next two hours, there was no sign of Officer Grant who I hoped would be first on scene. Instead, we had Officer Trent buzzing from one crime scene to the other like a mosquito.

Once the police and forensics team left, Merilee and I leaned against the fingerprint dust-covered counter to survey the damage. I'd taken photos of my own and advised Simon to do the same. I also sent a couple of them to Rex. Not that I wanted him to worry, more so I wouldn't get an earful for not telling him what happened. He'd worry more if he heard it through the grapevine.

"Where do we start?" Merilee asked.

Numb, I shook my head. "You take the quilting section. I'll start on the needlepoint."

When she hesitated, I was sure she was about to quit. "I don't know about you, but I need sugar and caffeine. Why don't I grab us lunch first?"

"That sounds good." I nearly sighed aloud in relief. "I'll pick Drake up later. Providing Simon doesn't drop him off first."

I locked the door behind her then turned to face the store. Who would do something like this? Someone was looking for something, but what and why did they think it could be in Stitch'n'Time?

My next thought was the voodoo dolls that lay scattered all over. I owed it to Simon and Miss Lavinia to take care of them. As I crouched to pick them up, I gazed at the back door recalling the gouges in the door jamb from where someone broke in. I doubted there was any way we'd ever know who'd broken into either store.

Then I found something on the floor near the back door.

A strand of the felted emerald yarn like Judy Wells was using to make the peacock shawl for her daughter. It lay in a small clump with a tuft of blue fabric. The same blue fabric as the shirt on Dave's doll. I had assumed Miss Lavinia created it. What if I was wrong?

"Interesting," I muttered, rolling the tuft between my fingers as someone unlocked the front door and came inside. "Does this remind you of anything?"

Merilee tiptoed through the carnage to set a paper bag on the counter. She moved closer for a better look then held it away from her face and squinted. "Is that the same green yarn Judy uses?"

"Yeah. I found it near the back door. Someone jimmied it open."

"You don't honestly think she could've…?"

I shook my head. "I have no idea what to think. The blue is the same colour as the shirt on Dave Spencer's doll, but there's no way Miss Lavinia would trash our shop or hers and leave it behind."

She set her phone face down on the counter before she took off her coat. "Let's have lunch then get this place back in order. You're overthinking things. That yarn could've fallen off the table on Wednesday and blown into the room when people opened the front door."

I slumped onto my stool as she took two Styrofoam containers with clear lids from the bag. My mother would criticize my posture, but I had bigger worries. "You're right."

After broccoli soup, grilled cheese, and

coffee, we procrastinated for ten more minutes before Merilee turned on Christmas music and we dug into cleaning up. We'd straightened all the merchandise and did a good clean up before I went to get Drake.

Still no sign of Officer Grant, which was just as well. I couldn't think straight.

As much as I wanted to spend time talking to Miss Lavinia, I was worn out and needed to go home and put my feet up. I'd just returned to Stitch'n'Time from picking up Drake when the front door opened. My dog whimpered and lay on the floor, covering his nose with both paws.

"Merilee. Audra." Officer Grant gave a nod as he walked in brushing fine flakes of fresh snow off his shoulders onto nearby fabric.

She nudged my arm. A signal to keep my mouth shut about the yarn and the dolls.

"Officer Grant," she said. "What can we do for you? Needlepoint kit? Knitting needles to keep the prisoners busy?"

He chuckled. "I'm just here to see if you've noticed anything missing after the break in last night."

"Isn't that job for the lead investigator?" I asked.

"Trent? He's tied up with heap of paperwork due to a couple break-ins. I told him I'd drop by."

Merilee closed the lid on the box of voodoo dolls. "We haven't noticed anything missing, not since the forensics guys left and let us back in."

"Forensics?" he asked. "Are we talking about the same thing? Trent said he caught someone in the store when you closed last night. Do you think it was the same person?"

"I doubt it," I laughed. "We'd left Drake in the store waiting for us before we closed yesterday afternoon. Trent was the one who broke in."

"Ah. I see. What's in there?" he asked.

"Baby clothes for the women's shelter," Merilee said. "You want to see?"

Drake sneezed twice before he got up and strolled to his bed by the heat vent. A sign there was too much cleaning and talking going on for his taste.

Officer Grant shook his head. "I'm good."

I tried not to be obvious as I snuck my hand into a drawer for an envelope. Instead, I found a small plastic bag for buttons. Perfect. While Officer Grant turned his back to me to chat with Merilee, I tucked the snippets of blue and green into the bag before tucking it into my right pocket. While it might be evidence, I doubted the police would consider an errant scrap of fabric in a craft store that intriguing, even after a break-in.

"The coroner says Dave Spencer might've been poisoned on top of everything else," Officer Grant said while he roamed through the store.

Merilee and I exchanged glances. Neither of us let on we already knew.

"So the gunshot and the knife in the back were just for show?" I asked as I suddenly remembered the belladonna.

He shook his head. "Not exactly. The bullet to the heart killed him. The killer covered the dagger blade with poison to make sure he was dead."

Officer Grant hesitated then added, "Doc also mentioned Dave had eaten Christmas cookies. The kind with the jam inside like Judy Wells makes. I'm on my way to see her next."

My eyebrows twitched. Judy again.

"I wouldn't eat anything at her house if I were you," Merilee warned.

He snorted. "I doubt it was the cookies or Judy that killed him. I'm trying to establish a timeline even though Trent's money's still on Miss Lavinia's nephew."

Merilee leaned on the box until she remembered what was inside. "Do you mean the one who arrived in town two days after the police called him?"

Officer Grant and Drake both sneezed at the same time.

When I handed him a tissue, he nodded. "I'm here to see that voodoo doll you found. The dead guy's doll."

"We have no idea what you're talking about," Merilee said, then turned to me and raised her eyebrows. "Do we?"

"Simon gave it to me last night." I pulled the plastic bag out of my purse.

Officer Grant took the box with gloved hands and opened it. "Could she make these things any smaller?"

Merilee reached beneath the counter for a magnifying glass. "Will this help?"

He examined the tiny blue sweater and the shiny needle stuck in the doll's back for a few minutes, before he said, "There's something odd on this needle. I need to take this to the lab as evidence."

"Go ahead." I shrugged. "It's not mine."

"Where did Simon get it?"

"It fell out of the cupboard in Miss Lavinia's shop and landed on him," I told them. "He tried to tell Officer Trent, but he was brushed off."

"I'll check it out. Anything else I should know?" he asked.

Merilee drummed her fingers on the bin. "Nope."

"Then I'm heading to Judy's to ask when she last saw Dave. Oh, and if she offers me cookies, I'll bring them back for you two." He grinned.

"I'm not sure how to take that." I put my hands on my hips.

Merilee gasped. "Seriously? After all the help we've given you?"

"I'll walk you out," I told him.

He chuckled. "Why? So you can make

sure I leave?"

"Absolutely. I'll even lock the door behind you."

Officer Grant paused. "You want to know what the poison was in case it was something off the shelf of her shop, don't you? Don't worry. We've searched her shop. If we had found belladonna, she'd be in interrogation. Simon's not off the hook either. He could've gotten rid of it after the fact."

I groaned. "Will you give the man a break? I'm sure you've seen his plane ticket. What more do you need?"

Startled, he met my gaze. "I'll think of something."

When I slammed the door behind him, a clump of loose snow cascaded off the awning above. Too bad it missed him by a foot.

"Let's close early today," Merilee said. "Under the circumstances, no one would blame us. Tony and I will give you guys a ride home."

"Is he done work already?"

She held up her phone. "He told his boss I was on the verge of a panic attack, so they're letting him go early. He's ordering dinner, then he should be here in half an hour."

"Sounds good."

Merilee draped her arm across my shoulders. "Let's finish cleaning up then go to your house. That way we can work on our suspect board. Rex doesn't get home until tomorrow, so that gives us time to research poisons. The one the killer used, not for your husband."

I reached to my pocket for my phone and realized I'd left it on the counter. When I lit up the screen there was a message from Rex saying they'd be snowed in until Friday morning.

"You already saw this, didn't you?" I turned to Merilee.

"I was beside it when he texted," she said.

As I lugged the bin of voodoo dolls back into the storage room, I realized aloud that we hadn't seen or heard from Simon since the police arrived. He wasn't in the store when I went to pick up Drake.

"I hope he's okay. Miss Lavinia said they heard a noise last night. When he went downstairs to check, he came back with a bruised eye and a cut on his head. He wouldn't tell her what happened."

"You have his number. Call him."

When I gazed at my phone, she snorted. "I knew it. You're not as worried about checking up on them as you are about snooping for belladonna or those cookies."

"Who me?"

Drake covered his eyes with his paws again while Merilee printed off our notes.

"Yeah, yeah." I texted Rex while we

waited for Tony, whoever came by first.

Rex and Andrew were stranded in Chicago but were able to keep the same hotel rooms for one more night. He was thrilled to have a hot tub and a bar on the main level. I was happy he was safe and not stuck in an airport overnight.

The second Tony's truck pull up in front of the store, Drake darted to the door and whimpered. If he had opposable thumbs, he would've been outside before I'd even grabbed my coat.

I made sure to lock both front and back doors. Since I'd be home early, maybe I'd make a batch of brownies for Simon and Miss Lavinia. Being a good neighbour didn't mean I was snooping, did it?

The pizza place was on the way to my house and in the opposite direction of Merilee and Tony's cozy home which stood on a hundred acres of prime real estate Andrew Laney would love to get his sticky fingers on. Well, Andrew and my husband, whom it seemed was now his right-hand man.

Once at my house, Tony rummaged through the kitchen to find paper plates and set out dinner. Merilee and I searched for the extra piece of Bristol board I'd tucked away the last time we'd made a suspect board. Drake yawned before he chose a spot in front of the fireplace to hint he was cold.

Tony handed us each a plate filled with pizza and salad and said, ""I have a buddy who installs security systems. I'll talk to him tomorrow and see what he can do to help secure the shop."

"I don't have money for that," I reminded him. "Craft shops aren't exactly high turnover businesses. Besides, we have stock to replace after the break-in."

He leaned down to kiss my forehead. "Silly, Audra, that's why you have insurance. Let me worry about the surveillance stuff. The guy owes me a couple favours."

"I can't let you do that," I insisted.

Tony flashed a wide grin. "Consider it an early Christmas gift. By the way, you don't have to let me. I have permission from the owner of the building."

"Thank you, but you guys don't need to do that."

Merilee gave me a hug then sat back with a black marker and a stack of brightly coloured sticky notes. "I work there too, and I want to feel safe. Start reading me the suspect list."

"The ex-wife," Tony called from the kitchen.

I had my doubts as Merilee put Joelle's name on a pink note. Best to stick to the facts. Technically, Joelle could've killed her ex-husband, but she had no real motivation that I knew of.

"Officer Trent. Just because Drake and I don't like him." I pointed to a green note. So much for sticking to the facts.

Tony burst into laughter as he handed us each a glass of wine. "That's not a good reason to add someone to the list."

"Have you met the guy?" Merilee asked, writing his name on a note. "To be honest, I don't like him either."

Another thought struck me. "Do you know what belladonna is or what it's used for?"

"Nope," Tony said, taking a seat at the dining table, "but give me five minutes and I'll be all over it."

We were halfway through the pizza and had made a significant dent in a bottle of wine when my phone rang.

Rex sounded exhausted even from hundreds of miles away. "Hi, honey. How are things going? Did you and Merilee get the store put back together?"

When my throat tightened, I realized how much I missed the big lug. "More or less. We have to order replacement stock, but insurance should cover it. Tony and Merilee are here having pizza."

"And wine," Tony added in the background.

"That sounds like more fun than being snowed in here," Rex said. "Andrew and his friends started drinking at lunch and haven't stopped since. They're still in the hotel bar."

"Why aren't you with them?" I asked.

He seemed to hesitate. "I thought I'd see how you were doing. That and I wanted to tell you how much I miss you. I've been a real jerk."

I pulled the phone away from my ear and stared at it. "You have?"

Merilee raised her eyebrows. "Is everything okay?"

"Rex either has hypothermia or dementia."

He groaned. "No, I don't. Look, Audra, I know I don't say it enough and I'm not home as much as you'd like, but it's a decent job and I want to be able to keep the house."

What had I missed? "Keep the house? Rex, what's going on?"

There was a long pause before he said, "Hopefully, I'll be home sometime tomorrow, and we can talk then. Why don't you spend tonight researching a security system for your store?"

"Oh. Tony already said…" I started.

A loud series of bangs filled the background. Muffled voices called out before Rex moaned. "I have to go. They found me. I'll call you once we get our flights sorted out."

As I hung up, I blinked back tears. Rex was keeping secrets. The thought those secrets were financial, not marital or health related, hadn't occurred to me until now.

"Are you okay?" Merilee sat next to me on the couch.

"Hey, did you know belladonna grows around here?" Tony interrupted. "It's from a plant called Atropa belladonna, or Beautiful Lady, but it's also known as Deadly Nightshade. We even have some in the field behind our house."

I blinked the tears away. "What?"

He pointed to my laptop. "Purple flowers. Red berries. According to this, it takes ten to twenty berries to kill an adult. Two for a child."

"That's a little unnerving," Merilee said. "And the police think someone crushed some berries then smeared the juice on the dagger that killed Dave?"

I skirted around her to sit next to Tony. "Wouldn't the berries have to be ingested?"

"That's how it sounds. Although I'm sure the berry juice on an open wound wouldn't feel so good. It causes blurred vision, loss of balance, staggering—"

"So someone who had a couple drinks could look and act like they were drunk, and it would leave a red stain on fabric."

"What's going on?" Merilee asked.

"Rex passed out on the couch the other morning. He had a red stain on his shirt and I…" Closing my eyes for a second, I tried to keep from overreacting. "I assumed he got drunk and passed out. What if the killer did a test run?"

Tony shook his head. "On Rex? No way. Who'd want to kill him?"

Merilee chuckled. "You mean besides his wife lately?"

"After all these years, I haven't been mad enough to poison him yet," I told them as I forced a smile. "Give him the silent treatment maybe, but poison requires more effort."

Tony slid the laptop toward me. "Are you okay?"

I hesitated then closed the laptop. "Maybe I'll watch a movie and give this murder stuff a rest for a while. You guys should get home before you get snowed in."

"As much fun as that would be, you're right. Promise you'll call if you need anything," Merilee said.

"Promise."

Tony scratched Drake's ears. "Make sure your mommy relaxes, will you, bud? She's not too good at letting things go when she's on the trail of a bad guy."

I walked them to the door before hugging them. "Thanks for coming over. I'm glad we were able to get things out of my head and onto paper."

"You bet." Merilee shivered as Tony opened the door. "Ooh, this is a good night for a roaring fire with a glass of wine. I'll see you tomorrow, Audra."

The roaring fire I was good with, but I'd already had too much wine. I tucked the suspect board under the couch then found a holiday movie and curled up on the couch with my needlepoint. I'd barely done ten stitches before Drake cuddled next to me. Just my luck, the movie ended and the next one began. It was about a woman who'd poisoned her husband.

I changed the channel.

# Chapter Twelve

### Friday, December 2

My phone rang as I let Drake inside from his Friday morning constitutional. I cradled the phone between my ear and shoulder while I pulled clumps of snow from his fur and tossed them back out the door. "Hello?"

"Miss Audra, I need your help," Simon said.

The urgency in his voice made me nearly lose my grip on the dog. A shiver ran over me as I asked, "What's going on? Is your everything okay?"

"My auntie and I are fine, although after the break-in, I fear we won't be that way for long. Can you come to the shop this morning?"

"Drake and I are leaving in a couple minutes. I'll see you soon."

I debated whether to bring the dog with me. After the mess we walked into at the store yesterday, I took one last look at the Christmas tree before I left him home and hoped for the best. I could come home at lunch to take him out.

Before I left the house, I texted Merilee to let her know I'd be late. A fresh layer of snow had fallen overnight. When I came to take Drake out, I'd have to shovel the sidewalk and driveway. There was no way Rex would be home before lunch anyway.

By the time I arrived at Miss Lavinia's shop, Simon paced the room scrubbing his head with both hands. The store was spotless, even if it still reeked of assorted spilled concoctions, but it was much tidier.

"What happened? You look upset."

"Oh, this is bad juju." Simon opened a drawer behind the counter.

I sighed. "I thought we agreed you'd…"

My words dissipated into a gasp when I saw what he'd found. A small fabric woman dressed in black with white hair. The doll had black button eyes and a thin strip of black electrical tape where the mouth should be. A piece of white string bound one hand to the other in front of her. Miss Lavinia.

"I found it after the police left yesterday," he said. "Please tell me she's playing cat's cradle. You know that string game you play with your hands?"

Leaning for a closer look, I winced. "If you take it literally, her hands were tied."

He met my gaze. "Or someone planned to kidnap her. Why didn't I see it before the break-in?"

My first thought was that someone

planted it and the break-ins were mere distractions. I didn't want to spook Simon any more than he already was. Instead, I snapped a photo of the doll before I found a plastic bag, turned it inside out over my hand and packaged the doll. Forget Officer Trent, I'd give it to someone else at the station who'd treat it as evidence.

"Why the tape and string?" he asked. "Do you think someone has a horrible secret and warned my auntie to keep her mouth shut?"

"If I knew that, the case would already be solved and I wouldn't have to worry about either of you," I told him.

"Me?" His eyes grew wide.

"By default. In case the guy comes back."

Simon leaned on the counter. "Maybe we should call the police. They need to know if someone threatened my auntie."

I hugged my purse to my stomach as though protecting the mini Miss Lavinia. "That's why they keep questioning her. They're hoping she'll remember something. I'm not sure who to trust. I haven't warmed up to Officer Trent and Tyler Grant once locked me in jail wearing only my pajamas."

Simon chuckled. "Why'd he nab you in your pajamas, *cher*?"

"It was Sunday morning. I was walking my dog and searching for evidence."

His laughter grew. "Ah! I wish I could've

seen that. I'm sure it was amusing."

"The judge sure thought so," I told him as my cell phone went off. Merilee wanted me to grab a dozen Christmas cookies on my way back to the shop. "I'd better go. Merilee's either bored, busy, or wants the latest gossip."

"My money is on the gossip," he said.

"Speaking of, you never told me what happened when you heard noises in the shop the night of the break-in?"

He moved his head back slightly and it felt like an invisible shield went up between us before he said, "I could use coffee and cookies, too. You have been so kind since I arrived. Why don't we make the trek to the bakery together? My treat."

"Simon, you don't have to—" I started as he ushered me to the door.

The door opened wide, and Judy Wells blocked less than half the entrance. "Where's Miss Lavinia? I have an appointment."

"Looks like you have work to do." I glanced at Simon then walked toward Judy. "Simon's taking over the shop until she's feeling better, but after yesterday he—"

"Well, he's doing a poor job." Judy snorted as she leaned on her walker. The door was still open wide behind her. "He hasn't shoveled the sidewalk and this place reeks. Young man, you need to open the windows and let in a little fresh air."

I folded my arms across my chest. No small feat in a parka. "He'll get to that in a minute."

"I need my prescription." Judy waved me off. "Where am I supposed to get it now?"

"The drugstore?" I suggested.

Her glare made me regret opening my mouth. "Lavinia makes me a fresh batch every week for my condition."

My initial urge was to ask what condition she had. This time I kept my mouth shut.

Simon nudged my arm then turned to Judy and asked, "What is your name, *cher*? I can make whatever you need."

Judy pressed her lips together while she studied me, then Simon. Finally, she blew out a breath that made her pink lips vibrate like a miniature pony. "Judy Wells. My daughter and I run a bed and breakfast. Where are you staying?"

"Here with my auntie."

"Too bad," she said. "We have nice rooms. I'll be back tomorrow. Make sure my medicine's ready by ten."

I waved to Simon. "I'd better go, too. Are you okay here on your own?"

He sighed. "Just drop off cookies and a large, black coffee, if you please. I'll look after Mrs. Wells before I talk to my auntie about her patients."

"Sounds good." As I walked past Judy on my way out, I flashed a smile.

She grabbed my arm. In a loud whisper,

she asked, "Should I trust that one?"

"Simon's a good guy. He'll take care of you."

Judy huffed. "That's what I'm afraid of."

I texted Merilee to let her know I was on my way to the bakery before I followed Judy out the door. At the bakery, I placed my order. "Three large coffees, one black, one with cream, and one with one sugar and one cream. A dozen holiday cookies. Oh, and I'll take three cinnamon rolls and a dog cookie."

"For sure." The girl behind the counter snapped her gum.

While I waited, I looked around and remembered Drake was at home today. I'd have to save his cookie for later. Only one bistro tables was occupied. I turned away before Joelle or Officer Trent saw me. The bakery was an odd place for an investigating officer and the ex-wife of a murder victim to meet. Just like he'd met Bree in the deli. What was he up to?

"Here ya go," Hilda, the owner of the baker, said. "I threw in the dog cookie for free. Bring Drake by later. I'm trying a new recipe and I'd love his feedback."

"He's at home this morning, but I'll bring him by next week."

She beamed. "Great, I'll make one Monday morning with his name on it."

I averted my gaze as I hustled back to Miss Lavinia's shop and opened the door. "I brought coffee and a fresh cinnamon bun."

Simon glanced up from something he was reading. He pinched his eyebrows together into one long, bushy caterpillar. "Thank you. I was thinking about those cookies I brought to your store by mistake. Did I mention I got in trouble when I got home? The blue tin was regular chocolate chip cookies. The cookies in the green one she'd made with…a more potent herb."

"That explains the ladies singing show tunes. Good thing marijuana's legal."

"For the record, those were the voodoo cookies the ladies spoke of. Should I learn to bake those?"

I tugged his cup out of the tray. "You'll have to ask your aunt. How did it go with Judy's medicine?"

He motioned for me to follow him to where two large filing cabinets stood in the back room. "Not well. Both of these are full of people. I may need my auntie's help."

"Wow. She's sure had a lot of clients over the years. Any one of these people could've been angry enough to… Where are you going to start?"

"At 'W' for Wells," he said. "I suggest you begin with 'A'."

I shook my head. "You're not as funny as you think. I have to bring Merilee her coffee before she comes looking for me."

"This must be where she stores her doll making supplies." He reached to the top of a set of cupboards to take down a brown tote box. When he opened the lid, he said, "Um, Miss Audra…"

The box was filled with embroidery thread boxes inscribed with a name and two dates.

He grimaced. "Either these people died young, or—"

"Or she started treating them then stopped for various reasons."

"Let's go with that. There is no way I'm going to open any of those little boxes, *cher*," Simon said backing away from the box.

"I glanced at the coffee and paper bag in my hands. "Yeah, I know. Bad *juju*. I'm going to bring these to Merilee. I'll come back to help you in a bit, okay?"

His eyes widened. "You're going to leave me alone with the little people?"

"You've been alone with them for days, why is it a problem now?"

Concern flashed across his face. "Now I know about them."

"I promise you'll be okay," I told him, glad his doll was in the box in our store. "I'll be back in fifteen minutes tops."

The second I walked into Stitch'n'Time, Merilee pounced. "What's going on with Simon? Is Miss Lavinia okay?"

Setting the coffee and bag of cinnamon buns on the counter, I filled her in on the files and Miss Lavinia's voodoo doll. "I promised to help figure out who hurt his auntie."

She waved a hand at the snow falling outside. "I doubt we'll be busy anyway. I think most of our regulars are snowed in. Besides, they started their Christmas shopping weeks ago. Oh, Tony's security camera friend is tied up until early next week. He'll give us a call when he can."

"Okay. Peace of mind would be nice." I checked my phone. Still no word from Rex. "I need to run home later to get Drake. Hilda has a new treat she'd like his feedback on. I have to bring him by on Monday."

Merilee raised her eyebrows. "Hilda knows he's a dog, right?"

"Yep. She also knows he's a regular who loves her cookies." I sipped my coffee before fetching paper plates from the back for the cinnamon buns. "Oh, guess who was at the bakery? Officer Trent and Joelle."

She frowned. "Why doesn't he question us in places like that?"

I shrugged. "You got me."

"Did they seem intimate?" she asked.

"What do you mean?"

Merilee met my gaze over her coffee. "Were they holding hands or gazing into each other's eyes or anything like that? I mean, she cheated on Dave. What's to stop here from stepping out on Chuck?"

I wanted to say fear, but I had no proof Chuck was the man Drake and I heard the other night. Joelle might've had questions for Officer Trent about Dave's murder, but if Chuck was abusive, she'd have two good reasons to talk to the police.

"No idea. I was more concerned with them not seeing me."

"I get it," she said. "What would you like me to do while you're walking Drake and helping Simon?"

Before I answered, I bit into the cinnamon bun. Against all odds, it was still warm and gooey. A gob of icing covered my lips and ran onto my chin. It helped that I'd stuck the bag next to the coffees on the tray on my way back to the shop.

"Oh, this is so good," I moaned. "Why don't you start looking for Valentine or Easter kits and fabrics? I know we have a few left from last year, but it would be nice to find fresh items, especially now that we have the sewing circle here."

She smiled. "Good idea. Maybe looking at flowers and bunnies will help me forget we're getting a big dump of snow in December for the first time in years."

Once we'd savoured our cinnamon buns, I wandered back to Miss Lavinia's to find Simon cross-legged on the floor surrounded by stacks of file folders. I wanted to ask why he took them out of the drawer in the first place, but he seemed flustered.

"Can you take those brown boxes down?" he asked. "I'm afraid to touch them."

Climbing the ladder he'd set up; I started taking down boxes. Ten banker boxes in all, each filled with dolls made from various mediums from felt to string. Drake would've been in his glory.

"Oh, shoot. Simon, I need to go check on Drake. I'll be back in a while."

I popped into Stitch'n'Time to tell Merilee where I was going and mentioned we'd found even more dolls even though I knew they'd freak her out. While I went to get Drake, Merilee headed two doors down to see for herself.

Drake danced in circles the second I opened the door. I grabbed his coat and his leash and  took him outside. Rather than do his business then head for the door, he trotted toward Stitch'n'Time so fast that I had to speed walk to keep up. I guessed he didn't want to be alone anymore.

Merilee was shoveling snow in front of our shop when we arrived. As soon as I got close enough, she passed me the shovel. "Those dolls were awful. I'm going to get comfort food before I completely lose my mind."

Before I said a word, she strode up the street toward the pizzeria without her purse. Good thing the guy who owned the place was one of Tony's hockey buddies. He'd put it on her tab.

I finished shoveling before Drake and I went into Stitch'n'Time. While he settled near the heat vent, I texted Simon to say I'd drop by later. I barely had time to run to the washroom before Merilee burst into the store armed with a large paper bag. She unpacked two personal-sized lasagnas in silver foil trays and a third tray containing garlic bread. She must've ordered ahead.

"Do you think having all those teensy bodies back there bothers Miss Lavinia?" Merilee asked. "I'd find it creepy. Do you think any of those were kids?"

Drake forgot about heat to sit between us and drool. Anything with gooey cheese was his second favourite food group. Right after fabric.

I stroked Drake's head. "You have food in your bowl. Those dates were when she started treating patients then the date of their last appointment."

"Or when they died," she said, unpacking the paper bag with our lunch.

"Then why didn't she just get rid of the dolls? She must've expected the people who left to come back." I glanced at Drake.

Her eyes grew wide. "She was creating zombies? Jason will love that."

Jason was her movie make-up artist son in Toronto.

"I mean the ones who followed up for another treatment."

"Where's the fun in that?" she asked, crunching on a piece of garlic toast.

"You'd rather have zombies prowling the streets of Sugarwood than her patients returning?"

"It would be just like any other Monday," she said.

We'd barely finished lunch when the door burst open. Simon flew in surrounded by snowflakes and held up a purple notebook. "I found what the cops were looking for. My auntie's day planner."

My eyes grew wide. "We looked everywhere for that thing. So did the police. Where did you find it?"

His face reddened. "Under the cushion of her chair at the little table. I went to sit down and missed. Me, the book, the cushion, and my coffee went flying. So did a set of tarot cards. When I sat up, the Death card and the book were on top of me. I figured it was some sort of sign."

Merilee chuckled. "Look before you sit down?"

"I figured the Death card had more to do with the day planner than with my aching posterior," he said, "but yes, that, too."

"Doesn't the Death card mean you're going to die?" she asked.

He shook his head. "Actually, the Death card is one of the most positive cards in the deck. It signals a major phase in life is ending, and a new one will start. In short, a major change or transformation.”

I met his gaze. “In this case you.”

“Heaven knows I’ve had enough changes lately,” he said. “I guess it’s time to put the past behind me, so I can focus on what lies ahead.”

“Like staying here and working with your auntie?” Merilee asked.

“That seems to be one scenario.”

I sipped my coffee before I said, “This must be scary for you. Strange country. Strange town. Strange people.”

Simon nodded. “The uncertainty, yes. A great deal depends on how well my auntie recovers. As hard as I try to welcome the change it’s tough to do things I never wanted to do again.”

Merilee picked at her garlic bread. “Shoveling snow and working in a store?”

“Casting spells and mixing potions,” he said with a sigh. “I thought I’d put that life behind me. My auntie tells me moving forward is one of the lessons Death teaches us. I was dying a slow death in that accounting office and the tarot knows it.”

Drake nuzzled Simon’s hand as if to give him a little support.

“You’re a good dog, Drake.” Simon patted his head. “Where did you get your lunch? It smells like something my auntie would eat. Lately, she hasn’t had much appetite, but I think she’d like that.”

"It's from a little pizzeria some friends own," Merilee told him. "Here's their flyer. Why don't I place an order for you and draw you a map how to get there. It's not far and the food is great."

Simon shook his head in amazement as he gazed from Merilee to me. "Once my auntie feels better, we will invite y'all over for a bayou dinner. Crawfish, gumbo, grits, jambalaya, and boudin sausage for starters, with a pecan pie to close. Ain't nobody going home hungry from that shindig."

"Mmm, that sounds delicious." I reached for a piece of garlic bread.

"I'm in," Merilee said. "My husband Tony loves to cook, and I love to eat. He'll want to learn every trick you can teach him. I have to run five miles a day to burn it off."

"That's why I walk. I love good food." I grinned.

Simon seemed pleased. "I'm sure my auntie knows where to get the ingredients. I'll let you know when she feels up to it."

Half an hour later, I tucked the three dolls Drake had dropped near the garbage can into my bag. I left him to protect Merilee while I returned to see what else Simon needed help with.

"Well, hello." Miss Lavinia glanced up from her reading table. "Simon mentioned you were coming. Oh, and thank you for the lasagna. We're saving it for dinner."

"That was from Merilee," I told her. "I thought you were supposed to take it easy."

She waved a hand. "A girl can only take things so easy before she gets bored out of her head. Besides, Simon says my patients are losing their patience."

"I'm glad you're here. I have a couple questions." I pulled out the plastic bag.

Miss Lavinia narrowed her eyes as she reached for it. "Now where did you get these poor things?"

Simon cleared his throat. "I may or may not have brought them to her shop."

"Yes, it wouldn't make sense to ask the woman who made them, would it?" His auntie laughed. "Why are they in a plastic bag?"

"The bin kind of fell over and Drake sorted these from the rest because they have a similar smell," I explained.

She pointed to each through the plastic. "Joelle Benson. Alister Trent. Judy Wells."

I hadn't recognized Judy's doll. Odd how Drake had never growled at her, although she'd been in the shop several times. Always with the sewing circle. Maybe the smell wasn't as strong when there were so many people in the room.

"Have you figured out who made a mess of my store?" Miss Lavinia asked.

"Not a clue." I sat across the table from her hoping she didn't smell the coffee on my breath. "I saw your ad in Saturday's paper. Why are you selling the shop?"

"Is that where that story came from? People have been calling all week. We had no idea what they were talking about."

I removed the photocopy of the order form from my purse. "According to this, Dave Spencer placed it."

"The man who died?" Simon asked.

Miss Lavinia shook her head. "That's not possible. Did you show the people at the paper his picture to be sure?"

"I didn't have one handy and the receptionist wasn't the one who took the order." I paused. "What was Dave doing here that day?"

She reached for the tarot deck then shuffled it. "I told you. He wanted an early appointment because he needed to go to Toronto after work that day. I was mixing him a sleep elixir that was more potent than the one I gave him before."

"And you said he was using it at an unusual rate. Is that what you were mixing on the counter while he was here?"

Miss Lavinia stopped and handed me the cards. Her eyes grew wide. "Yes. I had my back to him then heard a noise and turned around. All I remember is a flash then everything went dark."

As I clutched the cards, she held both my hands in hers and met my gaze. "I heard your voice, Audra, but I couldn't answer you. It was like I wasn't no longer in my own body. It was surreal."

Simon cleared his throat as he placed a stack of folders on the counter and said, "Audra hoped you could help figure out what smell makes her dog growl at people."

I nodded. "Whatever you're giving Rex makes Drake go crazy. He's eaten half my husband's wardrobe, including a suit jacket and pants. He also growls at Joelle and Officer Trent. Actually, he flat out hates Officer Trent."

"He is an unlikable guy," Simon said.

Miss Lavinia smiled. "I see. Is that what these files are for?"

My face grew warm. "I thought if I could figure out what Rex was using, I could cross-reference the list with the others and—"

"And invade the privacy of my patients. Even if one of them is your husband."

Simon placed a hand on the folders. "So that's a no?"

"No," she said.

Trying not to appear defeated, I shuffled the deck. I could find another way.

"Set the deck down," she ordered.

Sure I was about to get kicked out, I obeyed.

"Turn over the top card."

I reached for the deck and flipped the top card. The Fool. "How fitting."

Miss Lavinia smiled. "Don't be so quick to judge. The Fool represents new beginnings and adventure. Of course, when reversed, it can also mean recklessness and risk. How you interpret the card depends on your perspective. I see it upside-down whereas to you it is right side up."

"So what does that mean?" I asked with a quick glance to Simon.

He chuckled. "That means you may interpret the cards any way you want. You can still be a fool. Do you still want the information you seek?"

I met Miss Lavinia's gaze. "If I have the information, I won't be diving in recklessly?"

"But it may put you on a whole new adventure you may not be prepared for."

When I picked up The Fool, I blew out a breath. "'Fools rush in where angels fear to tread.' That's what my dad always said. Let's do some digging."

Simon placed the stack of folders in front of his auntie along with a notepad.

"You cannot lay eyes on the documents inside." Miss Lavinia smiled when I sighed. "But I will give you a list of the common ingredients that could be aggravating your dog."

"What should I do in the meantime?"

Simon handed me a duster. "You can get the bottom shelves. I can't reach them without making my knees crack."

I chuckled. "You got it."

* * *

When I returned to Stitch'n'Time, I waved my list at Merilee. "I got it."

"Is it contagious?" she teased. "How did you get so filthy? You've been gone an hour."

Brushing dust off my pants, I told her, "I helped Simon clean while Miss Lavinia made a list of the ingredients in the treatment oils she gave Rex, Joelle, Officer Trent, Judy Wells, and Dave."

Merilee stared. "That must be some list."

"You'd think so." I crouched in front of Drake before I pulled a few small brown vials from my pocket. "She gave me samples to test on Drake. I don't know the exact measurements or what they're used for, but these are the most common ingredients."

She lunged to grab my shoulder. "Um, maybe we should discuss this before you start waving vials under his nose and he trashes the place."

I gazed at Merilee then at Drake. The image of Rex's suit came to mind. Then of Drake pinning Officer Trent against the counter. I scratched his ears and changed my mind. "Good thinking. I'll do some research first."

"What are the main ingredients?" Merilee asked as she headed toward the computer.

I checked the labels on the vials. "Peppermint, myrrh, frankincense, lavender, chamomile, and tea tree oil."

"No belladonna?"

"Nope."

She scowled. "Darn. Are those in everybody's mixtures?"

I shook my head. "Yes, but in varying amounts. Come to think of it, Drake reacts stronger to some people than others. He barely notices Judy or Joelle yet flips out when Rex or Officer Trent are nearby."

"Did Drake ever meet Dave?" she asked.

"Not that I know of."

Merilee pulled up a list of essential oils and made little noises as she read.

My knees cracked as I stood. "Either let me see or read out loud."

Drake whimpered as he made his way toward the door.

Missing a bit of light reading was better than cleaning up puddles. Glad I hadn't taken off my coat, I grabbed his leash and followed him. "Let's go, boy."

"I'll print off a cheat sheet," Merilee said. "It'll be easier than reading how—"

Her voice was cut off when I closed the door behind us. Yes, I was being childish, but why did I always have to be the one on dog duty? I blew out a frustrated breath. It would be great if my husband were around to help out now and then.

"Are you Audra Clemmings?" a man spoke as we stepped outside.

A shiver raced down my back as Drake's hackles rose. While he didn't growl, he tensed and sidled closer to me. We both recognized that voice.

He walked toward us and handed me his card. "I'm Chuck Benson. I don't believe I've had the pleasure."

"I've seen you on the bus benches. Your ads, I mean," I said, shoving the card into my pocket before Drake led the way toward the park.

Grinning, he jammed his gloved hands into his pockets and fell into step with me. With my luck, he had a gun. Also with my luck, it would backfire.

"Is there something I can help you with?"

"My mom is part of your sewing circle," he said. "She's been gushing about your cozy little shop for weeks. I'd love to see inside your building sometime."

"The store's open six days a week. You're welcome to come in to do a little Christmas shopping." I paused to look at him, but Drake pulled me along. "Or are you one of those guys who need an invitation to step inside a building?"

"One of what guys?" he asked.

"A vampire."

Chuck grinned again. No long, pointy incisors. "My mom was right. You really do have a vivid imagination."

"Oh, yeah? What else did she say about me?" I asked, not sure I wanted to know.

He looked me in the eye and said, "That you're always up for a challenge and love a good mystery."

I clenched my fingers in my gloves so he couldn't see my hands shake.

"Tell Rex I said hi. I hope things are going well in Chicago for he and Andrew." With that, he turned and walked away in the opposite direction as Stitch'n'Time. Dropping my husband's name didn't exactly endear him to me. It freaked me out a little.

Drake and I both hustled back to the store and were panting by the time we arrived. When I unhooked Drake's leash, he headed for the vent. He kept looking back over his shoulder as though Chuck would come back. I didn't blame him. I wanted to lock the door and hide. Instead, I pulled down the window shade and peered around it.

"Can you believe all this snow's supposed to melt by the end of next week?" Merilee asked. "That's lake effect for you. I don't mind fall or winter, but I hate the constant... Are you okay?"

I took off my coat. "I ran into Chuck Benson. He's interested in seeing our store but wouldn't come in unless I invited him."

She narrowed her eyes. "Interested how? In shopping here or taking over?"

"He didn't say, and I didn't ask."

"Then why are you so freaked out?" she asked.

I stood guard near the door trying to figure out what to do if he did come inside. "Drake and I heard a guy yelling when we went for a walk the other night. It was him. Drake didn't go crazy barking like with Officer Trent, but Chuck made him—made both of us—uneasy. See. The fur on his back is still standing on end."

Merilee tapped the list on the counter. "Did you smell anything on him?"

"Like oils? I was too scared to notice," I admitted.

"Scared of what?"

"I couldn't swear it in a court of law, but I'm positive it was Chuck who was yelling that night. If it is, Joelle could be in danger."

She came around the counter and gave me a hug. "You should take the weekend off. You and Drake are burning out."

Before I could agree, my phone rang.

# Chapter Thirteen
### Saturday, December 3

It's never comforting to get a call from your doctor to come into his office on a Saturday morning. My first thought was that I'd gone from the early stages of breast cancer to having less than a month to live. The longer he took to shuffle through the paperwork in front of him, the faster those thirty days ticked away, and my anxiety grew.

When Doctor Angus Cook avoided my gaze, my heart sank. After a long silence, he cleared his throat. "It seems there was a mishap."

That odd sensation of freefalling several floors in a fast elevator swept over me and seemed to send my stomach straight into my throat. It took several seconds to catch my breath before I managed to whisper, "What kind of mishap?"

"Someone placed the wrong paperwork in your file."

Not the words I wanted to hear. "What do you mean?"

He sat back, but still didn't meet my gaze as he toyed with his pen. The clicking was starting to get on my nerves when he said, "Your test results were normal. You don't have cancer."

"What do you mean I don't have cancer? You told me I did," I reminded him. "I've been drinking green sludge, avoiding coffee most of the time, and drinking water until I've started to grow scales. I even had a biopsy and a ton of bloodwork."

He held up a hand. "You had your tests done at the same time as another patient and somehow the results got mixed up. Your lump is benign."

I closed my eyes as my vision twinkled with little stars. If I stood up now, I'd end up face down on the floor. I tried to focus. "I want to see my test results."

"Audra, I—"

"I want to see my test results," I repeated.

Dr. Cook held out a piece of paper. "I assumed as much. I made you a copy."

My hand shook as I took it. Before reading the page, I said, "I also want an apology."

"I'm deeply sorry."

I shook my head not sure I'd heard him correctly. "What?"

"Audra, my office has caused you and another patient a great deal of grief. You have every right to be upset, but keep in mind this was a horrible mistake. There was no malice intended."

"At least I didn't start chemo yet."

His face paled. "I need to make another call."

I left his office in a daze. Miss Lavinia was sure I had cancer when she saw me. Wasn't that what she said? Or did she say I had a lump? The one the doctor told me was malignant, but now was miraculously benign. Far from being relieved, I was confused and shaken. I paused in the middle of the hallway to stare at the test results. The word malignant jumped out at me once more. So did the name on the paper.

Emily Trent, Officer Trent's mom. Was she told she was fine? Either way, she'd have to face the same roller coaster of emotions and concerns that had robbed me of sleep and sanity for weeks.

Doing an about-face, I ran straight into Doctor Cook. I held up the page between us ready to accuse him of breaching patient confidentiality. "This isn't mine."

"That's why I came to find you," he said, his face reddening as he ushered me back inside his office and closed the door. "You must think I'm completely inept. I've tried so hard not to let my private life interfere with work, but I've been distracted and made mistakes I've never made before. These are your results."

My heart nearly stopped as I read my name then the word benign highlighted in orange near the middle of the page. A relieved breath rushed out as it felt like a boulder rolled off me. "Yes, it is. That's great news."

"Good."

When I looked back up, he was staring out the window with a frown. "Are you okay?"

"My dad has pancreatic cancer," he said softly. "I've come to realize how lightly I've treated my own patients when I gave their results. When my dad broke the news, I brushed it off with that same nonchalance until I saw how scared he was. You must've been terrified."

"That sums it up. Miss Lavinia had me doing Castor oil compresses and drinking green sludgy stuff to build my immune system. I couldn't give up the coffee though." I paused. "Part of me is still afraid you're wrong."

His frown deepened. "Miss Lavinia might be a comfort to my father. I hoped she'd be back at work soon. Do the police have any leads?"

"None that I know of." I hesitated. "Her nephew Simon is looking after her shop for now. He seems like a good guy, and he's met some of her clients."

Dr. Cook stiffened. "Does he have her dolls?"

"Excuse me?" That wasn't the question I expected to hear.

"Her voodoo dolls. Does Simon have access to them?"

Wary, I replied, "Yes."

"Do you think he'd be able to give my dad's doll a treatment until he can see Miss Lavinia in person?"

"I could find out."

He met my gaze. "You're positive he's trustworthy?"

"From everything I've seen, yes. Miss Lavinia trusts him with everything."

"I'll call him," he said. "He should have my doll as well as my dad's. Maybe we can get a group rate."

I chuckled. "I never would've guessed you were patients."

As I turned to leave, he took me by the arm. "Audra, I need your discretion on this. No one knows about my dad but our immediate family. I'd like to keep it that way."

"For sure." I gave him a hug for the first time ever. "Could I mention it to Miss Lavinia? I'm sure she and Simon could come up with a plan before you call and make things easier for you and your dad."

Dr. Cook hesitated then agreed. "Yeah. That might help. I'll talk to my dad."

I left his office feeling twenty pounds lighter. Most of my fear and anger had drained away and I was able to breathe easier for the first time since my misdiagnosis. I'd sleep like a baby tonight. Rex might want to sue the doctor, the clinic, the hospital, and the lab, but I just wanted—and needed—to move on.

Elated about the negative test results, I half ran to Stitch'n'Time. Merilee dropped a bundle of cloth and raced toward me the second I walked through the door. Drake scrambled off the vent and gave a couple yips before he licked my hand.

"Someone filed the wrong paperwork in my folder," I told her. "The lump's benign. I don't have cancer."

Merilee squealed as she hugged me. "I'm so happy to hear that."

Although Drake had no idea what was going on, he reared up on his hind legs and danced in a circle then sat expecting a treat to celebrate.

"Aww. Even Drake's thrilled." I wiped a tear from my eye.

"Of course he is, honey," she said. "He's worried about you. I read somewhere that dogs can smell cancer. I'll bet he knew you were scared."

I scratched his ears and hugged him. "Probably. I should tell Miss Lavinia she won't have to make me anymore green sludge. She may need to make it for someone else though."

Merilee's eyebrow twitched. "Oh. Right. Did you find out whose paperwork was in your file?"

For a heartbeat, I wasn't sure I should divulge that, but I'd never held anything back from my best friend before. "Emily Trent's."

"The cop's mom?" she asked, her eyes wide. "Do you think that's why he's been such a grouch?"

"You mean aside from having me trampling all over his case?" I thought about Dr. Cook and how mentally absent he'd felt lately. My impression of the cop softened. "I don't think he knows yet."

She hugged me again. "Oh, that's so sad. I'm happy for you though. This calls for celebration cheesecake. What did Rex say when you called him?"

Guilt flooded me. I'd been so focused on Emily and the doctor that I'd forgotten about my husband. He'd be just as surprised by the news as I was. At least I hadn't told the kids what was going on. I'd planned to wait for the biopsy results.

"I'll call him right now," I promised.

When a couple of our regulars came into the shop, I moved into the back room with Drake hot on my heels. Rex's phone rang once then went to voicemail. He must've been on a plane or driving.

"Hey, honey," I started then hesitated. Should I leave a voice message or tell him to call me later? I preferred the personal touch. "Call me when you get a minute.

When Drake whimpered and pawed at my leg, I shrugged. "You're right. I should just tell him the good news. He can call me when he gets a chance."

After I'd called Rex back and left a long-winded message, I texted Simon. *"Is this a good time to see your auntie?"*

*"Certainly,"* came his reply.

After I took Drake for a quick walk, I promised we'd go to the deli to grab lunch and see Charity then grab cheesecake from the bakery. We had lots to celebrate.

Simon met me at the front door with a wide smile. "Miss Audra, come in. My auntie is tired today, but she'll be happy to see you and hear your good news."

"Is it that obvious?"

"Your eyes are smiling. I take it your husband is home." He winked.

I shook my head. "I just came back from seeing the doctor. They misdiagnosed me. I don't have to drink green sludge anymore."

Simon hugged me and twirled me around, which caught me off guard. His laugh was deep and throaty. "She'll be thrilled to hear that. You might not want to give up on that nasty stuff so fast. It works wonders for the immune system."

"I'll keep that in mind." I straightened my coat with my face burning.

"Go on up," he said, pointing toward the red curtain. "I made a pot of tea."

By the time I got to the landing, Miss Lavinia waited in the open doorway. She had more colour in her cheeks than the last time I saw her. "Audra, what a lovely surprise. Come on in."

"You look like you're feeling much better today."

Her long, white hair hung loose around her shoulders, and she wore a bright peach robe that made her skin glow. "I just had a nap. I'm good to go."

"I won't keep you long," I told her. "I have news I had to deliver in person."

Once she closed the door, she took my hands in hers and gazed into my eyes. "Please tell me those silly doctors came to their senses."

"Sort of. Someone misfiled my paperwork. The lump is benign."

"Audra, that's fantastic." Miss Lavinia hugged me.

At first, I just stood there not sure what to do. First Simon hugged me, now his aunt, which had never happened before. Finally, I hugged her back.

"I'm so happy for you," she said. "Whatever you do, keep taking the green stuff. I know it tastes strange, but it works wonders for the immune system."

"That's what Simon told me."

"He's a good student." She winked then indicated the tea pot and a couple ceramic mugs. "Would you mind pouring the tea? I have a tough time lifting the full pot. It's the arthritis."

I poured two cups of peppermint tea then joined her in the living room. As I sank into one of the oversized chairs, I said, "I have other news I have permission to share."

"About Dr. Cook's father?" she asked.

"How did you…?"

Miss Lavinia chuckled. "Dr. Cook Senior called me as soon as he broke the news to his family. He wants to exhaust his options, even though he made it clear he still thinks I'm a witch doctor."

A sense of peace washed over me. I didn't have to say anything that might get me in trouble. "I'm glad to hear that. His son's taking it hard."

Miss Lavinia raised her mug. "And how is Rex taking your news?"

"I left him a message." When I sipped the peppermint tea, I realized another flavour mingled with it. "What's in this?"

"Peppermint and ginger. They're good for the immune system. I always drink this in case I come into contact with people who have colds or anything."

"Does it work?"

"I haven't been sick in twenty years. Of course, that could be the green powder."

After I took another sip, I met her gaze. "Good sales pitch. I should get a box of this tea for Officer Grant. He has an awful cold right now."

"Ask Simon for a sample on the way out," she said. "If I were you, I'd switch to tea instead of coffee. At least for a couple cups a day."

"You're right. Maybe it's time to not tempt fate and start eating healthier. One health scare was enough for me." This time, I meant it.

"But with Christmas coming and your love of sweets, we'll talk in January." Miss Lavinia waved a hand. "Are the kids coming home for the holidays?"

I could hardly contain my excitement. "December twenty-second. I need to do some baking and buy presents. Is Simon staying through the holidays?"

Miss Lavinia sipped her tea. "It depends on whether the government will let him. He isn't supposed to work here, but I can't run the shop alone. Besides, I'm getting used to having that boy around. Maybe I'll convince him to stay. Thank you, as well."

"For what?" I asked.

"I hear you and Merilee are sorting my dolls, so Simon can make heads or tails of my records."

"Oh, that." I took another whiff of the tea. "It was creepy at first, but interesting.

You're really good at details, but how do you tell them apart?"

She chuckled. "It's not easy. If that box ever gets dumped, we'll have a huge mess."

I bit my lip. There was no way we'd get the right dolls in the right boxes after Drake had dumped the bin at the store.

"That's one of the things I wished to speak to you about," she said. "You and Merilee could use my records to write the names on the right boxes. I wasn't going to do that out of respect for their privacy, but if Simon needs to perform a healing ritual, he'll have to find the right doll."

"Of course we can." I paused. "How many dolls are there exactly?"

"In the shop? Five thousand, two hundred and forty-five. I have another twenty-five hundred stashed in a storage room at the end of the hall."

By the time I left, Simon was gone. Leaving the store, I glanced at the piles of boxes in the back room and gasped. The enormity of doing the inventory began to sink in. It would take days and involve spending time with so many voodoo dolls.

Just as I was filling Merilee in on how I wished I'd never opened my big mouth, Simon walked into Stitch'n'Time. He carried a cardboard tray, three large cups, and a white paper bag that instantly made me drool.

"Have you figured out who killed Mr. Spencer yet?" he asked. "Judging by the number of people who come to the shop, my auntie's patients want to know."

"Not yet," I told him, "but we're not giving up."

"What did you bring?" Merilee leaned closer hoping for a peek.

"The coffees are black. I didn't know what y'all took." Simon set a small bag on the counter then pulled three chocolate-drizzled, almond croissants from the bag.

"Oh, those look so good," she sighed.

My pants were already snug from an overabundance of comfort food, and it wasn't even December yet. By the time my kids came home for the holidays, I'd be asking Santa for a fur-lined muumuu.

I frowned. "Oh, darn. I forgot to ask who her last few patients were."

"That's gonna be like going through a snowbank to find a diamond, *cher*. She has trouble remembering things. The only name she had in the little book was Dave's."

"What about video surveillance?" I asked. "Are there cameras in the shop?"

His eyes grew wide. "Oh, I hope not. The police might not like some of the herbs my auntie packages." He paused before adding, "For personal use, mind."

Merilee and I exchanged glances before she raised an eyebrow. "Are we talking about the smoking kind that's legal in

Canada?”

Simon sipped his coffee. “Just double checking. Those herbs work best to take away the pain. My leg was crushed in a car accident. Some days, it’s like someone’s stepping on my voodoo doll. Believe you me, *cher*, I wouldn’t cook up wacky cookies or brownies if I didn’t need them to sleep. I hate cooking.”

“How are things going in the shop?” I steered him back to the reason he came.

“She’s mad I took down the blackout curtains,” Simon said. “The only reason she kept it dark was so no one could see how much dust there was. I had to go outside to breathe after all the cleaning.”

Merilee laughed. “That makes sense.”

“What happened with that chalice?” I asked. “Is it back on the shelf?”

“No, ma’am. The police took it and then drove me to the station. I’m not sure why since I couldn’t tell them what I didn’t know.”

I frowned. “What did they want to know?”

“What my auntie used that chalice and dagger for.”

Merilee squirmed. “Does she actually make all those voodoo dolls, or does she buy them in bulk?”

“Those are handmade. She taught me how to stitch them when I was a guppy,” he said. “My father thought I was too good to be one of *them*. My mother won that

229

argument. She sent me to Louisiana to live with my auntie and learn all I could."

"Where did you live before?" I sipped my coffee still trying to resist the croissants.

Simon shrugged. "We moved around. My father was in the army and my mother… She was a bit off her rocker, as they say. When my father was deployed, he asked my auntie to stay with us, or sent Mama to hospital so she couldn't hurt herself."

"Oh, Simon, that's so sad," Merilee said.

When he bit into a croissant, a dusting of icing sugar settled on his chin. "It wasn't so bad. My auntie knew people who lived in the bayous and had farms where they grew all the things to make what she needed for clients. I hated the chicken farms. Nothing worse than chopping the heads and feet off any creature. They are tasty though."

I softened. "You love animals that much?"

"No, I am a chicken. I faint at the sight of blood," he said with a smirk.

"Maybe you should come to our sewing circle one Wednesday and teach them how to make their own dolls," Merilee suggested. "Not right away since you're so busy, but I could see that going over for Valentine's Day. All we'd need is a love potion or spell to add to them."

"Would you make a doll of Tony?" I asked.

"Nah. George Clooney. Would you make

one of Rex?"

I considered the possibility. "Only if I could find a way to make him pick up his socks and underwear. Poor Drake's going to get sick if he keeps eating them."

Simon chuckled. "I'll think about it. We might have to get everyone to sign a waiver saying they will use the dolls for good instead of evil. A love potion is a clever idea."

"For the dolls?" I picked at the croissant. So much for willpower.

"For the ladies who make them, *cher*. We want to keep it positive. No pins through the hearts or nether regions allowed." He shuddered, adding, "I'm not into the black magic nor do I want to get pulled into a divorce because of a fabric doll."

I laughed. "No doubt."

Merilee grinned. "Guess I'd better not make a George Clooney doll then."

"Any time you want to start labelling my auntie's dolls, feel free," Simon said. "I can use the company."

Merilee nudged me. "It's quiet today. If you want to take advantage and go, I won't be offended. I planned to do some online shopping anyway. I'll find some new ideas for the stitching group when they finish what they're working on. What about making a Christmas ornament?"

"Ooh, I saw some great mini needlepoint ideas in a magazine that only take a couple hours." I glanced at Simon. "I'll start today if that's okay with you."

He nodded. "I love Christmas ornaments. You're right. Maybe when my auntie feels better, she can teach everyone how to make dolls to bring in love and peace."

"I didn't know there was such a thing."

"Of course, *cher*. It's all about your intention."

Merilee chuckled. "That's great, but I think Audra meant about her going to your shop this afternoon."

Simon slapped his forehead and left a powdery white mark of icing sugar. "Come on by after lunch and I'll show you what I've found. I'm still figuring what to keep and what to throw away. An extra set of eyes will help."

I stopped pretending and dug into the croissant with gusto. "Then I'm going to need some fuel to do some serious labeling."

Simon grinned as he raised his coffee cup. "I'll go dust a path for you."

Once he left, Merilee patted me on the back. "You're a good friend. I just hope you know what you're getting yourself into."

"Trouble," I muttered. "I'm getting into trouble. Again."

Due to the decadent croissants, we kept lunch light and simple. Soup and grilled cheese sandwiches, which Drake insisted he needed to sample. It was just after one when I pulled on my coat and headed to Miss Lavinia's shop after making Merilee swear she'd text me at three.

Simon wasn't joking about the amount of dust. Sharp lines cut the grit where he'd stopped wiping. A clean path stretched from the front door to the counter where he'd mopped. The dark spots in the wood where I'd found Dave had faded to dark gray.

I backed away from a spider web on one of the wooden shelves. "Your auntie keeps that Halloween vibe going on all year round, doesn't she?"

"Yup, I even thought about hanging tinsel on the cobwebs," Simon said, handing me a pair of gloves. "You might want to use these."

"Right. I don't want to get fingerprints on anything."

He raised both eyebrows. "Silly girl. I thought you might keep your hands clean. You get right into this whole crime-solving thing, don't you?"

"Some days a little too much. My husband thinks I'm obsessive," I told him.

"And are you?"

My face burned. "Completely."

"Sounds like we'll get along fine then." He lifted a plastic box from behind the counter. "Some of her patients are in here."

"Her patients. I don't think I'll ever get used to that."

Simon set the box near the table where

Miss Lavinia normally treated people for various ailments. "I'll let you take over the table so you can be comfortable while I wash the grime off this place. I'm still trying to figure out how to clean the smells out after someone smashed bottles everywhere."

As I reached for the plastic box, I understood the need for the gloves. The lid was greasy with various daubs of oils with fingerprints of dirt smudged through them. Most of the spots looked old, but a couple seemed fresh.

"Did you touch this?" I asked.

"Just to see what was inside," he said. "I wore gloves. Heaven knows what that stuff on the lid could be."

I reached over to turn a Tiffany lamp on. "You don't happen to have tape, do you?"

He tossed me a roll of packing tape. "This is all I found so far."

"It'll work." I found a pair of scissors then cut off a two-inch piece of tape. Gently, I pressed it to the fingerprint, careful not to smudge it before I lifted the tape away and stuck it on a small white card.

"What did you find, *cher*?" Simon asked, leaning over the table.

"It looks like a fresh fingerprint. I thought I'd take it to someone I know on the police force to take a look."

He raised his eyebrows and asked, "You mean, Officer Trent?"

"Officer Grant. I helped him solve a murder at Halloween. Suddenly, we're best friends. Well, friends. Best might be pushing it."

Simon made a face. "Careful. Those cops are tricky. He might be looking for a chance to lock you away for life."

"He tried that when he arrested me in my pajamas." I smirked.

While he walked away laughing, I opened the lid. Miss Lavinia was well organized. I knew each doll had their own boxes, what I wasn't prepared for was the full card catalogue of patient files in the box. A few were in a folder labeled, "Archived." Did that mean they were dead, had left town, or both?

As I thumbed through the file folders, part of me winced with discomfort. I'd be miffed if someone aside from Miss Lavinia read my personal information. Not that it stopped me. Surprised to see my name, I headed straight to my file first. Notes in her spidery handwriting detailed my eczema and perimenopause.

"Oh great," I grumbled, wanting to take my files and shred them. No one needed to read all that. One notation sent a chill through me. Possible preliminary stages of breast cancer. Miss Lavinia's comment was dated last July. I'd only found the lump this fall. How did she know?

The next file was Rex's. Nothing unusual

there, just comments about his sleep apnea, his snoring, and his… My eyes grew wide. Since when did my husband have angina and why didn't he tell me?

"Are you alright?" Simon asked from across the room.

"Yeah, why?"

He pointed. "You dropped the scissors. That's not a good omen, *cher*."

Sure enough, the scissors had fallen from the table and stuck point down into the floor. My gaze darted back to Rex's file. I took out my phone and took a picture of the page that made my palms sweat. The one I wasn't supposed to see.

As I stuck Rex's file back in the box, I noticed one for Alister Trent. The words "invasion of privacy" struck me upside the head, but they bounced off as I reached for the folder.

The front door opened before I got my gloved fingers on his file.

"Good afternoon, Officer Trent," Simon stepped between us. "What can I do for you?"

He peered around Simon. "Audra, what are you doing here?"

I replaced the lid while I swung my feet beneath the chair. A feeble attempt to look innocent. "Simon asked me to help."

"I'm sure he did," the officer said, taking a step closer. "And what exactly are you cleaning?"

Simon slid the box behind the counter. "Things my auntie uses for her spells. Chicken feet, feathers, that sort of thing. Audra isn't squeamish, so I begged her for help."

"Chicken feet?" I gagged.

Officer Trent's cheek twitched. "I'm sure she is. I came to see if you've found anything that might help our investigation into Dave's murder."

"Didn't the crime scene guys dust for prints and take samples?" I asked, joining Simon.

Simon slapped his forehead. "That's why this place is so filthy. Here I am thinking my auntie is a bad housekeeper. The whole time it was the police who left the mess."

Fingerprint dust. That was the goop on the plastic bin. I reached for the card I'd left on the table behind me and stuck it in my pocket.

"What's that?" Officer Trent asked.

I pulled a mint from my pocket. "Candy. You want one?"

"Pass."

"I promise to have my auntie call you when she wakes up," Simon said. "She's become a sound sleeper since the attack and doesn't like to be disturbed."

Officer Trent scowled then huffed, "That's fine. I'll be back."

Simon locked the door once the officer left. "Besides that the other cop was here this morning. What is it with that man? My auntie was attacked, and he seems convinced she's managed to stab that man in the back before she had a stroke."

"Then who shot him in the back?" I asked.

His eyes grew wide. "Dave the Butcher was shot?"

I forgot I'd held back that part. "He was shot before they stabbed him."

"And my auntie was shot before she had a stroke," he said. "Do you think he missed Dave with the first shot or meant to frighten her?"

"That's a really good question."

"Simon?" Miss Lavinia called down the staircase. "Could you come up? I need help with that darn window again."

"My cue to leave," I said. "I'll come back Monday. Call if you need anything."

By the time I got home, I still hadn't heard from Rex. I tried to call him before I made dinner with still no answer. After slapping together a peanut butter and jam sandwich, Drake and I curled up on the couch while I watched a movie.

When I still didn't hear from my husband by nine o'clock, I let the dog out for a romp in the yard. He jumped up on the bed while I went into the bathroom for a bubble bath. If I didn't hear from my husband soon, I'd never get to sleep.

Or so I thought.

# Chapter Fourteen

### Sunday, December 4

Rex was supposed to be home Friday night, but I hadn't heard from him since he'd boarded his plane in Chicago. His Air Canada flight had arrived right on time at five after nine that night, yet my husband was still unaccounted for, and my calls went directly to voice mail. While Drake had managed to sneak in naps, I hadn't slept much since Thursday night and was bordering on hysteria. So much for thinking I'd sleep.

Had Andrew taken him on a joyride to Niagara to gamble away our life savings? Had he been kidnapped? Worse, had he left me and planned to send divorce papers via courier Monday morning? I closed my eyes and tried to calm the hysteria that threatened to bubble over after simmering all night.

For a lazy Sunday, neither Drake nor I could sit still let alone relax. My head throbbed like all nine drummers were drumming inside my skull. It was a good day to do some needlepoint since I wanted to finish Drake's stocking before the kids came home for the holidays.

I caught my breath and realized I'd nodded off and dropped my needlepoint on the floor. Turning it off the crime show on television, I chose a music station to listen to. I had to find something better to do than solve crimes from the couch.

Then I remembered the Christmas ornaments Merilee and I discussed. My plan for the next sewing circle was to offer everyone a small kit to create a Christmas ornament. No time like the present to start organizing since I needed something to keep my hands and mind busy.

I put on a pot of coffee then went to rummage for scraps of Aida cloth. I found two chunks of dark blue and about a dozen three-inch squares of white. I'd always thought of Aida cloth like graph paper I could stitch rather than draw on. Over the past couple of years, Merilee and I had managed to find several great colours for cross-stitch pictures. I'd kept every scrap in case I ever found a use for them. Call me a hoarder, but the habit that made Rex cringe might just pay off. Eventually.

Next, I pulled out as many festive skeins as I could find in my craft bin. Blues, greens, whites, yellows, and reds of every shade. Even black for outlining and browns for tree trunks and branches. That's where I found just what I was looking for.

A couple years ago when I had the flu, Merilee gave me a magazine filled with dozens of pages of miniature needlepoint patterns. Everything from owls wearing Santa hats, to Christmas stockings featuring penguins, and even mistletoe.

Grinning as I hauled my treasures to the couch then plunked them onto the coffee table. Choosing a dark blue fabric square, I decided to make a snowman raising his twig arms into the falling snow. My phone rang as I put in the final stitch for his orange carrot nose. The screen read unknown caller. I hesitated for a couple rings before I answered.

"Hey, honey. How's your Sunday?" a familiar voice asked.

I bit back my impulse to get upset and released a sigh. At least he was okay for now. "Rex, where are you?"

"Windsor."

"Did you get on the wrong plane?" I stared at Drake like he was a stand in for Rex.

"Andrew's driver had a family emergency. He forgot we were in the backseat of his limo and left Pearson Airport heading toward Windsor. We were halfway there when he remembered."

"Are you telling me neither you nor Andrew realized you were going the wrong direction?"

Rex sighed. "It was snowing, and we were discussing the meetings we had in Chicago." He paused. "Anyway, the driver dropped us off at a hotel while he went to the hospital. It's a girl, by the way."

I lay my head back on the couch. "This happened Friday night?"

"Uh-huh."

"And it didn't occur to you to call me or check your messages? Or that your wife might be worried about you?" I asked.

Silence, except for the grinding of my molars while I tried not to scream.

"Our suitcases were in the trunk," he said. "So were all my power cords."

My heart beat so fast and hard with anger that my entire body bounced against the couch cushions. "Where are you calling from now?"

"There's a phone in the limo. The driver asked his brother to drive us home while he spent time with his wife and new baby."

I wanted to be mad, but thoughts of crafting baby gifts filled my mind. "I guess I'll see you when you get home then."

"We'll hit town in about four hours. I can't wait to get a good night's sleep. You have no idea what we've been through," he said before he hung up.

His voodoo doll was still in a box in my purse. I gazed at the needle in my hand and itched to test out his voodoo doll. Instead, my gaze darted to the clock. He was due to arrive around dinner time. I'd better work fast if I wanted to get one ornament ready to show the sewing circle on Wednesday.

Before I could start stitching the snowman's arms, my phone rang again. Skipping any niceties, Merilee asked, "Any word from Rex?"

I filled her in on the story of the limo driver taking them to Windsor.

"And you buy that?"

"It's either that or I convince myself he's cheating on me and stick a needle in his doll," I told her.

"Those are both crappy options," she said. "Okay, let's go with the Windsor story, but if he comes home with lipstick anywhere on his person, you can forget the voodoo doll. I'll sic Tony on him."

I chuckled. "Thanks. I think."

By two o'clock, I had completed half the snowman, but had nothing to show for it. The instant I nodded off, the Aida cloth fell off my lap. Drake ate it. Thankfully, without the needle. His belch woke me.

Rather than sit around feeling sorry for myself or being angry at Drake or Rex, I grabbed the leash and dragged the dog out for a walk. The park glistened with snow on the tree branches and a fresh white blanket draped over the grass and benches. Footprints and dog tracks dented the pathway. The fresh air could work to my advantage. Once we got home, Drake would fall asleep and ignore me and the cross stitch.

We walked for over half an hour before he made a beeline for the house. As the porch came into view, Drake let out a low growl. Someone in a pink coat sat waiting for us. I was surprised Joelle knew where to find me.

"Hi, Audra, sorry for dropping by like this." She flashed a smile as she stood. "I spoke to Andrew Laney earlier. Your husband said you'd be home. I wanted to know how Miss Lavinia's doing."

"She's doing well. Head injuries can take time to heal." I cleaned the snow off Drake's paws before letting him in the house.

"That's right. Officer Trent mentioned she got a bad blow to the head."

I bit back the parts about Miss Lavinia grazed by a bullet and having a stroke, and that I thought Officer Trent was a jerk. I also didn't ask why I'd seen her having coffee with him in the bakery. Not yet. "How are you and the kids doing?"

Joelle shrugged, looking more tired than the last time I saw her. "It's been a rough week. My oldest insists Chuck had something to do with Dave's death, but that's not possible. He was in Toronto for a conference and didn't even know what happened until I called him."

"I take it the kids don't like Chuck much."

She stared at her gloves. "Only in small doses. He can be a lot to take. He's larger than life, if you know what I mean, and likes things done his way."

"I've seen his ads. How did they get along with Dave?"

A small gasp escaped her before she met my gaze. "I suppose you've heard the rumours and you're curious what I'll tell you."

My eye twitched. How had I not heard any rumours? Merilee should've caught up on all the gossip by now. If she had, why hadn't she shared? "Actually, I haven't heard anything. I've been helping Simon tidy up Miss Lavinia's shop."

"Simon? Is that her nephew's name?" she asked. "He's a big man. I hear the police think he was involved."

Officer Trent did, which is probably what he spoke to her about.

"That's not possible," I told her. "He was in New Orleans at the time."

Her shoulders fell slightly. "I see."

"Do you want to come inside for tea?"

She shook her head. "I have to go. Chuck promised to bring home pizza so we could we'd watch a movie together. I'm a sucker for sappy Christmas movies."

"Me, too. Do your kids like them?" I continued fishing.

"Not like they used to. My middle son, Jared, is in the military. My oldest, Mike, lives in Toronto with his girlfriend and two dogs."

I waited while she applied lip balm from a plain container. A local brand the drug store sold.

"Bree, my daughter, is between jobs right now," Joelle said softly. "She used to work at the butcher shop and was furious when Dave sold it. She's dealing with things as well as she can. I guess that's all I can ask for."

"I ran into her at the deli the other day. She seems like a sweet girl." I hesitated then asked, "Why didn't Dave use his father's last name?"

She averted her gaze as she twisted her wedding rings around her finger. "He did. It was his father who changed his last name."

"I don't understand."

"Dave's father, Jake, not only ran a costume and rental shop, but he worked for a local theatre for years. He did props and costumes mostly. Now and then, he'd even perform. He loved to be on stage and could quote any Shakespeare play you asked."

"Sounds like an interesting man."

"He really is," she said. "Anyway, he met someone during one of his shows. They had a torrid love affair for a couple weeks, then closing night, he packed a bag and took off. Dave figured he was too embarrassed to tell his wife and kids."

I frowned. "He was too embarrassed to explain falling in love with another woman?"

Joelle shook her head. "Another man. Things like that weren't as acceptable then as they are now. Dave's mom was devastated."

How would I take the news if Rex ran off with Andrew, or his new secretary Armando? It might feel like a total blow to my womanhood.

"Why did his dad change his last name?" I asked.

"A year after he left, he sent Dave's mom divorce papers in the mail," she explained. "Once the divorce was final, he married his friend and took the man's last name."

"Ossington. That must've been tough for Dave, especially when his dad moved back to town."

Joelle nodded. "He nearly lost his mind. His mom raised him and his sister on her own. She hadn't seen or heard from his dad in twenty or thirty years. Suddenly, the man buys a building down the street and opens a costume and rental shop."

"I can't even imagine."

She flashed a weak smile. "Me neither. Then I go and cheat on Dave even after I knew the whole story. It must've destroyed him, and I never even gave it a second thought until after he…" She paused. "Now it's too late."

While I wanted to comfort her, I didn't know the whole story. "I've never seen anyone with Mr. Ossington. He's always been alone."

"His partner died of AIDS before he came back to town. Jake tried to reconnect with Dave, but since he hadn't bothered to contact his kids in decades it was a hard sell. When we separated, Dave shut himself off from everyone. The last person he wanted consolation from the father who'd abandoned him." She glanced at her watch. "I'd better go. Chuck will be home soon."

I narrowed my eyes. It sounded like there was more to the story, but I'd have to go to a different source to hear it. Namely Charity Wells. Whatever gossip Merilee wasn't aware of, Charity would have on the tip of her tongue.

"Chuck stopped by asking about our store the other day. Do you know why?"

"No, sorry. I just know he's always looking for new investment opportunities. Thanks for listening." She got up then glanced back at me. "Maddie suggested I check out the sewing circle this week, but I have no idea what to make. I'm not exactly the crafty type. Not like she is, anyway."

An idea hit me like a snowball. "I might have a good project for you. If you do join us on Wednesday, I'll have a counted cross-stitch ornament for you to make."

Joelle's eyes lit up. Suddenly, her demeanor seemed even warmer. "I have no idea what that is, but I'll give it a try. Thanks, Audra. I'm already looking forward to it."

So was I. The way the ladies in that group talked, it could be interesting. Merilee and I might learn more about Dave and his ex-wife, which might help solve his murder.

After a little more research about Chuck, which proved less informative than I thought, I settled back with my needlepoint and a movie. Keeping my hands busy meant I could ruminate on everything I'd learned so far. I still couldn't piece everything together. Two movies later, I pulled out the suspect board for another look.

The doorbell rang around six o'clock startling both of us. Drake let out a bark as he headed for the door. Rex stood outside holding a bouquet of roses in one hand with his briefcase and an empty plastic bag in the other. A light snow fell behind him as the empty grocery bag flapped in the wind.

"Can I come in?" he asked.

"From what I remember, you still live here."

He flashed a sheepish grin. "Yeah, but after what I've put you through lately, I was worried you changed the locks."

"It wasn't your fault the guy drove you all the way to Windsor." I paused. "Was it?"

Rex shook his head and whispered, "No."

"You're home earlier than I expected."

"Yeah. Andrew insisted I come home and spend time with you."

My mouth fell open before I barked a laugh. "He insisted? Wow. That's heartwarming. I feel much better now."

When he reddened, his ears darkened in the porch light. "That didn't come out right. I brought flowers."

"They're pretty. Thank you."

We stood in awkward silence with the falling snow dancing in the gust of a breeze that sprang up. After a long minute, Drake nudged my backside like he expected me to do something. Anything.

I glanced back at my cozy spot on the couch. "Look, if you're not coming in, I'm closing the door. I'm cold."

My husband brushed the snow off his wool coat then reached to his left to pick up his suitcase. Once he stepped inside, he handed me the roses. "I asked the driver to stop at the store. I wanted to pick up flowers and something for dinner. I hope you're hungry."

"I am. What did you get?"

"Frozen pizza." He held up the empty grocery bag. "What the...? The bag must've torn when I got out of the limo. I'll be right back."

While he set off in search of the missing pizza, I strolled to the kitchen to turn on the oven and smiled. At least he was trying. I checked the fridge and found half a bottle of chilled wine inside. I set it on the counter then glanced toward the door. He should've returned by now.

Drake raised his head off his large paws as if he'd heard a noise outside. We both watched the door expectantly with still no sign of Rex. Andrew must have changed his mind and carted him off to the office.

Or Rex changed his mind and left.

My stomach sank.

When Drake whimpered, I grabbed my coat, slid into my boots, and told him, "Two dog treats says he's on the phone with his boss. I'm going to make sure he didn't forget why he went outside."

I didn't have to go far.

Rex lay on his back on the snowy sidewalk ten feet from the front porch clutching a vacuum-sealed, store-made pizza to his chest. He waved a hand but didn't get up. "Watch out for the ice."

"Are you okay?" I crept forward holding onto the railing.

"Aside from the fact I can't move? So-so."

I grabbed the pizza then backed away. "I'll call an ambulance. Stay right there."

"Where am I gonna go? I can't get up."

Once inside, I kicked off my boots, stuck the pizza in the fridge, and turned off the oven before I reached for my phone. "Sorry, buddy. Daddy fell on the ice. I need to call an ambulance. I'm taking your blanket to keep him warm."

The dog yawned then moved to lay in front of the fireplace. He shot me a dirty look when I grabbed his favourite blanket off the couch. I stepped back into my boots while I called for an ambulance.

"Are they on their way?" Rex asked when I draped the blanket over him.

"No one's answered the phone yet."

"What were you doing? I could've frozen to death."

"But you didn't." Juggling the phone as the nine-one-one operator answered, I sat in the snow next to him to peer into his eyes. Nope, no dilated pupils. Yes, he still had a pulse. As I replied to the operator's questions, Rex began to shiver, which I reported promptly.

"It's okay, honey, the ambulance will be here soon," I told him as I patted his chest.

"Please tell me you put that pizza in the fridge."

I blinked back tears. This wasn't how our reunion was supposed to go.

"He's forty-nine," I told the operator. "Yes, I think he's still alert."

"Audra?" Rex suddenly sounded even

more worried.

"What?"

"I think I broke my back."

The operator spoke in my left ear, "Keep him calm, ma'am, and tell him not to move. The ambulance is on its way."

When I repeated her words to Rex, his gaze met mine. "If I die, I want you to find someone new. Someone who will be there for you and cook you breakfast in bed and not gripe if you want to start a silly little craft shop."

"Silly little what?" I asked.

"I'm in shock," he said. "I'm babbling because I'm going to die."

I pressed my hand to his cheek as Drake began to howl. "You're not going to die, Rex. Not yet, anyway."

He flinched. His eyes grew even larger. "Is that a hell hound?"

"It's Drake. He's worried. You're starting to talk like you have hypothermia."

"Oh, no," he groaned. "I was right. I'm dying. We should've bought that lot on the hill."

"What does that have to do with anything?" a man asked. A tall figure in a thick parka strode toward us. Harry peered out from beneath a dark wool cap. His hands were in his coat pockets. "Rex. Audra. Is everything okay?"

"I fell and broke my back," Rex told him. "Now I'm going to freeze to death right here

254

on my own sidewalk. Can't you hear the hell hound?"

I rolled my eyes. "The hell hound in question is Drake who's inside and wants to help. The ambulance is on its way. I'm on the phone with 9-1-1."

Harry crouched next to Rex. "Have you been drinking?"

"Not since I got out of the limo," he said.

"Uh-huh. Can you move your toes?" the judge asked.

"No," he replied. "They're numb. I can't feel my arms or legs."

Placing my hand on his cheek, I reminded him, "You're lying on a sheet of ice surrounded by snow. Odds are you're cold. Try to relax and think warm thoughts."

Rex met my gaze. "Honey, you should have me cremated. I'd be a whole lot warmer than I am right now."

"I'd say he's in shock," Harry confirmed in case I had any doubt.

A siren pierced the evening air growing louder until an ambulance approached our house with its lights flashing.

"The siren stopped. Where did the ambulance go?" Rex asked.

"They're in front of your house," Harry said.

"Am I dead?"

Harry grimaced. "Not yet."

He groaned, "You're not helping."

Sliding past them both, quite literally, I

greeted the ambulance and answered any questions I could while the paramedics rolled out the gurney and grabbed their kits. It took mere minutes for them to check Rex over, slide him onto a bodyboard they place on top of the gurney, and load him into the ambulance.

As they headed toward the hospital at the north end of Sugarwood, I released a slow breath. A small crowd of neighbours had gathered along the sidewalk to see what was going on. I avoided their questions and returned to the house.

Harry waited on our porch with Doc sipping from a steaming mug. The two spoke in hushed tones before I approached. Their conversation came to a halt as they each gave me a hug.

"We did Rock, Paper, Scissors," Doc said. "I'll drive you to the hospital."

I glanced from one to the other as he handed me a mug. Hot chocolate. I had no idea where it came from, but I was grateful for the sugar. "Did you win or lose?"

Harry chuckled. "That depends how you look at it. Doc has to put up with Rex whining in the backseat all the way home. Unless you'd rather go alone."

"Company would be great, thanks," I told them. "Rex still has the car keys. Let me lock up. I need to talk to Doc anyway."

While I ran inside, Doc pulled his SUV into our driveway. Harry spread a thick layer of salt on the sidewalk from the bin on the porch before anyone else fell. He opened the passenger door for me then waved us off.

On the way to the hospital, I filled Doc in on my lunchtime conversation with Miss Lavinia. Including how she'd used belladonna in Dave's ointment for sciatic pain. "After years of being a butcher and being on his feet all day, that poor man must've been in constant agony."

Doc nodded. "Ah. Now the belladonna makes sense. It's the dose that's puzzling. I'd understand if someone smeared it on his skin, but his killer dipped the dagger blade in it before stabbing him."

Just like the pin jabbed into Dave's doll. I gazed out the window as we drove past Stitch'n'Time. "Why does it feel like we're not getting helpful answers?"

"Welcome to the world of mystery solving," he said. "Are you and Merilee working on a suspect board again?"

"Would you be mad if I said yes?"

"Add notes about the belladonna. It might not be a major cause of death, but it is a clue. Did you ask Miss Lavinia about the dagger?"

I shook my head. "I was so distracted by the poison, I forgot about the dagger."

Doc drove past the Wells' bed and breakfast and crossed the highway toward the hospital. "I may be able to help with that. The dagger is called an athame. It's a ceremonial blade used in magic rituals that usually has a black handle. It's one of four elemental tools in witchcraft or the occult. The athame represents fire, a wand for air, the chalice or cup symbolizes water, and the pentacle for earth. If you've ever seen tarot cards, they appear as the four card suits in each deck."

"Swords, cups, wands, and pentacles," I said. "That explains the cup I found near Miss Lavinia that day. It was a ritual chalice."

"A cup? Are you sure?" Doc asked as we pulled into the parking lot. "Sarah and I went over the crime scene photos several times with Officer Grant. There was no cup."

I turned to face him so fast I got a sharp, burning pain in my neck. "But I saw it next to Dave. It was upright. Like someone had placed it beside him."

He slid the car into a vacant spot and turned off the ignition. "That would make sense. Was there anything inside?"

"There was some kind of liquid inside, but I don't know what it was. Do you think it was the belladonna?"

Doc placed a hand on my arm. "Don't say a word of this to anyone. For now, let's keep it between you, me, and Miss Lavinia until I chat with Officer Grant."

As I glanced toward the hospital, I

swallowed hard. My only logical conclusion was that someone had tampered with the crime scene after I stumbled into it, but when? "Do you think someone intentionally left it out of the crime scene photos?"

"One thing I did read was that the athame is the male principle and the chalice is female," he said, avoiding voicing the same thoughts I had. "Using the two together evokes procreation or universal creativity."

"Procreation? Do you think this has to do with someone wanting a baby? Now I'm really confused." I placed my hands on each of my elbows and hugged my body for warmth. Or for comfort.

Doc gave a nod. "I was leaning toward creativity. Come on. Let's see how Rex is doing. They may keep him overnight for observation."

"For observation? Why?"

He smiled as he opened his door. "Don't worry, Audra, it would only a precaution in case he has a concussion. Nothing to worry about."

"Unless he actually does have a concussion," I reminded him. "Then what?"

"Then we'll deal with it." Doc walked me into the hospital right past the nurses' station and into the emergency room. He chatted with one of the doctors while I tried to get a glimpse of my husband who lay covered with blankets and groaning on a bed near the far wall.

A petite, brown-skinned woman nodded. Her chin-length bob shimmied around her jaw like dark fringe. "Hello, Audra, I'm Doctor Davinder. I haven't had a chance to examine your husband yet, but the nurses have covered him with heated blankets to warm him. I understand he fell."

My eyes welled as my initial shock wore off and I suddenly lapsed into a surge of emotion. "He went outside to get the pizza he dropped and slipped on a patch of ice."

"I received the notes from the paramedics," she said. "You did a great job keeping him warm and still. I understand he thinks he's dying. Something about hell hounds?"

Wiping a tear away, I laughed. "He heard our dog howling and thought Drake was a hell hound."

She smiled. "Ah. I will assure him the hellhound has not followed. Why don't you and Doctor Griffith take a seat? Once I examine Rex, I will let you know my findings."

"Thank you." I nodded and leaned into Doc when he put one arm around me.

He handed me a box of tissues from the counter. "You haven't eaten yet, have you?"

I shook my head. "No, I stuck the pizza in the fridge. It seemed wrong to cook while he was lying there."

"Let's see what's in the machine then we

can discuss your friend Simon." He led me down the hallway to where the vending machines hummed.

"Why's everyone so obsessed with Simon? He wasn't even in town when Dave… You know."

"He does check out, you know," Doc said. "Even though Officer Trent did everything he could to discredit him."

"Have you met Simon yet?" I asked.

"No," he admitted as he bought us each a chocolate bar and a coffee. Jet fuel for the brainstorming I sensed was coming. "I've been trying to come up with an excuse to visit Miss Lavinia, but things have been busy at work. Dave and Molly have the police and the lab in a twist. While Trent insists their deaths aren't related, Grant isn't convinced."

"Are you?"

He nodded. "No. I think someone had a reason to get rid of them both."

While we waited for Doctor Davinder, Doc filled me in on Molly Lavier. The seventy-three- year- old woman was found in a wooded area lying on a cloth pentagram in the snow. A stick whittled to look like a wand was in one hand and a set of keys in the other. She was shot in the temple.

"Now I'm spooked," I said with a shudder. "Why didn't I know this until now?"

Doc met my gaze. "The police swore me

to secrecy. The more I've learned about Miss Lavinia's rituals and tools, the more it makes sense the two are connected. You'll have to talk to Officer Grant to find out more. I'm on the fringe."

"Did you find belladonna on her?" I asked.

He hesitated then lowered his voice even more. "She wore a small glass flask around her neck that contained a trace amount. She also had some in her wound. Enough to make her ill, but not to kill her. The bullet did that job."

"Then the two deaths are related."

"So it seems."

Were Miss Lavinia and Molly working together or part something bigger? I'd need to do research when I got home. What I knew about witches could fill a tarot card.

"I might need to bring Miss Lavinia lunch again," I thought aloud.

Doc looked me in the eye. "What I would suggest, young lady, is that you take your husband home and worry about him rather than Dave or Molly. I know you want to help, but the last thing I want is to find you on my table at work one day."

"I'll be careful."

"Don't be careful," he said, wagging his finger. "Stop digging. Our friend Grant will tell you the same thing. Again."

Footsteps sounded in the corridor as Doctor Davinder approached. Her dark eyes scanned the waiting area until she met my gaze. "Mrs. Clemmings, may I have a word with you?"

"Is he okay?" I walked next to her while Doc followed us down the hall toward the examination room.

"His back is bruised, and he'll be sore for a day or two, but he seems fine otherwise. I would like to keep him in overnight for observation. I'm concerned he may have a mild concussion, so I'd like to keep an eye on him for symptoms."

"No broken bones?" I asked.

"None at all," she replied. "I'm sure it felt like he did though. His body temperature is normal and he's hungry, which is a good sign. One of the nurse's went to find him dinner. We're awaiting a room before we get him settled for the night."

Doc placed a hand on my shoulder. "Can we see him before we leave?"

"Of course. Follow me." She led us into the examination room. "Mr. Clemmings, you have company."

Rex lay with his eyes closed, his breathing slow and regular. As he opened his eyes, he broke into a grin. "Hey, guys. You were right, Audra, no hounds of hell and no broken back. I'm fine. Even better after the meds they gave me. I might get a good night's sleep for the first time in months."

"That's good. I hear they're keeping you

overnight.”

His response was slow. “I need sleep. Apparently, I work too much, and they want to hook a machine to my heart or something.”

“Your heart?” I suddenly found it hard to breathe.

Doctor Davinder cleared her throat. “Ah, yes. There was a note on his chart that he’s suffered an angina attack recently. The chest pain he’s had lately may be stress, but I’d like to rule out anything concerning.”

My mouth fell open. “Chest pain? Rex, why didn’t you tell me?”

He lifted a hand but didn’t seem to have the strength to move it. “It’s nothing.”

“No. Just your heart,” I growled.

Doctor Davinder sidled between us enough to make me take a half-step back as she said, “We’ll make him comfortable and keep a close eye on his vitals. We’ll have more answers in the morning. In the meantime, Doc can take you home, Mrs. Clemmings. There’s no need for you to sit at your husband’s bedside all night.”

“But what if…?”

Doc draped his arm across my shoulders. “Rex will be sleeping. You might as well go home and do the same. Come on, I’m craving a burger and fries.”

“Ooh, I want fries,” Rex mumbled.

Doctor Davinder chuckled. “You get what the nurse brings you. Nothing fried, I assure you."

My stomach growled. "Okay. I'll come back in the morning."

"I would expect nothing less," she said with a warm smile.

Once we left the hospital, Doc made a beeline for the nearest drive-thru. Armed with burgers, fries, and milkshakes, we returned to my house. Thankfully, everything was intact although Drake seemed sullen.

Before we could sit to eat, Harry let himself in the front door. "Hey, how's Rex?"

Suddenly, I couldn't speak past the lump in my throat.

Doc filled him in on the possible concussion and the angina.

The judge turned on the fireplace while I nibbled my fries. When he sat in the armchair, he met my gaze. "Don't worry, Audra. It's nothing serious."

"What if it is? Here's me with the whole cancer scare and now Rex with heart problems. The kids will be home soon, and I don't know what to tell them."

"You're a strong woman and Rex is a better man than he's been acting lately," Doc said. "Between you both, you'll get through this."

Harry agreed, "And I guarantee neither will slow you down when it comes to figuring out what happened to Dave."

"Or Molly," Doc added.

His face paled. "You told her? What were you thinking?"

Doc raised his milkshake. "It was only a matter of time before she figured things out anyway. I just saved us both the aggravation."

"You know all about Molly's death, too?" I stared.

Harry shrugged. "What can I say? When you hang out with the local coroner, you're bound to hear the latest gossip."

Doc chuckled. "Except my gossip has a foundation in fact."

"And you're willing to share it with anyone who feeds you," the judge said. "Where's your suspect board, Audra?"

I reached beneath the couch and hoped Drake hadn't snacked on it while we were at the hospital. It was intact. "What else can you tell me about Molly?"

Harry groaned, "You mean aside from the fact she's appeared in my courtroom monthly for the past decade? Once a week when she was fighting a cause."

"I've only seen her in passing before this week," Doc said. "I'm not an activist by any stretch of the imagination. Looks like you believe Dave and Molly were killed by the same person, too."

"The dagger, the wand, the pentacle, and the chalice are all good clues."

"What chalice?" Harry asked.

Doc shook his head. "I keep telling you,

there was no chalice at the crime scene.”

I fished out my cell phone to pull up the photo I’d taken. “Yes. There was.”

“Did you take that before you called the police?” Harry asked.

“No, I’m not that morbid. I took it after. Right before Miss Lavinia came to.”

Doc reached for my phone as he raised his eyebrows. “She came to?”

“Briefly. She didn’t say anything though.”

While he and Harry took a look at my photo then texted it to themselves, I took the opportunity to ask, “What do you know about Chuck Benson?”

When they both looked up at me, I knew I was onto something. “What? He’s a big, strong guy. He’d be able to do commit both crimes without breaking a sweat.”

Harry nodded. “You’re right, he could. The question is why? Chuck has everything to lose if he got caught.”

“Good point,” I grumbled. “What about Andrew Laney?”

“Rex and Laney were out of town when each murder occurred,” Doc said.

I stared. “How do you know that?”

“Officer Grant told me.”

“So Rex was a suspect.” I snorted. “I knew it.”

Harry scowled at me. “Don’t get too high and mighty, you were a suspect, too.”

My eyes grew wide. “Me? I didn’t know Dave or Molly. What motive would I have?”

"You don't , which is why you're no longer a suspect."

Doc tapped the Bristol board. "Why do you have Emily Trent on here?"

"She's a question mark. I don't know much about her aside from the fact she's the lead investigator's mom who left town under mysterious circumstances."

"She's also a forensics investigator," Doc added.

I fumbled my pen. "She's what? Please tell me she wasn't at both crime scenes."

Doc and Harry exchanged glances before Doc said, "I can find out."

After they left, I studied the suspect board for another hour. How was I supposed to fall asleep with so many thoughts rambling through my head? I started to pour a glass of wine then reconsidered. A bubble bath would work much better.

# Chapter Fifteen

Monday, December 5

The bubble bath didn't work. I tossed and turned all night.

Drake and I both walked in a sleepy daze to the shop the next morning. He was lucky enough to get to curl up on the heat vent while I slumped over the counter and filled Merilee in on the latest.

"Rex did what?" she asked as she stood across the counter with a coffee in one hand. "Was he hurt?"

I shook my head. "His back is bruised, and he might have a concussion. The doctor was concerned he had an angina attack, so they kept him in overnight."

Her mouth fell open. "Oh, Audra, why didn't you call me?"

"Doc and Harry were there, they—"

"What are you doing here? You should be at the hospital."

I blinked back tears. "I called there before I left the house. Rex was in and out of tests all night, so he was asleep. His doctor won't be in to go over his results until three. I'll call a cab at noon and hang out with him until then."

Merilee sipped her coffee before she asked, "You don't have the car?"

"The keys are in his coat, which is at the hospital."

"You need to hide a set in your purse," she said. "Don't you have a spare?"

"Knowing Rex, they're in his desk at work again. Good thing I like to walk." I pulled suspect board from my tote bag. "On the upside, Doc and Harry rolled up their sleeves to brainstorm and gave me a new perspective on some things."

Merilee grinned. "Ooh! Did they add any names?"

I unrolled the suspect board and watched for her reaction. I knew the instant she read about Molly Lavier's connection to Dave.

"Doc and Harry told you this?"

"It's a matter of public record," I told her. "Those two did everything short of pulling out crime scene photos."

"Too bad. We could've used those."

We spent an hour going over the poster before Merilee sent me to grab food for Rex. We'd both sampled hospital food and knew he'd be ravenous. On my way out the door to head to the deli, my phone rang.

"I have an appointment in Toronto," Simon said. "Could you bring my auntie lunch today? I'll be back as soon as I can. Thanks."

He'd hung up before I could even respond.

Merilee raised her eyebrows. "Now what?"

"Simon has to go to Toronto, so he asked me to bring Miss Lavinia lunch. I would've just told him I was busy but didn't get the chance."

She shrugged. "We could close the store for a while. I can run up to see Miss Lavinia while you go to the hospital."

Behind me, the front door opened, and a couple of white-haired women wandered inside. Drake raised his head and whimpered before he settled back on the vent. Scratch that thought.

"I'll bring her lunch then call a cab. Is it okay if I leave Drake with you again?" I asked. "I should've left him home, but…"

But I was exhausted and not thinking straight. My mind was scattered over everything. Rex's fall. Dave and Molly. The store. The sewing circle.

"Go." Merilee waved. "Feed Miss Lavinia then go to the hospital."

* * *

"Audra." Doc stood in line just ahead of me in the deli his voice was harsh like he had borderline laryngitis. The lines on his face seemed etched a little deeper than last night. "I was just thinking about you. I

271

suppose that's why I decided to get a sandwich and a container of pickles."

I gave him what I hoped was a much needed hug. "I'm good. I'm picking up lunch for Miss Lavinia. Her nephew had to go out of town and asked me to look in on her. I'm also getting something for Rex and Merilee."

"Ah. Rex is fine. Harry and I brought him breakfast and checked in on him earlier. How's Lavinia?" he asked. "Fully recovered, I hope."

"You guys saw Rex this morning?" Disappointment washed over me. "Why didn't you call me? When I called the hospital, they said he was sleeping."

Doc smirked. "Nope. Harry and I both had meetings in the area, so we carpooled. Rex was sitting back with a lukewarm coffee on a call with his boss. He seems to think he'll rest when he dies."

"That sounds like something he'd say. How are you? You look like you need to sleep for a week."

"If that's your subtle way of saying I look like crap, I'll take it. Let's just say I'm keeping busy. Sarah's off sick this week. That flu that's going around has her so sick she can barely get out of bed."

"That's awful."

Charity Wells glanced up. "Hey, Doc, what can I get you today?"

I stepped back to wait while he placed

his order.

"What are you getting?" he asked before he paid.

I waved a hand. "That's okay, I'll get it. It's not just for me."

She raised her eyebrows. "I wouldn't turn down free food if I were you, especially not from Doc. He's the biggest cheapskate around."

"Gee, thanks." Doc scowled. "I'm aware who you're having lunch with, Audra, and I insist. After all the sandwiches you've brought me, the least I can do is to treat you lovely ladies to lunch."

"That's really sweet of you," I told him.

I ordered three butternut squash soups, three grilled cheese sandwiches, and passed on coffee in favour of herbal tea since Miss Lavinia would give me grief. Despite her advice to avoid caffeine while I was using her green powder, coffee had been my lifeblood since my kids were little and I refused to give it up completely.

He steered me toward a table near the front window while we waited. "Bumping into you works in my favour. I need information."

"From me? Now there's a switch. What do you want to know?"

"I had a curious question from Officer Trent earlier about a suit that belongs to Rex," he said. "Where'd the red stain on his shirt come from?"

"Why are you asking?" I asked suddenly
wary of his motives, which was likely how
he felt about me on a good day.

Doc leaned closer. "The officer thinks it
could be blood spatter and has asked the
lab to examine every speck on the suit.
When one of the techs tested it, he
discovered it was a poison."

"Let me guess. Belladonna."

"Bingo. How'd you know?"

"Rex said he ran into someone coming
out of Miss Lavinia's shop the day before
Dave died and he felt unwell later, like he
was drunk. I found him passed out on the
couch the next morning. When he saw the
stain later, he thought he'd spilled red
wine."

Doc frowned as he shook his head. "That
boy needs to stop drinking. You can tell him
I said so. Neither of you wants to see what
cirrhosis of the liver does to a body. It's
never stopped me from enjoying a glass of
brandy now and then, but still."

Charity saved me from further medical
ick. "Here's your lunch, Doc. Audra, I put
your food in separate bags. I threw in a
treat for my favourite doggie, too."

"Thanks, Charity." I considered getting
Drake before I saw Miss Lavinia. I never
asked if she was okay with dogs.

As Doc walked me out, he asked, "Is it
possible that's what stained Rex's suit?"

"You don't believe him?" I raised my

eyebrows in surprise.

"Did Miss Lavinia see it happen?"

"I can find out. I'm going there now."

"Do that and get back to me," he said. "Oh, and if you happen to see a bottle of belladonna in her kitchen, I'd run."

"Why would she…?" I started to ask, but Doc was rounding the corner and heading back to work before I could finish. "That was odd."

I stopped by Stitch'n'Time to get the key to Miss Lavinia's from Merilee then took Drake with me. Hopefully, he'd sniff out the scent that drove him crazy as we walked through the shop. Or he'd be distracted by lunch. Worst case, he'd amuse Miss Lavinia.

With the lunch bag balanced precariously on two steaming paper cups, I let us inside. We'd barely reached the counter when someone cleared their throat behind us. I hadn't locked the door. My heart raced like I'd run across town.

"You know I could arrest you right now for entering a crime scene." Officer Trent stood in the entrance with his hand hovering over his gun.

Drake growled. His hackles rose as his torso vibrated against my leg.

I turned around slowly. If my hands weren't full, I would've patted his back. "It's okay. He won't hurt us. First of all, it's no longer a sealed crime scene. Secondly, I have a key. Simon's out of town, so we're bringing Miss Lavinia lunch."

Officer Trent flared his nostrils. He moved his hand a couple inches away from his weapon as he took a couple steps forward.

Drake's growl grew louder. More menacing.

"Let me set this stuff down. I'll lock the door when you leave."

I hoped he'd take the hint, but he remained rooted in place. His feet didn't move, but his gaze swooped around the room like a hungry bat. Drake continued to growl while I kept a tight grip on the leash. One moment of weakness and Officer Trent could become Drake's next chew toy.

"Tell Miss Lavinia I'd like a word with her when she's up to it," Officer Trent announced as he turned to leave.

Just as I started to release a relieved breath, he paused in the doorway letting a spray of snow inside. "And tell Simon I'd like to talk to him, especially if he plans to stick around Sugarwood."

"Okey, dokey."

Officer Trent's cheek twitched as he stepped outside then pulled the door closed.

I dropped the leash on the floor, clutching the food against my chest. As I lunged to lock the door, Drake stopped growling in favour of snuffling the area where I'd discovered Dave's body. Too bad he couldn't tell me what he smelled. It would've made things easier.

"Okey, dokey? Really? Oh, brother. Come on, boy. Let's go see Miss Lavinia." I led him to the staircase.

Drake gave a whimper as we walked past shelves lined with jars and bottles. He didn't seem interested in any of them. Although he hesitated at the staircase, he climbed to the top and sat in front of the apartment door with no further growling.

"That's a good start." I rapped on the door twice then opened it as I called out, "Hi, Miss Lavinia. Drake and I brought lunch."

No reply. My entire body tensed. The apartment was so still I heard a mouse chewing the wall from the inside. That is until Drake let out a soft whimper. He moved away from my side to sniff the floor.

I set our lunch on the counter while he meandered. Just as I pulled out my phone to call Merilee, Drake padded down the hallway toward me, his nails clicking on the floor.

Miss Lavinia, dressed in tie-dyed leggings and a long, gray sweater, walked behind him with a grin. Her long graying hair hung in a thick braid. "Your dog was worried about me. He has no concern for privacy though. Walked right into the bathroom like he owned the place."

"That sounds right."

Miss Lavinia sank into her cushy armchair and tossed her braid over one shoulder. When Drake sat near her, she stroked his ears. "He's a lovely animal. Why haven't you brought him by to meet me before now?"

"He has a lack of discretion when it comes to his diet. He'll eat anything."

"Then we have a lot in common, don't we, doggy?" She chuckled as I fetched our lunch from the cupboard. By the time I returned, Drake had his head in her lap and moaned while she made small circles above his eyes. "This poor boy is stressed out. Fabric gives him comfort. Is everything okay at home?"

I shooed Drake aside as I pulled out a container of soup and the warm foil packet with Miss Lavinia's sandwich. "No worse than usual."

"That explains it then. To what do I owe the pleasure of your company?"

"Simon asked if I could bring lunch since he had to go out of town."

She gave a nod as she said, "Ah, so you're my babysitter. My poor nephew's afraid I'll burn the place down if I make a sandwich."

"He was probably more concerned that you'd be alone all day. He asked me to deliver lunch and make sure you didn't need anything."

"Uh-huh. We know better. Don't we, Drake?"

"Do you need anything?" I asked.

"Nope." When Miss Lavinia reached for her soup, my dog craned his neck toward her sandwich. She tapped his nose with her fingertip. "Don't even think about it, doggy."

I picked up the bag with my lunch and motioned to Drake. "Okay, then we'll get out of your way. Come on, Drake, time to go."

She stared. "You're leaving already?"

"You're right. You don't need a babysitter. I'm going to the shop."

Drake didn't move. His gaze was laser-focused on her grilled cheese sandwich and drool pooled at the corner of his mouth.

"I'd rather not eat alone," she said. "Besides, I need help with this huge sandwich."

Right on cue, Drake smacked his lips.

Taking off my coat, I grinned. I wasn't ready to leave yet. I still had time to get to the hospital before Rex's doctor released him. "If you insist."

Miss Lavinia snuck Drake a small piece of her grilled cheese sandwich as she said, "Simon told me he found the voodoo dolls."

"Um…yeah. He showed us. They're a little spooky." She knew I had my doll as well as my father's, but I'd never told her Merilee and I snuck into her shop after the cowboy died. And again after I'd discovered her and Dave on the floor. Would she be

279

upset I took Rex's doll?

"They get the job done."

My eyes widened. "What job is that?"

"Healing people." Miss Lavinia fed Drake another chunk of her sandwich.

"Oh. That." As much as I wanted to bring up Rex's fall, I wasn't sure what to ask.

She leaned over to touch my arm as she said, "You seem awfully distracted today. I've told you those dolls are meant for good, not evil. I use them to heal. I've never used one to kill and I don't plan to start now."

Then who made the doll with the needle in its back? My appetite waned.

Drake seemed to sense my sudden lack of hunger. He inched toward my sandwich with a string of drool seeping from his mouth.

"Don't even think about it, buddy," I warned.

He lay on the floor and buried his nose beneath his paws.

"You have a sweet dog," she said. "He must be great company."

"When he's not eating fabric or knocking over the Christmas tree."

Miss Lavinia smiled. "Is this his first Christmas?"

"Yes, it is." I paused and patted Drake's head. "I keep forgetting that he has no idea what all the shiny stuff is or why a tree suddenly appeared in the living room. He doesn't like the cold, but he loves the snow.

If I let him, he'd play in the park all day."

Her eyes lit up. "Maybe I'll have to join you for a walk one day. Playing in the snow sounds fun."

Another thought struck me. "If you're looking to get out of the apartment, you should drop by our store Wednesday afternoon and join our sewing circle.

"What do I have to do?" she asked.

"If you have a needlepoint or knitting project you're working on, bring it along. The circle meets from one o'clock until three."

She slipped Drake another piece of her sandwich. "I might take you up on the offer. Did Simon mention why he went to the city?"

"Just that he had a meeting, and the cab would cost a fortune."

Miss Lavinia smiled then sighed. "The doctor said it might be months before I can work in the shop alone all day. Simon's trying to get a work visa so he can stay to help me out. I don't have anyone else I trust to mix treatments for my clients."

I sat up a little straighter. "That's great. I mean about Simon staying longer. I'm sorry you're having a rough time getting through this."

"It's not so bad," Miss Lavinia said, patting Drake's head. "This is the first time I've had company for lunch in years."

Doc's comments came back to me. "Do

you happen to sell belladonna in your shop?"

Her neck cracked when she faced me. "Belladonna? I do keep a little under lock and key. It's lethal in large doses."

"What about in small doses?" I asked.

"It's not to be taken internally. Mostly, I use it in salves or plasters."

"Plasters? Like for broke bones?" I frowned.

"Not quite. In the old days, most people used pieces of cloth soaked in various mixtures for colds and the like," she said. "The patient would apply it to the skin and relax while the medication soaked in. These days, people prefer to pop pills, but I still swear by the plasters. They make people slow down and take deep breaths."

A lightbulb seemed to flicker on in my head. "Like the castor oil you told me to use."

"Exactly. I have clients who use a tiny bit of belladonna to stop bronchial spasms during asthma attacks and for colds and hay fever. Even as a painkiller."

"Did Dave Spencer use it?" I asked.

She frowned. "Audra, you know that's privileged information."

"Right. Sorry."

"I never told you this," she lowered her voice, "but he used it for sciatic pain. After years of being on his feet all day, the poor man was in constant agony."

Now the belladonna made sense. Just not on the tip of a dagger. I'd be obligated to give Doc the heads up. Privileged information or not.

"Maybe this will give you a glimpse into what I do." Miss Lavinia got up and went to a narrow bookshelf draped in lush ivy growing from a ten-inch round black cauldron. She handed me a book with a dark purple cover.

"*A Guide to Witchcraft*," I read aloud and tried not to recoil. Rex's worst fears were suddenly confirmed in paperback form.

She chuckled. "Don't look so scared. I'll bet it's not what you're expecting."

"No eyes of newt or wings of bats?"

"We celebrate nature, Audra, not chop it to bits for amusement like some people."

"Laney Developments." I didn't even have to ask.

Miss Lavinia tapped the end of her nose. "Read the book. You might learn things you don't expect."

After taking Drake for a quick walk, I returned to the store. I started to help Merilee with customers before she asked when I was going to see Rex.

I slapped a hand to my forehead. "Rex. Oh, my goodness. I got so distracted, I forgot to call a cab. I'd better call the hospital."

Luckily, I had the number on speed dial. The nurse who answered said, "Mister

Clemmings went home. He was discharged an hour ago."

"Oh crap. Why didn't anyone call me?" I was torn between guilt and outrage.

"A tall, distinguished gentleman picked him up. I believe his name was Harry."

I'd barely hung up before my phone chimed with a text from Rex.

*"Harry drove me home. See you after work."*

Guilt grabbed me by the throat. "Merilee, I have to go home."

"Home? Not to the hospital?" she asked.

"Harry took him home an hour ago and neither of them bothered to call me. I'll talk to you later."

Drake and I did a fast walk to the house and stomped up the front steps. Why didn't he call me? Why was I the last one to know everything? I might have to use that doll after all.

By the time we burst through the front door, Rex lounged on the couch with a burger and fries. On the coffee table, stood an orange pill vial and an extra-large drink sweating water droplets. Harry sat on the armchair reading the newspaper while he munched his own fries.

Rex grinned and asked, "Hey, honey, how was your day?"

"Why didn't you call me?"

"You have enough on your plate without me causing you grief."

I scowled and reminded him, "I'm your wife. You're supposed to cause me grief."

The judge folded the paper and crossed the room to get between us before I threw anything. "Now that you're here, I'm heading to the courthouse. I'll be home around six. Let me know if you need anything."

"Thanks for bringing him home, Harry." I walked him out to the porch.

Once I closed the door behind us, he paused. "Don't be mad at Rex. Doc and I stopped by the hospital early this morning and spoke to one of his doctors. Rex's test results were good. He's bruised and needs to take it easy for a while, but he's fine other than that."

"What about his heart?"

"They kept monitors on him all night and didn't see anything abnormal," he said. "Doctor Davinder wants to see him in a couple of days. For now, she prescribed him painkillers and medication for anxiety."

"Anxiety? You mean it wasn't his heart? That's a relief."

Harry grinned. "That doesn't mean he won't play it up a little. He's supposed to take up a hobby or find ways to relax. I doubt he'll do either, but it's worth mentioning."

I chuckled. "I expect he will. He's a lousy patient. This could be a long afternoon."

"With any luck, he'll take a couple

painkillers and sleep for hours." He hugged me. "How's Miss Lavinia? Doc said you brought her lunch."

"Pretty well, all things considered."

"I've been meaning to meet her nephew while he's here. It's Simon, right?"

"Yeah, he seems like a good guy. I'd better get back inside. The last time I left Rex and Drake alone, it didn't go well."

Harry grinned. "Good luck."

"Thanks. And thanks again for everything." I waited until he'd reached the gate then paused at the door and took a deep breath. If it wasn't so chilly out, I would've stalled even longer.

By the time I stepped inside, Drake lay on the couch curled near Rex's feet. My husband snored with the remote control in one hand. It hovered precariously above the floor.

With a grin, I took off my boots and coat then crossed the room to drape a blanket over Rex. I guessed he'd taken painkillers already. Heaven knew how long he'd be out.

Rather than do anything to disturb them, I pulled out the stocking to finish the tip of the toe. Before I got to work, I thought about the book Miss Lavinia loaned me. Now would be the perfect time to read it. I could work on the stocking when Rex was awake. He might not be as open-minded about a book on witchcraft.

I made a cup of tea then settled back with the book on witchcraft. I was about to crack it open when I realized two things.

One, the cover looked brand new.

Two, Lavinia Brevil, Molly Lavier, and the Sacred Sisters Coven wrote the contents.

What had I gotten myself into this time?

# Chapter Sixteen
### Tuesday, December 6

While Rex nested on the couch surrounded by pillows and cushions and watched the Tuesday morning news, Drake and I walked to work. The less my husband had to get off the couch for a while, the better.

I watched the snow fall outside the large window that spanned half the front of our shop and sighed. Moody Mother Nature seemed intent on blanketing us with a thick layer of white. It was pretty to look at, but the mere thought of cleaning snow off Drake every time he went outside made me tired.

Doc had hinted at a connection between Dave and Molly's murders, but neither of us had any proof. I hadn't even seen Dave's footprints that morning or I might've had a hint something was wrong. The killer had used a chalice, a pentacle, and a dagger as part of Dave's death, then a wand and pentacle for Molly's. If there were more people on the killer's list, I had no idea where he'd find more tools. They might've only been there because of convenience. Although, who just happens to find a pentagram in the woods or knows how to make one? More than likely, they were used to throw off the police—and me.

"What am I missing?" I whispered as I returned to the photocopies Simon made of Miss Lavinia's calendar. Doc had mentioned keys. Had anyone figured out what they keys were for?

Judy Wells was the last person to see Miss Lavinia on Tuesday before she closed. I wanted to ask Charity if her mom said anything odd after her visit, even though Judy was at the bottom of my suspect list. The woman needed a walker and had arthritis. In order to shoot anyone, she'd need to let go of the walker. Her daughter, on the other hand, could've done a dandy job of either, but was likely at the deli.

"That's ridiculous. They both loved Dave." I crossed them off my list.

"Uh-oh. I know that look." Merilee paused with a bundle of fabric in one hand. "You're trying to figure out who killed Dave and Molly. This calls for a hefty dose of sugar."

I waded through article after article of the media circus that stemmed from an argument between Molly and one of the town's former mayors. She was a member of One Healthy Green Earth. That group's name had come up when the cowboy died. Could that be the connection?

Digging into their website, I found a membership list. Only a couple people chose to remain anonymous. The rest seemed thrilled to let the world know they were part of the group protesting every decision the mayor and council made. Miss Lavinia and Molly Lavier weren't only members, but founders of the group. They'd put up a good fight against the mayor, council, and Laney Developments to protect what was now a hundred acre conservation area outside of Sugarwood.

Finally, one puzzle piece fell into place. But how did Dave fit in? Judging from the brutality of the attack, he was no innocent by-stander. The deeper I dug, the more great online bargains I found, but still no connection between Dave and Molly.

"You look frustrated." Merilee handed me a large paper cup and a small paper bag.

I frowned. "I didn't realize you'd gone out."

"Sure you did. You even looked up at me."

"Did I?"

She pulled me away from the computer. ""Oh, that's it, you need a break from that thing before you can't even see straight. How's Rex?"

"Good. I think. He keeps texting for me to bring him things."

"Okay, then it's the case. What's got you so confused?" she asked.

"I can't find a link between Dave and Molly," I admitted. "Dave was no tree-hugger. Molly was vegan with no reason to go to the butcher shop. Neither of them were part of the Rotary club, the Probus club, or even the Legion."

She sighed. "Did they use the same dating app?"

I closed my eyes and rubbed them. "How am I supposed to know?"

"You're not. It was a bad attempt at making you laugh."

"Dave Spencer wasn't on Miss Lavinia's schedule for Wednesday, but Molly and Judy Wells were. There has to be a connection. I just can't figure out what."

Merilee shrugged. "Maybe the killer only thought there was a connection."

"What do you mean?"

"What if the only thing they have in common is the killer?" she asked. "If we can figure out how they knew him, we can solve this case."

I rolled my eyes. "Gee, if only we knew who the killer was, we could figure out the connection between them all."

"Drink. You're becoming hostile." She shoved a cup toward me.

The aroma of whipped cream and peppermint wafted through the hole in the lid. Peppermint hot chocolate wasn't on my recommended foods list from Miss Lavinia, but this was a time of crisis. Comfort food was my best means of solving stress. That and thoughts of jabbing Rex's doll with a big needle.

"Do you remember that tree-hugger group we read out about when the cowboy died? One Healthy Green Earth. Molly and Miss Lavinia were founding members." I reached for the keyboard and pulled up a photo.

"Them again?" She leaned over to take a closer look at a photo that popped up. "Hey, wasn't that guy the mayor of Sugarwood years ago? Right before they turned the forest into a park."

The door opened before I could take a look.

Bennie from the sewing circle strode across the room. Her blue hair sparkled with melting snowflakes and the lenses of her red-framed cat's eyeglasses glittered with droplets. She marched straight toward us before she announced, "I know who killed Molly Lavier."

Drake gave a low growl but kept his distance. He seemed torn between barking and staying near the heat vent.

My eyes felt like they grew as big around as my cup lid. "You knew Molly?"

"Of course, I did. We're part of the same group," she said.

"One Healthy Green Earth." I took a wild

guess.

Bennie shook her head. "No, the Sacred Sisters Coven."

Merilee sat on her stool next to me. "Now that didn't come up in my research."

"It did in mine," I muttered, hoping there wouldn't be any spells cast in my direction. From what I'd read in Miss Lavinia's book, it explained why Bennie was making a wedding quilt to manifest a man for her granddaughter.

"Relax," she said. "We don't do black magic, especially during Yule."

"That's a relief. What's Yule?" Merilee sipped her hot chocolate.

"A celebration of the winter solstice, which is the longest night of the year and marks a return of the sun," I explained.

Bennie raised her eyebrows as she peered over her red frames. "Very good."

My cheeks warmed. "Miss Lavinia gave me a book to read."

"The coven's witchcraft book? Informative read. We had fun writing it."

When Merilee frowned at me for withholding information, I averted my gaze and asked, "We'll get back to that. Who do you think killed Molly?"

Bennie put her hands on her hips. "I don't think. I know. About a month ago, this woman showed up at a meeting and said she wanted to be part of our coven. Molly nearly lost her mind. She didn't want her in the group, but Miss Lavinia suggested we give her a chance."

Merilee held up a hand. "Wait. They're both in the coven? Who else is involved?"

For a split second, it didn't look like Bennie would give up any other names. She released a long sigh. "Me, Carol, Molly, Miss Lavinia, a couple women from Barrie, and three sisters from Collingwood. Then this new woman wanted to join us.

"Why haven't we ever heard of Sacred Sisters Coven?" I asked.

Bennie smirked. "Do you practice witchcraft or worship nature?"

"I don't practice anything, and I avoid nature as much as possible," Merilee said.

"Audra?" She turned to me.

"I enjoy a good walk in the park with Drake, but…" I waved a hand.

"There you go." Bennie grinned.

I still had questions and couldn't let the opportunity slip away. "What makes you think this woman killed Molly? Just because Molly didn't want a new member to join the group doesn't mean that's why she died."

She rummaged through her purse while she said, "No, actually it was because of the heated conversation Molly had with the woman after the meeting. I have no idea what was said, but Molly's turned tomato red and she clenched her hands so tight her fingers were white. The other woman was just as upset and left in a huff."

"Do you know her name?" I asked.

Bennie handed me a sheet of paper. "I'm the secretary, so I get all the new member information. I printed hers off after they found Molly in the woods. I figured the police would be asking questions before long."

"What was Molly doing in the woods alone?" I asked.

"Forest bathing."

Merilee's eyes grew wide as she recoiled. "That, you're going to have to explain."

"We worship the forest and trees, especially the area we rescued from Laney Developments that's thriving," she said. "Anyway, bathers walk slowly through the woods to admire the world around them. Every leaf, every bug, every tree—"

"You lost me at bug." Merilee cringed.

Bennie shook her head as she continued, "It's about using all of your senses to develop a connection with something outside of yourself, and your cell phone. About celebrating life in its many forms."

"Drake has that one down pat. He definitely uses all his senses when we go for walks." I chuckled, I unfolding the paper she gave me. As I read it, my hands grew oddly cold. All I could do was focus on breathing.

"What's wrong?" Merilee asked, nudging

my arm.

"It was Emily Trent," I whispered.

Her cheeks paled. "Oh crap."

"I'm sure you've heard about her," Bennie said. "She was Mayor Roger Trent's wife."

Merilee gasped. "That's the guy in the news story you were reading. He was the mayor who died in office who wanted to sell the conservation land to Laney Developments for new condos and was going to get a big kickback for it."

Bennie said as she puffed out her chest like a proud mother hen. "The one and only. Thank goodness for Molly and Miss Lavinia. Those two sure set him straight."

My head began to swim. "Do you think she came back to get revenge? What would she have to gain by killing Dave?"

"I don't know," Bennie said, "but she must be involved somehow. Anyway, after all that's happened, the coven's taking a break. We need time to figure out how to continue."

I met her gaze. "The police found a wand and a pentacle with Molly. Was she using them for forest bathing?"

Bennie closed her eyes and bowed her head for a moment. When she looked up, her eyes shone with tears. "Molly never went anywhere without her wand. Her son hand-carved it out of willow for her. As for the pentacle, anyone could've made one.

Do know what it was made from?"

Doc had mentioned a piece of cloth, but I had a feeling Officer Grant would be the best person to ask. As long as he was feeling better.

"Are you okay, dear?" Bennie asked. "You look a little pale."

Merilee nudged my cup of hot chocolate. "She just needs a lot more sugar, then she'll be right as rain. Er…snow."

"You should get your iron levels checked," she suggested. "Women your age tend to have issues with iron."

Iron wasn't my problem. Two murders and my husband falling on ice troubled me more. "I'll do that."

Bennie glanced outside. The small wet flurries had become large, puffy flakes that looked more like down from a pillow than snow. "Oh, look at that. Molly would say there was a giant chicken in the sky spreading feathers everywhere."

"I would've told my kids the same thing. I wish I'd known her," I sighed.

Bennie patted my hand. "Enjoy your hot chocolate. I'm going to check on Lavinia."

Hopefully, she wouldn't mention the abundance of sugar. As soon as Bennie was gone, I opened the little bag and smiled when I saw a Santa cookie inside. "I won't tell Miss Lavinia if you don't."

Merilee, who'd just taken a bite, covered her mouth. "My lips are sealed."

While I munched, I texted Rex for an update before I returned to surfing the web for more information. This time, I focused on Emily Trent, widow of the former mayor.

Judging from social media there wasn't much to tell. Emily was a devoted wife, mother, and philanthropist. She'd appeared at every gala and grocery store opening her husband Roger was a part of and seemed to always have her picture in the paper. Until the day Roger died. After that, she ranted to the media how the old witch gave her husband a potion that killed him. She just couldn't prove it.

The day of his funeral, Emily and her son left town unexpectedly—right before the burial. They never even showed up at the cemetery. For years, the local papers and national media offered wild speculation about their sudden disappearance. If anyone in Sugarwood knew where they'd gone, no one shared the information with the police.

I vaguely recalled the svelte brunette with the Farrah Fawcett haircut. Doc and Harry were friends with Roger. They played poker the last Friday of every month with a group of men at the local Legion, including Andrew Laney. Back then Rex worked at the car dealership and had nothing to do with most of them.

"Find anything?" Merilee leaned her chin on the heel of her hand while resting her elbow on the counter.

"Not really."

"Too bad the sewing circle only meets once a week," she said. "They're a good source of comic relief."

I nodded. "And of information. Despite that membership form from Bennie, I still can't find much about Emily Trent. It's like she fell off the planet until recently."

She chuckled. "I'll bet she was abducted, and the aliens finally got tired of her."

"It's possible, but I'm willing to bet she took off before she could humiliate herself or her family any more than she thought she had. Speaking of, do you happen to know her maiden name?"

Merilee glanced at her watch. "Nope. She wasn't a local. Think anyone would notice if we snuck out ten minutes early?"

"Today? No one would notice if we left ten hours early," I grumbled.

"Go home. It'll give you time to check up on Rex and work on the suspect list. Who knows, maybe Rex knows more about Roger and Emily."

That got me to smile. It was right up there with cookies and hot chocolate.

Once we'd locked and double checked the doors, Drake and I took the long way home through the park while I thought over what Bennie told us. She, Molly, Miss Lavier, and others in the sewing circle were witches and Emily Trent wanted to join the club. Had she been a part of any other covens? I doubted they kept membership lists on websites, but it was worth digging around online for.

I called out when I opened the front door, but Rex was nowhere in sight. My first guess was he'd gone to the office to see what he'd fallen behind on. Rather than start making dinner right away, I let Drake into the backyard then called Officer Grant.

One thing was for sure, he didn't seem thrilled to hear from me. "Please tell me you're not still poking into Dave's murder."

I flashed a smug smile even though he couldn't see me. "Nope. Molly Lavier's."

"Oh, brother. Audra, why can't you just drop this?"

*This?* I straightened as I stood near the counter. "You mean the two are related?"

"I never said that."

"I know, but it's the way you never said it."

Drake barked to come back in. I didn't blame him. The temperature had plummeted ten degrees over the past three hours and was dropping fast. The weather felt more like January than the end of November. I hoped Rex hadn't gone for a walk.

"Do yourself a favour," Officer Grant said. "Light the fireplace, make a cup of tea—hell, pour a glass of wine if it makes you feel good—just stop meddling."

"Where did you find Molly?" I asked, rubbing Drake's fur with an old towel to get the snow off. Did he really have to roll in it? "I know someone found her body in the park. I just want to know where."

He grunted. "Please stop talking to Doc."

"I can't. He lives two doors down. He'll worry if I stop asking questions, and I don't want to be responsible for giving him health issues."

There was a long silence where the clock hands ticked to four-thirty. The fact he was thinking it over was encouraging. Nerve-wracking, but encouraging.

Finally, he said, "A jogger found her near the pond where there's a clearing in the trees. It's where the Sacred Sisters Coven meets. I'm sure you've learned all about them from your sewing circle, so I'll leave it at that."

I hung the towel on a cabinet drawer knob to dry. "Man, I never want to start jogging. Too many joggers find bodies. How do they run in all the snow? The Conservation staff doesn't clear the trails in winter. Wait, are you saying the coven has permission to do rituals there?"

"I didn't say that, but that was an interesting thought progression."

"You didn't not say it." I followed Drake to the couch.

He sighed. "Part of the deal when the Conservation took over management of the forest was that they'd allow the coven to keep and maintain their sacred space for the next hundred years."

"That's a long time. Was she nude?"

Officer Grant coughed then cleared his throat. I'd caught him off guard, then cleared his throat. "No, she wore her usual winter coat and a pair of boots. They save the dancing naked under the light of the full moon for warmer months."

Rolling my eyes, I groaned, "That's not funny. I just wondered if she'd been assaulted in any way, that's all."

"Nothing but a bullet through the heart, and a wand coated with belladonna protruding from the wound."

"Just like the dagger," I mused. "Do you have any suspects?"

"Would I tell you if I did?" he asked.

I hesitated before chose to share what I'd learned, "Bennie said Emily Trent might know something. Emily was trying to join the coven and Molly wasn't happy about it and refused to let her join."

"Why is that?"

"None of us had any idea."

Officer Grant gave a reluctant, "Thanks. I'll look into it."

"One more question. Have you figured out what the set of keys she was holding belonged to?"

There was a long silence before he said, "Not yet. They seem to have disappeared from the evidence locker. Once I find them, I'll let you know."

I crossed my fingers he actually would tell me. Maybe since I'd given him a lead, he'd be nicer to me. Or share something he knew. A girl could dream. I fed Drake then picked up my phone once more. When Rex didn't answer, I called Merilee. "Rex is gone, and I need a ride."

She didn't ask questions when I called around quarter to five. She just offered to drive. Once I'd saddled Drake with his cozy blue blanket coat, we enticed him into the back of the SUV with treats.

As I buckled into the passenger seat, Merilee giggled. "This is just like an old buddy movie. So what are we doing? Going to a country bar? Breaking into Rex's office to search for clues he's having an affair?"

"Why would you say that?" My mouth dropped open.

She shrugged. "Oh, sorry, I thought we were hunting him down. What's up then?"

"Ever since we talked to Bennie, I haven't been able to get the thought of those woods out of my head, so I called Officer Grant. A jogger found Molly in the clearing near the pond. Apparently, the town and the Conservation made a hundred year allowance for the coven to use it."

Merilee met my gaze. "You know the park's closed after dark, right?"

"Which is probably why they meet there," I said. "There's a small parking lot a few hundred feet from the pond. I used to bring the kids there to swim, back when it wasn't so overgrown."

She drove toward the highway then—following my directions—turned left and past the hospital. The entire hundred acres formed a barrier between the hospital and farmland beyond. At the far end of the forest, I directed her down a dirt trail that ended in a parking lot barely big enough for ten cars. On a good day, about twenty squeezed in. Tonight, it lay deserted except for Merilee's SUV.

"I hope you brought a flashlight," she said, turning off the ignition.

I handed her a flashlight then got out to open the back door for Drake who cowered on the floor. "Even better, I brought two. Come on, you big chicken. Let's go explore."

Drake refused to budge.

Merilee opened the door behind him. "Do I need to push?"

I tugged on his leash while she shoved his rear. With a whimper, he crawled toward the exit before stepping gingerly into snow. Out of breath, I wound his leash around my hand then turned on the flashlight.

"This place gives me the creeps at the best of times," she said as she shone her beam around like a lighthouse beacon.

"Good thing I never knew there were witches hanging out here before now. He didn't happen to mention how Molly died, did he?"

I blew out a puff of air that crystallized in the dim light. "Just like Dave. She was shot then stabbed with the wand with belladonna on it."

"Have the police figured out if it was processed or homemade?" she asked.

My step faltered. "What?"

"The belladonna. I'm sure there's a market for the stuff. I just wondered if they were able to track down where it came from. Different places must use a different process."

One more thing for us to research tomorrow since I didn't have my phone handy. I was on the lookout for anything that moved. Something rustled the bushes off to our right. I swept the beam of my flashlight toward the sound. Since Drake never barked, I assumed either hadn't heard anything. Either he sensed it was nothing that would harm us or was downright terrified of making a sound.

"The pond's up ahead." Merilee pointed with her light.

"That means the clearing should be to the left."

There was a loud crack ahead of us. Like someone had stepped on a dry tree branch. This time, the hackles on Drake's back rose and he growled. My eyes grew wide, and I forced myself not to run back to Merilee's SUV. Since this was my idea, it wouldn't look good if I abandoned them.

"Please tell me that was just a big bunny," Merilee whispered.

With my hands shaking, I continued moving forward. "It sure sounded like a big bunny to me."

"Good thing we're doing this on an empty stomach, or I'd hurl," she said.

As we neared the pond, the far edge of the clearing came into sight. The place was pretty during the day. By night, it was downright spooky with the light of the waning moon peering through the bare tree branches. The twentyish metre circular field of glittering snow surrounded by trees and shrubbery, appeared more like a fairy kingdom than the site for coven meetings.

"Where do you think they found her?" Merilee asked.

"I'm not sure." I kept Drake on a shortened leash as we strolled to the centre of the packed down clearing. The last snowfall was no longer fresh and pure but filled with dark lumps and boot impressions.

After a few minutes, Drake wandered toward a large, flat rock and sat thumping his tail in the snow as if he'd found something important.

I gazed around us and fished for a dog treat. "Good boy, Drake. That kind of looks like an altar."

"You mean where they cast spells and stuff?" Merilee took a large step back.

"Yeah, exactly. I'll let you read the book Miss Lavinia loaned me," I said, slipping the leash off my arm. I handed it to Merilee before approaching the flat rock. "From what I read; the right side of the altar is the God side. People place phallic symbols like the athame and the wand here, as well as a God statue and candle."

"Phallic symbols, huh?" Merilee mused. "Maybe I should give this witch thing a chance."

Drake groaned and wandered around behind her.

"The left side of the altar is considered the Goddess area. Things like the bowls, chalices or feminine statues go there." I pointed.

"Gods and goddesses. I can get into that," she said. "Where was Molly found?"

"Probably on the altar as a sacrifice. Doc said she was holding a whittled wand and a set of keys. Apparently, the keys have gone missing from evidence."

Drake whimpered.

Merilee hugged her arms around her torso. "I agree with the dog. I'm all for a good mystery, but this is getting creepy. We need to get out of here before that giant rabbit comes back."

As I turned away, the beam from my flashlight reflected off something near the rock. Moving the light back over the rock, it shone again. I crouched near the rock to dig whatever it was out of the snow.

"Did you find something?" she asked.

"It looks like a bus token or a medallion." I wiped the snow off the object as I held it beneath the light. "On one side it's carved with trees a moon and stars with the number ten in the moon. The other side says, 'To Thine Own Self Be True.'"

Merilee made a small noise before she whispered, "It's an AA token."

"A what?"

"From Alcoholics Anonymous. It's a sobriety token." She started toward me then stopped. Drake refused to budge. "Can you bring it here? He and I are not going near that rock."

After illuminating the area one more time, I gave a nod. "Let's go back to the truck and warm up."

Drake was heading back up the trail before I even got near them.

"Traitor," I mumbled handing Merilee the token.

She passed me the leash then paused to examine the token in her flashlight beam. "From what I can tell it's a ten year token. That's a long time to be sober."

"How do you know?" I asked.

Merilee fell into step beside me. "My dad was an alcoholic. I kept his tokens after he died. They're good reminders to never let life get the best of me."

With no signs of big bunnies, or even little ones, Drake attempted to yank my arm out of my shoulder socket as he picked up his pace. I had no choice but to pick up my pace and follow.

"Is there any way we can find out who it belongs to?" I asked. "After all, it was in a crime scene area and could be the killer's."

Merilee shrugged. "It was in a public park next to a rock. It could belong to anyone. Besides, I'm sure the police scoured every inch of this place. Someone must've lost it after they found Molly."

"Why can't people commit crimes in low traffic areas?" I opened the back door for Drake who jumped in and curled up like we'd just finished a ten kilometer hike.

Once we got inside her SUV, Merilee took photos of each side of the token. "Why don't you hang onto it? I'll talk to people I know and see what I can find out."

I stuck it in my coat pocket. "I'll take photos when I get home and send them to Officer Grant. He might've seen something similar before."

"In a crime scene?"

"Anywhere."

* * *

When my husband appeared on the front porch wearing slippers and a bathrobe, Merilee dropped Drake and I off, then drove off into the night. From the look on Rex's face, I wished I could go with her.

"Hi, honey. We're home." I tried to sound cheerful as Drake and I walked past him into the house.

"Where were you? I tried to call, but your phone rang in the couch cushions."

I patted the pockets of my coat. "Oh, that's where it is. I was in a hurry. Merilee needed a hand with something."

"Is that why Drake's covered in snow and shivering?" he asked.

I gazed longingly to where the dog dropped onto the carpet in front of the fireplace. "It was something outdoors. Do you want a cup of tea? I need something to take off the chill before dinner."

"Audra." There was a warning in his tone that set my teeth on edge.

"Earl Gray or chamomile?"

He grabbed my upper arm. "Why do you have notes about belladonna, and several people we know on a big piece of cardboard?"

My stomach sank. He'd found the suspect board. "We're trying to help the police. Doc gave me an idea and—"

"About poisoning someone?"

"Someone was already poisoned. Two someones actually. I was just trying to figure out who did it and why." I was babbling but couldn't seem to stop. The disbelief on his face was sending me over the edge like a chattering lemming. "After I found Dave, it seemed like someone was actually after Miss Lavinia and he got in the way. Then a jogger found Molly Lavier, her keys have gone missing, and things got more complicated. Now we think their deaths have to do with a local coven, but I have no idea how Dave was involved."

"Dave Spencer was in a coven?" Rex asked.

"No. Miss Lavinia and Molly are. Were. Didn't you hear a word I just said?"

He shook his head. "Not really. I was too busy thinking you must have hypothermia. Why don't you sit near the fire while I get the tea? The pizza will be ready soon, so you don't start hallucinating on top of everything."

I bowed my head and mumbled my thanks before stumbling toward the couch. As I sat, Drake shot me a look like he'd told me so.

"Oh, be quiet," I growled, then turned to ask Rex, "Where were you this afternoon?"

"I left you a note. Harry took me to my appointment with Doctor Davinder. She wanted to make sure I was recovering after my fall. Unlike my wife, who was off playing

Nancy Drew.”

I closed my eyes. I'd been so focused on this case I didn't even pay attention to the note or his medication. “Is everything okay?”

“Healthy as expected.”

Dinner was a brief, silent affair. Drake pouted because I refused to share my pizza, Rex zoned out after taking his painkillers, and my gaze lingered on the television while my mind wandered back to our adventure in the woods.

When Rex announced he was going to soak in the tub before bed, I told him where to find the Epsom salts and tried not to show my relief. He inched his way up the stairs with Drake close behind. Half-way up, the dog seemed to reconsider. He returned to the fireplace with his gaze on the Christmas tree.

From the way his gaze darted from me to the tree, I guessed he was plotting how to get rid of it. Why had he been so proud to find the altar then couldn't wait to get out of the woods?

The token.

I darted to the closet and dug into my coat pocket. Any remaining dirt had rubbed off and, with the added light from overhead, I could clearly make out the carved with trees with a crescent moon and a dozen stars. The number ten I thought was inside a full moon was inside a triangle surrounded by a circle.

After making sure Rex had made it up the stairs and hadn't passed out halfway up, I fetched my laptop. At first, I had no idea where to start looking, then recalled Merilee telling me it was a token from Alcoholics Anonymous. A sobriety chip.

"That's as good a place as any."

It took a while to find a duplicate of the one in my hand. I wasn't surprised to learn it was handmade and created from a mix of pewter and stainless steel. What I wasn't expecting was there could be hundreds or hundreds of thousands exactly like it. With a sigh, I examined it for more clues. *"To Thine Own Self Be True."* That was the slogan that appeared on the other chips I found. The circle and triangle were a thing, too. I was getting nowhere.

As if he read my mind, Drake snorted.

"You're right. I'll send photos to Officer Grant. Chances are he's seen one like it before or knows who this one belongs to."

He moaned then rolled over as if satisfied he got his point across.

I set my laptop on the coffee table then took photos of both sides of the token. I imagined he wished he'd never shared his phone number with me, or that I'd go bother someone else. Or both.

Less than a minute later, my phone dinged. My pizza did a somersault in my stomach. He probably wanted me to back off and leave him alone. Instead, I was greeted by, *"Call me."*

Intrigued, I hit the phone icon.

"You went to the park, didn't you?" Officer Grant asked.

"Yes."

"Where was the chip?"

"Wedged next to the flat rock." I glanced toward the staircase worried Rex might overhear me before I realized Officer Grant had called it a chip. "You know what it is."

"Yes, and I suppose your grubby fingerprints are all over it," he said.

Guilty. I closed my eyes. "I needed a better look. Merilee told me it was a sobriety chip from Alcoholics Anonymous. Do you know whose?"

"It might be Dave Spencer's."

My head started to spin. "That was fast. But he was dead before Molly. How would his chip end up in the woods near the coven's altar?"

He groaned. "Since you're not going to let this go, you might as well brainstorm with me. Come by my office in the morning."

"With you? I thought Trent was the lead on this case."

"On Dave's case. I was called in when they found Molly and there was more overlap than expected. I don't want the junior guy messing this up. You have a way of getting more information than he does. Oh, and bring your suspect board with you."

"How did you…?"

"Judge Harry." His voice seemed to soften when he added, "Don't worry, he doesn't tell me everything. He's just worried you're getting in over your head, especially after the break-in at your shop."

I smiled. "That makes sense."

"I'll see you at nine o'clock tomorrow morning if that works."

"Nine is great," I told him. "Do you mind if I bring Drake? Rex is still home after his fall, and I can't seem to leave Drake alone with him these days. All he does is growl."

"Rex or Drake?" He chuckled.

"A bit of both. See you in the morning."

* * *

I'd finally fallen into a deep sleep when the house shuddered with a crash followed by small tinkles. I sat upright gasping for air in the darkness. I guessed what had happened without even being able to see through the walls. Drake had found a way to take down the tree again.

I slid out from beneath the quilt my grandma had made by hand and tried to get out of bed as quietly as possible without waking Rex. I didn't need to worry. He wasn't there anyway. Had he fallen down the stairs and landed in the Christmas tree?

"Oh, no." My heart continued to race as I ran across the bedroom and down the stairs. I forgot all about my robe and fluffy pink slippers.

Drake was nowhere near the tree. In fact, he lay at the bottom of the stairs with his gaze glued on Rex who lay sprawled among scattered presents, broken ornaments, and garland. I knew the painkillers made my husband loopy, but I hadn't expected him to sleepwalk.

Stepping over Drake, I turned on the light then crouched near Rex, mindful of the broken glass. "Are you okay?"

He grunted. At least he was alive. I went into the kitchen to grab the broom before anyone else got hurt.

"Honey? You still there?" Rex moaned.

"I'm here. Don't move, there's glass everywhere. Are you okay?"

Rex tried to laugh but ended up groaning. "I heard a noise. When I came downstairs the tree attacked me."

"The tree attacked you," I repeated, too tired to even act surprised. Leaning the broom against the wall, I reached out both hands to help him up. "Okay, let's get you back up to bed before your happy pills wear off."

"You don't believe me, do you?"

Nope. "Of course I do, honey, but it's the middle of the night and we're both exhausted. Why don't you tell me all about your tree attack in the morning?"

Rex pointed toward the patio door. "He went that way."

"The tree?" I asked. Those painkillers weren't doing him any favours.

"The guy who pushed the tree."

Despite what Rex said, the patio door remained closed. With a sigh, I crossed the room to double check the lock and stepped in something wet. I would've preferred one of Drake's puddles over a set of boot-shaped prints any day. I glanced toward the staircase wishing I hadn't left my cell phone plugged in near the nightstand.

The door remained closed but unlocked despite me whispering beneath my breath, "I swear I locked it last night."

"What did you say?" Rex still lay on the floor.

Closing my eyes, I replayed the evening in my head. I'd returned from the lake with Merilee and Drake. We'd had dinner. Rex went to bed. I called Officer Grant then let Drake outside and…

Had I forgotten to lock the door when he came in? Locking it now, I closed the blinds then returned to Rex's side to help him to his feet. My plan was to lead him to the stairs.

"Who was it?" he asked, swerving toward the couch.

"I didn't see anyone. Are you sure you didn't dream it?"

Rex sat then grabbed the throw blanket off the back of the couch. "Positive. My dream people don't smell like alcohol."

"I'm calling Officer Grant." I headed toward the stairs to get my phone.

"Don't bother," he said. "Call him in the morning. At least he won't be cranky because we woke him up in the middle of the night."

While he did have a good point, I ran upstairs to grab my phone anyway. I also tugged on the pink bathrobe and slippers while I tried to shake off the chill that had settled over me.

# Chapter Seventeen
Wednesday, December 7


I awoke from a restless sleep to a gust of bad breath and a soft tongue licking my face. I pushed Drake off my lap and stretched the kinks out of my back while he pranced around me. Falling asleep in the armchair wasn't as great an idea as it seemed at the time.

Rex lay sprawled on the couch, his hair damp and face sweaty. He appeared oblivious to Drake who whined to go out.

Shuffling half-hunched over to the patio door, I froze. What if I opened the blinds and the man who'd attacked Rex was out there waiting for me? It wouldn't be the first time I'd come face to face with an intruder, but I'd make darn sure it was the last. We'd move to a high-rise condo.

"It was all a dream," I said aloud. Giving my head a shake, I brushed the excitement of the night off to Rex's painkillers and was glad I'd set the tree upright before trying to sleep. Although I still had no explanation for the wet spots on the floor. I counted to three before I peeked through the blinds. No sign of anyone in the backyard.

Drake seemed to hesitate, looking around for a split second before he shot out into the yard. When he raced toward his favourite tree, I shrugged off my paranoia and went inside to make coffee. Rex and I would both need some. Besides, it was an effective way to appease my husband, whether he remembered what happened last night or not.

Once I let Drake back inside, I locked the door before going upstairs for a shower. I decided to leave Drake home to keep Rex company since I had an appointment at the police station anyway.

"You really didn't see anything last night?" Rex asked,

I set a steaming cup on the coffee table then helped him to sit upright. "By the time I got down here, he was long gone."

His hands shook as he said, "We should've called the police."

"To tell them someone broke into our house and assaulted you with a Christmas tree? They already think I'm crazy." I handed him his cup before sitting next to him. "I'll stop by the station this morning and talk to Officer Grant. I doubt there's much he can do, but I'll see if he can stop by later to take a look around."

Appeased, Rex reached for the painkillers and shook one into his hand.

"Okay. I planned to go into the office today, but I'll wait."

"You want to go into the office?" I tried not to laugh in surprise. "You can't even sit up without help let alone leave the house alone."

He frowned. "We have a big meeting on Friday that I can't miss. I need to gather numbers for spreadsheets and talk to Andrew."

As much as it irked me, I told him, "Why don't you ask Andrew to come here? Or better yet do a video call. I can set up your computer here or on the kitchen table and—"

"You really don't want me leaving the house, do you?" he snapped.

I flinched. "What? No. The doctor said you need to take it easy."

"For a few days."

"You fell on Sunday and came home Monday. Today's only Wednesday. It's not good to push it, especially after last night." When his jaw tensed, I sighed. "Why don't you start with a shower and see how it goes?"

I had a feeling by the time he climbed the stairs, took a shower, and dressed, he'd collapse across the bed anyway.

"That's a good idea. I'll let you know what time I'll be home." He set down his coffee then tried to stand. After a couple minutes, he grunted, "Could you give me a hand instead of just watching?"

* * *

As I grabbed my pink parka from the closet, I smiled. The colour never failed to give me a lift, so I paired it with my favourite pink hat and black gloves. I left Drake home to babysit Rex who, as predicted, fell asleep on the bed, and still hadn't returned to the couch. I was at the deli before I realized I could've taken the key and the car and then he'd be stuck there. Darn it! I was such a creature of habit.

At nine o'clock on the dot, I set a large black coffee on Officer Grant's desk and asked, "Did you find out who owns that token?"

He scratched the stubble on his chin as he reached for the cup.

I moved it out of his reach. "Not so fast. I want answers."

"And I want coffee," he said, meeting my gaze. "If you think we're at an impasse, keep in mind I'm the one with the gun and the handcuffs."

"Good thing I'm not wearing my pajamas then." The words sounded better in my head than they did aloud.

A nearby officer smirked.

"Get your mind out of the gutter, Jacobs," Officer Grant snapped. "Last time I arrested her, she was wearing her pajamas out in public."

Handing him the coffee before he bit anyone, I decided to consider it my good deed for the day. I sat across from him and asked, "So?"

He sipped the coffee. "Needs cream."

"You're welcome."

With a grunt, he shuffled through a stack of papers on his desk until he found what he was looking for. "That sobriety chip is a custom piece made in the UK. It took several phone calls and emails to prove I was a cop before I learned it was made for Joelle Spencer who bought it as a gift for her husband."

"You were right. It was Dave's." I sat up a little straighter.

"Actually, she bought it for Chuck."

I released a gush of breath like he'd sucker-punched me. "Oh."

"That's what I said, which is why I pulled his files."

Suddenly, I was almost giddy with anticipation. I was about to hear information I was never privy to. "Chuck Benson's a respected member of the community. From what I've heard, he's a nice guy."

Officer Grant shook his head as he recited, "Domestic violence, speeding, jaywalking, theft over a thousand dollars...but I never told you any of that."

My scalp tingled as my first thought went to Joelle. "Is his wife in danger?"

"I haven't had any calls yet."

I was outraged. "Can't you just check in on her?"

"You know as well as I do that not all abuse victims call the police until it's too late." His eye twitched. "Until I do get a call, there's nothing I can do. Even a wellness check has to be initiated by a concerned third party."

"Like me?"

"Are you a friend or family member who hasn't seen or heard from her for an unusually lengthy period of time?" he asked.

I deflated. "She came to my house the other day. Friday, I think."

"Then no. I never should've told you any of that. Just because I let it slip about Chuck's past, doesn't mean you can become even more of a vigilante." He sat back and gazed at his coffee cup before he said, "I've already talked to Chuck."

"About Joelle?"

"About Molly Lavier. He's also the jogger who found her body. He and Andrew Laney run in the park three times a week. At least they did before the last snowfall."

"So maybe he killed her before he went for a run." Suddenly, another thought struck me. "Or they killed her together. I'll be she was trying to stop a development."

Officer Grant held up a hand. "Or it's just a coincidence he went for a run and found her. Trust me, Andrew Laney's far too busy to waste time killing people. Between his business and his mistress, he's got his hands full. You need to stop overthinking everything and focus on your own problems."

My eyes grew wide. "What mistress?"

"I'm surprised you don't know. He's been seen with Emily Trent several times now. Oh, and I know about the cancer," he told me gently. "Let your husband take care of you and stop worrying about chasing bad guys."

I took a gulp of my latte and tried to catch my breath. Emily and Andrew? "I don't have cancer. That was a mix-up with another patient's files. Emily's in fact. Besides, how's he supposed to take care of me when he was in Chicago for the past week, then stranded in Windsor? When he came home Sunday night, slipped on ice, and injured his back. He's been on the couch ever since he got home from the hospital. Well, except last night when he insisted someone attacked him with our Christmas tree."

He chuckled as he made notes on the paper in front of him. "Windsor, huh?"

"Did you miss the part about the tree?" I asked, trying to see what he'd written. His handwriting was as bad as Doc's. "Why are you laughing? What's going on?" I asked as a wave of nausea swept over me.

"I'm not getting involved in anything to do with Andrew Laney until I have enough evidence to lay charges."

Tears welled in my eyes. "Charges against Andrew? Is my husband caught up in something illegal?"

"I'd love to say no, but since he and Laney are glued at the hip these days." He paused. "Laney may try to incriminate Rex. Just keep your eyes and ears open."

"For what?"

Officer Grant leaned his forearms on the desk as he met my gaze. "Anything."

"Here I thought all I had to worry about was the belladonna on his shirt."

He narrowed his eyes. "Was that the shirt you gave Officer Trent?"

I pressed my lips together before I said anything I'd regret. Was he trying to send me down a different path just to get me off the trail of a murderer? He'd definitely been quick to steer me away from Emily.

"The spot wasn't blood, it was red wine," he said. "They found specks of belladonna. A few drops splashed on his shirt. I got the lab report. "

Cradling my cup in both hands, I asked, "So he didn't ingest it?"

Officer Grant shrugged. "Only if someone slipped it into his wine. But we wouldn't know if he consumed the belladonna without a blood sample. Do you think someone tried to poison him?"

"Why would they want to? Unless he saw or heard something he wasn't supposed to. He does know what Andrew Laney's up to. It could have something to do with Chuck." I leaned toward him and lowered my voice. "I could ask Rex to wear a wire."

Officer Grant blinked. "Excuse me?"

"If you want evidence against Laney or whoever he's dealing with, Rex could wear a wire and get Laney to incriminate himself." I paused. "What do you know about Emily Trent? I think she might be involved. Bennie said—"

"You can't just come in here and accuse people of things, especially without proof."

I held up my index finger. "Number one, Emily had access to Rex's keys at his office. You're the one who said she's been having an affair with Andrew Laney."

"Alleged affair," he said.

"Number two, she's Dave Spencer's older sister and was probably angry he'd inherit their father's building and left her out of the will."

He shook his head. "She hadn't spoken to Jack or Dave in over fifteen years and wanted nothing to do with either one."

"Three, she had grudges against both Miss Lavinia and Molly. Neither could give Roger a treatment that would help his headaches. When she came back to town recently, she wanted to be part of the Sacred Sisters Coven, but they wouldn't let her."

Officer Grant shook his head. "Roger Trent had a brain tumour and took his own life with a handful of drugs. Doc did the autopsy."

"He did?" I averted my gaze. "Oh."

"Are you done yet?"

The thought that had haunted me since Rex's Christmas tree incident popped out of my mouth. "I think she plans to kill me next."

His eyes snapped open as he gawked. "Are you serious or just trying to get my attention?"

"Someone stole Rex's second set of keys from his desk at work. Then someone broke into our house and attacked Rex with the Christmas tree. It's only a matter of time before—"

"You were serious about the Christmas tree?" He rubbed his eyes. "Audra, we've strayed a long way from you coming in here to ask about a sobriety chip. Look, just for laughs today, why don't you take care of your store and I'll chase the bad guys?"

"I get it." A bit embarrassed by my enthusiasm, I stood to leave.

He cleared his throat as I turned to leave. "Um, Audra."

When I faced him, he held his hand out with his palm up. "The sobriety chip, please.

I don't care who found it, that chip's evidence because of where you found it."

With a huff, I dug it out of my coat pocket and placed it in his hand. At least I still had the photos to show Joelle.

Hopefully, I didn't have long to wait.

* * *

Still reeling from everything I'd learned at the police station I was glad for the distraction of customers at Stitch'n'Time. I took off my coat to ring in sales and chat with people seeking gift ideas. Once everyone left, except a woman in a camel wool coat, blue jeans, and black Caterpillar work boots, Merilee and I both paused for sips of tepid coffee. We'd barely set down our cups before she approached the counter.

"Did you find what you were looking for?" Merilee asked.

"That depends. Are you Audra?" Her green eyes met mine. Her blondish-gray hair was damp with the remains of snowflakes. Something about her seemed so familiar, yet I couldn't place her.

I flashed a smile. "I am. This is my partner, Merilee."

The woman gave me a quick once over. Her face hardened just for a second. "My son told me you might be able to get a message to an old friend on my behalf. I've tried to call but haven't had much luck."

Merilee frowned. "Oh really? Who's your friend?"

"Lavinia Brevil."

"Uh-oh," Merilee said so softly I doubted the woman heard her.

My senses went on high alert. The scent she wore reminded me of Rex. The same smell that drove Drake crazy. I knew I'd seen her before. "Who's your son?"

"Alister Trent. He's a local police officer."

While I tried not to act surprised, I desperately needed to sit before my legs gave out. After my chat with Officer Grant, I wasn't sure how to react. Maybe I should be the one wearing a wire.

She bit her lower lip as she toyed with her gloves. "Alister says you and Lavinia are good friends. Please, I really need her help."

The cancer. The affair. Roger's apparent suicide. My stomach sank. This was one of those times where I knew way more than I should've, and it wasn't a good feeling.

"I've tried going to her shop, but the man behind the counter says she's not seeing patients right now," she said. "I'm desperate, Audra. You have to help me."

I slid a note pad and pen across the counter toward her. "If you write down your name and phone number, I'll deliver it when I get a chance."

Emily grabbed my hand in hers. "I need

you to do it now. I don't have much time."

"Okay. I'll ask." I knew exactly how she felt.

She smiled, patting my hand before releasing it. Tears welled in her eyes. "Thank you so much. It really is a matter of life and death."

"Weren't you were married to Roger Trent?" Merilee asked. "I thought you'd left Sugarwood years ago."

Emily's face reddened as her jaw tightened. "I came back to see family and ended up moving back now that Alister works here."

Something about her seemed to have changed since she'd introduced herself. A sense she'd won something. Considering all my suspicions, I was hesitant to bring her information to Miss Lavinia.

"I hope we'll see you in the shop again soon," I told her trying to keep the fear from creeping into my voice.

"Maybe. I'm not one for crafts, but I have people on my Christmas list who'd die for some of the things you have here." She paused. "Thanks again for your help, Audra."

As the door closed behind her, Merilee and I blew out twin sighs of relief.

"You'd better get that over to Miss Lavinia. We know exactly what her life and death situation is," Merilee said. When I didn't move, she nudged my arm. "Audra?"

I picked up Emily's note. "I'll be back in a few minutes."

"Are you okay?" she asked.

"She smells like Rex."

Merilee started to brush me off, then gasped. "Are you sure? Too bad Drake isn't here then we'd know for sure. What are you going to do?"

"I don't know. If Miss Lavinia won't take her calls, how did she get that same blend of oils?" I asked, thinking aloud more than anything. "Do you think Emily could be the person who broke into Miss Lavinia's shop and gave Simon that bruise?"

"Maybe he made her medication under duress after she threatened him," she said. "I think you have more to talk about than that note."

"Yeah. I'll try not to be long." I grabbed my coat and left.

Simon nodded toward the stairs the second I set foot in the shop. He was on the phone and seemed agitated enough for both of us. Even though I had questions for him about the night of the break-in, I wanted to talk to his auntie first.

I pushed back the red velvet curtain and trudged up the stairs. Before I'd even reached the top, Miss Lavinia opened the door. Out of breath from the climb, I asked, "How do you do that?"

"You're wearing heavy boots," she said. "How could I not hear you?"

Flashing a smile, I stepped inside her apartment. "I can't stay. We have the sewing circle at one. I was asked to drop this off against my better judgement."

She held the note at arm's length and paled. "Emily Trent. What does she want?"

"Emily's test results were mixed up with mine. She's the one with cancer and it doesn't sound good."

Miss Lavinia sighed. "I vowed to never deal with that family again."

I shifted my weight not ready to leave yet. "Do you remember that night you and Simon heard noises in the shop? When he ended up with a bruise and a cut on his face. What happened that night?"

"Nothing. He tripped over a box," she said quickly.

"That's not what I think. Emily Trent just stopped by my store. She smells exactly like whatever it is you mixed for Rex. If she just moved back to town and you haven't seen her yet, how did she get it?"

"Audra, I—"

"She threatened you into making her what she needed, didn't she?" I asked. "I'll bet she even accused you of not helping Roger before he died."

Miss Lavinia folded the note and tossed it on the counter. "I warned them my treatments could only ease the pain, not cure him. His case was too advanced. According to the autopsy, he had a massive

333

tumour and—"

"Why did they do an autopsy?"

"Doc felt it was in the best interests of both the family and physicians involved," she said. "The tumour had shrunk a little since his last MRI, but it wasn't enough. He was in constant pain."

"Then the tumour killed him, not your treatments."

Miss Lavinia pursed her lips and nodded toward the door. "You'd better go tend to your circle ladies."

Her sudden abruptness made me shiver.

"You thought he took an overdose of pain medication," I spoke softly. "Is that why Doc asked for the autopsy?"

She closed her eyes. "Yes. On my insistence. I also think that's why Emily and her son left town suddenly. Roger's family blamed her for his death and didn't want her there. Her coming back to town has stirred up a hornets' nest."

That I could relate to. As I walked past Simon, I tried to fit all the crazy pieces of the puzzle into place. Was Emily Trent out for revenge? If so, why did Alister keep hanging around scaring me silly? Gut feeling told me Chuck and Andrew were a part of the grand scheme as well. Which part, I had no idea.

The second I returned to the store, Merilee whizzed past me saying, "Picking up lunch and cookies. Be right back."

I took off my coat and stumbled around like a zombie and tried to ignore my phone from eleven o'clock on, which was when Rex started texting every twenty minutes to ask what was for lunch, where Drake's food was, and how often the dog actually needed to go out. He also asked three times if I'd figured out who broke into our house.

Finally, I stuck my phone in a drawer not ready to share my suspicions yet.

* * *

Maddie and Judy were the first to arrive for the sewing circle. Oddly, they stood outside in the cold for several minutes with their heads close together while serious expressions played on their faces. By the time  they entered the store with their noses red and cheeks rosy.

"Hi, ladies," Merilee chirped. "I'm glad you made it."

Judy wheeled her walker to her seat. "It's nice to make it anywhere these days. People are too darn lazy to shovel their sidewalks. The cab dropped me off at the deli and I had an awful time from there."

"Oh no," Maddie said, patting her arm. "Next time call me to pick you up. Chuck reserves a parking spot for me at the real estate office."

Judy waved a hand. "No thanks. Then I'd

335

have to walk around the building and over that heap of snow in front of their building. I'd rather walk from the deli."

Maddie laughed. "Who goes around? I walk through the building, grab a coffee and whatever treats they've left out for their clients, and get one of those handsome agents to help me across the street. Most of them are real boy scouts."

Why didn't that surprise me?

Carol arrived next with Bennie and Rena close behind. They'd barely settled into their chairs before the door opened once more. When Miss Lavinia stepped inside and closed the door behind her, all eyes turned in her direction. It had been two weeks since the attack and I doubted she'd seen any of the women since then.

She gazed around the room then locked eyes with me. "Is this the sewing group you told me about?"

"Yes, it is. Come on in." I pointed out two empty chairs. One next to Maddie and the other near Bennie.

"Ladies." Miss Lavinia gave a nod before she sat next to Bennie. At least there was someone she felt comfortable with. A fellow coven member.

"What'cha working on?" Bennie leaned closer as Miss Lavinia placed a quilted tote bag on the table.

She paused then gazed sideways at Bennie in a deadpan way that reminded me of Morticia Adams. "Voodoo dolls."

Bennie chuckled before pulling out her own project. "Of course, you are."

"Am I late?" Joelle Spencer-Benson opened the door just as the women were getting settled. She wore her bright pink parka with a matching hat and glossy, pink hiking boots. She reminded me of a Barbie I'd always wanted as a kid.

"Depends on what you're here for, honey," Carol said.

Merilee waved a hand. "Come on in. There's a chair beside Maddie."

Joelle stiffened and seemed to hesitate before she took a seat. Since I'd already filled my partner in crime solving in on my porch chat with Joelle, Merilee vowed to get to know her before we added her to the suspect list.

I brought a dozen plastic sandwich bags to the table and set them on the table. "I made ornament kits for you to choose from. I'll show you how to get started."

"Needlepoint?" Maddie scoffed. "Don't waste your breath, Audra. I've tried to get her into quilting, and she has two left thumbs. She'll only draw blood."

"It's actually cross-stitch," I told her. "Fewer types of stitches."

Joelle's face reddened as she bowed her head slightly and took off her coat.

"Audra's cross-stitch kits are adorable." Merilee said. "They don't take forever to make either."

When Joelle met my gaze, I was determined not to let her wallow in the self-pity imposed by her mother-in-law. "Do you see one you like?"

Her expression softened as she chose a red candle in an old-fashioned gold holder. "This would be nice."

"I'd like one of those. May I?" Rena asked.

Before I knew it, each woman reached over to claim an ornament kit, tucking them into their craft bags for later. Even Maddie who grumbled that her granddaughter might like to try one. Miss Lavinia chose one with a dog that looked similar to Drake.

Joelle didn't bother to hide her grin as she mouthed, "Thanks."

For the first twenty minutes of the circle, I showed whoever wanted to watch how to start a thread and tuck its tail behind their work so it didn't stick out later. Then I taught them how to do a full stitch and a half stitch with the promise of scrounging up glittering silver thread for tiny snowflakes if anyone wanted.

"That sounds easy enough. What do I do when I'm done?" Joelle asked.

I smiled. "Bring it back and I'll show you how to turn it into an ornament."

She placed her hand on mine. "I'd like that. Thank you, Audra."

Once the group got to work, Merilee and

I huddled around the counter to read the suspect notes I'd made while we ate lunch. The women chatted about everything from the price of lettuce at the local grocery store to Christmas plans. Even Joelle relaxed enough to strike up a conversation with Bennie.

Miss Lavinia kept to herself while she created miniature people. We all wondered aloud who she was making, but she refused to say. There were no shortage of guesses until finally Joelle asked, "Is it Chuck?"

"Chuck Benson?" Miss Lavinia raised one eyebrow as she studied the younger woman whose face reddened.

Joelle shrugged. "Sorry. I just figured my husband was the only person no one's guessed yet. What do you do with the dolls after you make them?"

"Much like a doctor, I keep my patients' confidentiality." She paused with a dark blue thread in one hand. "We haven't met before, have we?"

"No, ma'am."

Miss Lavinia placed the doll on the table. "I create oils, tinctures, salves, and poultices to treat my patients with, then I treat the doll in between visits."

"You treat the doll?" Joelle asked as her eyes grew wide. "That's interesting. What do you do when the patient moves away or doesn't come back? Do you destroy the doll?"

"My dolls live in storage until the patient returns."

"You must have a lot of dolls," she said. "Did Dave Spencer have one? He's my ex-husband."

Miss Lavinia glanced toward us then back to Joelle. "Yes, he did."

Merilee leaned closer to whisper, "That's not creepy."

"What do you do with them when the patient dies?" Joelle asked.

Everyone in the room went so still and quiet I was afraid to breathe. When all eyes turned to Miss Lavinia, I expected her to walk out. She picked up the doll she was working on and studied it for a minute.

"The body dies, but the soul lives on," Miss Lavinia spoke softly. "Some dolls are returned to family members. Most remain in storage until I need to make space."

Judy Wells seemed transfixed. "Then what?"

"Then I take them near a body of water and build a funeral pyre."

Merilee and I both shuddered.

Rena whimpered before she asked, "So, did anyone else watch The Bachelor?"

Just like that, the goosebump moment ended. Miss Lavinia had established her place in the group and told them not to mess with her without having to say the words.

Joelle shrank back into her seat looking

deeply disturbed.

"I'm going to see how everyone's doing." Merilee patted my arm then went around the table to check on everyone's progress to lighten the mood.

I bowed over the counter to transfer the suspect notes we'd made on assorted sticky notes to add to our poster, including Miss Lavinia's latest revelation about Roger and my chat with Officer Grant about Emily. My mind churned, but my eyes needed a break from making notes on the brightly coloured squares of paper.

The variety of projects and conversation topics that made up the sewing circle sessions never ceased to amaze me. While part of me wanted to bring up what had happened to Dave, Molly, and Miss Lavinia, I bit my lower lip hard to force the notion out of my head.

"How's your head, Lavinia?" Maddie asked. "I hear you took quite a thump when that man was killed."

There went that plan.

Joelle cleared her throat. "That man was my ex-husband."

Miss Lavinia peered at me over the rim of her thin reading glasses. "Yes, it was quite a thump, as you call it, which was caused by a mild stroke. I'm doing better, thank you. It's lovely to have my nephew here so I can rest when I need to."

I bit my lower lip, determined to listen

more than speak.

"That nephew of yours is a looker. Is he single?" Bennie asked.

Rena snorted. "It doesn't matter. You're too old for him anyway."

Bennie smacked Rena's knuckle lightly with a ruler. "I have a single granddaughter. Why do you think I'm making a wedding quilt? To manifest a man for her."

"Right. I forgot you're one of those witches," Jenny said. "You need one of Miss Lavinia's voodoo dolls wearing a wedding dress."

"Witches?" Joelle raised her eyebrows.

Merilee hid a smirk behind her hand.

Miss Lavinia seemed amused. "Simon will stop by later. You can ask him if he's single then. He checks up on me ten times a day."

"Is he bringing more voodoo cookies?" Carol's face lit up. "They sure made that meeting fun, didn't they? We never got those at the church."

"I haven't had the energy this week," Miss Lavinia said.

Jenny patted her hand. "After what you went through, I'm glad he checks up on you. Head injuries are nothing to take lightly."

No one mentioned her stroke.

"Neither are knives in the back," Maddie mused. "Do those bumbling cops have any suspects yet?"

Bennie shrugged as she finished cutting more pieces for her quilt. "The usual. Ex-wife. The kids. Her new man. Her new mother-in-law."

"Very funny." Maddie scowled as her face darkened.

Joelle's face grew as pink as her coat.

"Sorry, honey. I'm just saying," Bennie said. "Dave wasn't worth much after you took him to the cleaners then hooked up with Chuck."

Joelle's gaze darted to the door. The way she shifted on her chair I expected her to bolt into the cold at any second.

"Maybe Dave's new girlfriend killed him," Maddie said, sounding a titch defensive.

My ears burned for more, but I didn't miss Joelle's flinch.

"He doesn't have a girlfriend," Jenny announced. "That woman he was with dumped him a couple months ago. She said he was boring. That her kid didn't like him."

"Who was he seeing?" I asked, breaking my no meddling vow, which wasn't lost on Merilee. When seven sets of eyes turned on me like I'd insulted Elvis, I swallowed hard and wished I could take back my question.

"Emily something," Jenny said.

"Emily Trent," Maddie piped up. "Her son's a cop."

My stomach seemed to go into freefall.

For someone I'd only met once, she sure popped into a lot of conversations lately. None of them good.

Rena scowled. "Her son's that nosy cop who gave me a ticket his first day on the job. He's been poking around Lavinia's shop, which makes me think he's up to no good."

"It's a crime scene. That's his job," Miss Lavinia reminded her.

Merilee wrote both Alister and Emily Trent's names on fresh sticky notes with question marks. She turned to the computer and tapped the keyboard.

"Well, if you ask me, Dave was killed by that sneaky kid who used to work in the butcher shop." Judy set her emerald felted wool project on the table. "He always overcharged me when I bought pork chops."

Joelle finally forced a small smile. "Jesse's a good kid. He moved to Guelph and went back to school when the butcher shop closed. I think he's becoming a mechanic."

"Better than that delinquent daughter of yours," Maddie said. "What's Bree up to these days? I've seen her skulking around town. I'm surprised she's not sponging off my son like her mother."

Before Joelle could pack up and leave, I jumped into the fray. "Wow, you've made great progress. I'm starting to think you've done this before.”

She gazed at me with tears in her eyes and whispered, “I should go. Coming here wasn’t a good plan.”

With a nod, I packaged her project while she pulled on her coat then walked her to the door. I would’ve loved her to stay but understood. Maddie was out for blood trying to make it clear this was her turf and Joelle wasn’t welcome.

“Why don’t you drop by my house once you finish the needlepoint,” I suggested. “I’ll help you turn it into an ornament. I can make you another kit if you enjoy doing them. I have more than enough supplies at home I need to use up.”

Joelle pulled a pair of pink leather gloves from her coat pocket before she asked, “Why are you being so nice to me?”

“Because you seem like you could use a friend.” I reached for a sticky note. “I’ll give you my number. Call me if you need anything. Even just to get out of the house.”

“Thanks, Audra. I’ll let you know when I get the candleholder picture done,” she said. “Do yourself a favour and watch out for Maddie. Her bite’s even worse than her bark.”

“I appreciate the heads up. Have a safe drive home.”

Joelle grinned. “Oh, I didn’t drive. I decided to walk like you. A little snow never hurt anyone, am I right?”

"Good for you. Enjoy your walk home then."

Once I closed the door behind her, the circle grew quiet. Without an easy target, Maddie lost her steam and her outburst had put a strain on the mood in the store. It certainly wasn't as merry as when there were voodoo cookies involved. The women began to leave shortly after Joelle.

It took Merilee and I the next hour to pack away the tables and chairs and sweep up before we closed. I was eager to get home to my laptop and more research since Emily's visit had left me rattled. After everything I'd learned about Alister and Emily, I needed to finish piecing things together.

When the door opened, Officer Grant looked even more somber than usual. He hesitated in the doorway and seemed at a loss for words as he closed the door. "Audra. Merilee."

"What's wrong?" I asked.

Merilee gave a nod. "Too bad you weren't here sooner. You could've helped us tidy up. That sewing circle's murder. I have no idea how they find all of that gossip about Dave, Joelle, Chuck, and…" She trailed off when he didn't react. "What is it?"

"They're about to have more," he said. "Someone ran over Chuck Benson's wife."

"Joelle?" I stared. "Are you serious? When?"

"Thirty minutes ago near your house. She was walking across the street when a car hit her then sped off. Rex had Drake out on the front lawn and saw everything. He thought—"

"She was just here. She walked here because of me," I whispered. "She was even dressed like me."

Merilee hugged me. "Don't do that. It's not your fault."

"Why was she here?" he asked.

I folded my arms across my stomach fairly sure I was going to be sick.

"Joelle joined the sewing circle today," Merilee said. "She stayed until Maddie Benson started poking at her. They were discussing suspects in Dave's death and Maddie brought up Joelle's daughter, Bree. That's when Joelle left. Actually, they all left."

"So Maddie couldn't have run her down," he said as though in thought.

A chill ran over me. "It's possible. She parks in the real estate office lot."

Merilee jumped in. "It wasn't necessarily a member of the circle."

"You think someone thinks Joelle knows something?" I asked.

"We thought it was an accident, but there's not much ice on that street," he said. "Whoever hit her drove away. They can't say they didn't see her. She was wearing a bright pink coat. Rex thought it was you,

Audra, since you have a similar coat."

I sat on one of the stools and closed my eyes as a wave of dizziness washed over me. "That's not good."

"Can we see her?" Merilee asked.

"They rushed her into surgery," he said. "It could be hours before we can talk to her."

I met his gaze. "Did someone call Chuck?"

Officer Grant nodded. "Yeah, and for the record he has an alibi. He was with a client looking at a property near Barrie. He'll be at the hospital as soon as he can."

"What about her kids?" I asked. "They're all in town, but I'm not sure Chuck will tell them right away. Not after what Maddie said."

Merilee shot me a scowl. "Audra."

"What did Maddie say?" he asked.

"She called Bree a delinquent," she said with a sigh. "That's what made Joelle pack up and leave."

Officer Grant turned his gaze to me. "Thank you. I want to hear the minute either of you hears something. Anything."

"Got it," I replied softly.

He rubbed his face with one hand. "I'll call when I get any updates on Joelle."

Merilee locked the door when he left and returned to give me a bone-crushing hug. "I'm texting Tony. We're driving you home. You know as well as I do that whoever ran over Joelle must've thought she was you."

"And Rex saw the whole thing. He must've been terrified." I started the search for my phone wondering why I hadn't heard from him.

My phone was still in the drawer where I'd put it before lunch. Rex had sent about twelve texts while the sewing circle was here. Four of those were about Joelle. The other eight asked where I was and if I was okay. By the last one, I sensed his panic.

*"I'm good. Merilee and Tony driving me home,"* I texted him.

*"Thank goodness. Can you pick up more wine?"*

Tony arrived less than ten minutes later. He not only hugged us both but searched me for injuries as though I was the one who got hurt. Finally, he gave me one last hug and said, "Let's get you home."

When the truck crept toward the corner near our house, I sucked in a sharp breath as bile rose in the back of my throat. The tire tracks near our driveway were slushy and pink. Narrow wheel paths from a gurney cut through the street from where Joelle ended up to where the ambulance had parked near the end of our driveway.

As I got out of Tony's truck, I doubled over and gagged.

"Audra?" Harry called from his driveway.

Merilee hopped out behind me. "Are you okay?"

I was far from it. After all the shouts Drake and I had heard over the past two weeks, all I could think was that Chuck Benson had tried to kill his new wife. He also might've been involved with getting rid of Dave and Molly.

# Chapter Eighteen
Wednesday, December 7


Harry assured Merilee and Tony that he'd look after me while I vomited cookies and coffee into the pink snow near the fence. Once my stomach was spent, he walked me to the front door away from the bloody, trampled snow.

"Doc's keeping an eye on things at the hospital," he said. "Sarah and Joelle are good friends. Since Sarah's sick, he'll make sure she's okay."

I nodded, too weak and shaken to speak.

The front door opened before we even reached the front steps. Rex stood in front of us, his face ashen and hair rumpled like he'd awakened in the middle of a bad dream.

"I'll call when I hear something." Harry gave me a one-armed hug before he left me shivering on the walkway.

Rex blew out a loud, relieved breath as he stepped aside for me to enter. "You have no idea how happy I am to see you."

That's when I finally dissolved into tears.

My husband closed the door and held me until I stopped sobbing then gently helped remove my boots and pink coat. If it caused him physical pain, he didn't show it as he locked the door behind us.

"Go sleep by the fire, buddy. Mommy needs to get warm," Rex said as he led me to the couch where Drake lay on the throw blanket.

Drake yawned, but obeyed, vacating the couch for us to sit. He moved slower than usual, and I wondered if all the excitement had worn him out.

"I saw your pink coat missing when I took Drake out this morning," Rex said. "This afternoon…I looked up when…Joelle looked just like you. Her coat was pink, but I thought that…" He leaned his head against mine. "I thought I'd lost you for good."

Meeting his gaze, I sobbed, "I'll stop. No more snooping. I'll keep my phone in my pocket and—"

"It's not that. Ever since that accident, all I've been able to think of was your cancer scare and the kids and how I haven't been upfront with you. I'm meeting with Andrew this evening to work out a new schedule. That new development on the edge of town needs someone to oversee the sales team, and I think I'm just the guy."

I hugged him. "I like that idea."

"I'd travel less and wouldn't have as much stress," he said. "Plus I can have dinner with my best girl most nights."

"Your best girl, huh?" I stroked his graying temples. "I'd like that."

He pulled me close and kissed me like he hadn't seen me in months. Technically, I suppose that was true. We'd been ships in the night for a long time. While parts of me began to grow warmer, my hands were freezing, and I couldn't seem to stop shaking due to shock.

"I made chicken soup with vegetables, your favourite." He kissed the end of my nose. "I figured we'd need something warm that wasn't too heavy. It's from a can, but that's the best I could do."

Throwing my arms around him, I announced, "It's perfect. I've missed this, Rex."

"Me, too, honey." He tucked me beneath the blanket and scurried to the kitchen. He returned a couple minutes later carrying a tray with our dinner.

My phone vibrated on the coffee table before he could set the tray down. "It's Doc. Joelle's out of surgery and in recovery. She'll be fine."

"I'm glad to hear that," he said. "I don't know her, but you seem to like her."

After soup and warm crusty rolls, we snuggled on the couch to watch a sappy movie. Drake gazed at us from the fireplace but didn't come to join us. He gave a deep sigh and closed his eyes.

"I set up a Zoom meeting with Andrew at seven, so you're not alone tonight. Is it okay if I do it here? I'll use my ear buds. That way you don't have to listen to him beg and plead for me to change my mind."

"That's fine." I chuckled.

The first thing Andrew asked once they started the call was if he could record it. "Just so we can get all the details typed up in a transcript and you get exactly what you deserve."

"That's fine," Rex said, fumbling with his ear buds.

I waved. "Hi, Andrew."

He smiled. "Hey, Audra. Long time, no see. Have you heard how Chuck's wife is doing?"

"Doc texted to say she's in recovery. She'll be fine."

Rex kissed my cheek as the recording in progress announcement came on. "Are you sure you're okay with this?"

"Just give me a nudge if I start snoring." My eyes were heavier than ever. I nestled against a cushion and closed them trying to focus on the soft voices from the television rather than Rex's call. Gradually, my mind began to wander, and I thought about what would've happened if...

Across the room, Drake raised his head and gave a low growl.

Before I opened my eyes, I heard a soft click. The door lock?

"That's enough, boy, calm down," Rex told the dog. "Sorry about that, Andrew. Not sure what he's freaking out about."

"I heard something, too," I said softly as I reached out for his arm.

"Hang on a sec, Andrew. I think someone's at the door." Rex tilted the screen down half-way and started to stand just as the front door opened, then closed. There was another, more metallic click.

I struggled to sit up while my husband took a couple steps toward the intruder.

"Who are you? What do you want?" Rex asked.

The figure in the doorway stepped forward into the lamp light. Dressed in black, right down to a wool balaclava, gloves, and Caterpillar work boots, it was enough to make my heart hammer and my breath come in short gasps. I'd be useless if I hyperventilated.

Drake snarled. He continued to growl but didn't leave the fireplace. That wasn't like him at all.

"I'm here to clean up some loose ends." The intruder's voice was low. More feminine than Chuck Benson's. "I'm sorry it's come to this, Audra. Thank you for handing the police all the evidence they needed to make their case. All I had to do was add a little of Dave's blood to Rex's clothing. No one will be surprised when your husband kills you for turning him in."

Rex's shirt. I never saw that coming. "You killed Dave and Molly, didn't you?"

A soft chuckle escaped the intruder. "Yes, and I would've killed Lavinia if it wasn't for you. A little belladonna in a gunshot wound goes a long way. Even a graze."

That's when I realized I knew that voice. I'd heard earlier today. "That shot grazing her head was no accident, was it, Emily? You wanted her to suffer the way Roger had."

She shook her head. "You're pretty clever. I doubt you were clever enough to figure out I put poor old Roger out of his misery. Do you really think I wanted to deal with a sick husband?"

I glanced to Drake who still hadn't moved. Although he appeared alert, his eyes were glassy, and a strand of drool inched from his lip. "What's wrong with Drake?"

"Poor little doggie shouldn't take treats from strangers when he's out in the yard. He'll think this was all a bad dream, especially when he wakes up and you two are dead," she said.

"You stole my other second set of keys," Rex said. "I'll bet it was you behind the Christmas tree the other night. Wait, who are you?"

"Rex, this is Emily Trent," I told him. "She killed Molly Lavier because she used to be

Miss Lavinia's business partner and helped with Roger's medication. Since neither of them could cure him, she decided to get even."

Emily shook her head. "On top of that, Roger wanted to sell the conservation land to Laney Developments for new condos and was going to get a big kickback for it. Those two stood in the way and cost us a lot of money. I tried to make it look like they killed him, but I heard Lavinia pushed for an autopsy."

"You tried to frame me too, didn't you?" Rex asked. "Too bad I wasn't even in town when Molly or Dave died."

Emily peeled off the balaclava. Her chin-length hair was disheveled. "Don't you think I knew that?"

"You!" Rex gasped. "You're the woman Andrew brought to the town council meeting. What did you slip in my drink that night? I didn't drink that much."

She chuckled. "Honey, if I would've known how much trouble you and your wife would be, I would've doubled the dose."

I wanted to run over to help Drake, but we needed to stall her in case Harry saw her come into the house. "Rex was in Chicago when Molly died. How did you plan to pin that one on him?"

"Easy. Her time of death was the day before he left town. All I had to do was plant the keys I stole when I ran into him at Miss

Lavinia's near her body and stage a struggle. Heaven knows I've seen enough crime scenes to make it look good. With the fresh snowfall, no one found her for a couple of days aside from a couple coyotes. That token you found was a bonus."

"Officer Grant told you," I whispered.

"No. I followed you that night and ran ahead to plant it to make sure you found it."

"What token?" Rex asked.

His computer made an odd noise. That's when I remembered it was still partly open and Andrew was recording their video call. My husband stepped to one side to block it from view.

"What was that?" Emily rushed toward us and the coffee table.

As she reached for the laptop, she lowered the gun taking her focus off us for a split second. Rex didn't hesitate. Pain or no, he dove around the coffee table into her midsection knocking her to the floor while I reached for my cell phone. Emily raised her arm and pulled the trigger. I covered my head and ducked next to the couch as dust rained down on them as they struggled.

"Get off me, you creep!" she shouted.

Rex wrestled the gun away from her and tossed it toward the front door. By the time he pinned her to the ground, I started to dial the police. Just as I punched in the second one, the front door flew open, and Officer Grant raced inside with his weapon drawn and three other police officers close behind him.

"Whoa, that was really fast. They're already here," I said as the operator answered. One of the officers helped Rex to his feet while I gave the operator my name and information.

"Well, how about that," Officer Grant said, "today's my lucky day. I arrested your son and another forensics investigator earlier today for tampering with a crime scene. Now I've got the ringleader red-handed."

"If you search her, you'll find our house keys in her pocket," I told him as I rushed to hug Rex and make sure he was okay. "I'll bet those were the keys you found with Molly that went missing. She planted them to frame Rex."

Across the room, Drake moaned as he placed his muzzle on his paws. If it wasn't for the culprit sprawled on the floor between us, I would've run to check on him.

Emily growled as an officer rolled her onto her stomach and handcuffed her. "You can't prove anything, Grant. It's your word against mine."

"Rex, are you there? Is everything okay?" Andrew asked from the computer.

"Yeah. We need to reschedule our meeting. Audra and I need to go to the police station. I'll explain later. Can you send a copy of the recording to Officer Tyler

Grant."

"Will do," Andrew replied. "No need to explain, I heard every word. Take a few days off. I'll see you Monday."

"What recording?" Emily paled.

Officer Grant grinned. "Rex was on a video call with Andrew Laney, who was going to hang up when he realized what was going on. Since they were recording the call to transcribe later, he heard every word of your confession and called us. In short, we have your recorded confession. Plus we have two witnesses who came forward saying they saw you run down Joelle Benson."

"You did that? But why?" I stared.

Emily scoffed. "Don't get me started on that one."

"What did Dave and Joelle ever do to you?" I asked.

Officer Grant held up a hand. "Save it for interrogation."

Emily shrugged him off as she met my gaze. "Dave and Roger had an arrangement when Roger was mayor. He took care of parking tickets and permits, while Dave supplied us with meat. Then Roger got sick. Dave suddenly stopped bringing us anything. When he decided to expand his business, Roger was useless."

I shrugged. "That seems fair. If Roger couldn't help Dave with tickets, then why give him freebies?"

"When I came back to town, I looked him up," she continued. "We met for dinner at some dive out on the highway. He couldn't even spring for a nice meal for an old friend. Just greasy burgers and limp fries."

Rex shook his head. "Of course he couldn't. He was flat broke."

"Which is why you ran Joelle down," I added.

Emily raised her eyebrows then laughed. "Funny thing about that. I've never even met the woman. I actually thought she was you and wanted to teach you to keep your nose out of my business. Imagine my surprise when I saw her face up close and realized I'd made a mistake."

Suddenly, I couldn't breathe. My head spun and I thought I'd pass out. "What?"

"Let's go, Emily. I've got a boring interrogation waiting for you." Officer Grant took her by the arm and led her out of our house before I could come to my senses. He paused to instruct another officer to bag the gun and the balaclava.

A younger officer remained crouched next to Drake. "Is your dog normally like this? He doesn't look well."

I shook my head. "She said she drugged him."

"Then we'd better get him to the vet clinic and get his stomach pumped." He scooped Drake into his arms and gave us a nod. "Meet me at the cruiser, I'll give you a ride."

Rex sat up front while I rode in the back seat cradling Drake's head in my lap. Tears cascaded down my cheeks and I couldn't stop thinking what I'd do without my faithful companion.

# Chapter Nineteen
### Saturday, December 10

The fire licked at the carefully stacked wood sending sparks and yellow-orange flames into the night sky. If the weather was twenty degrees warmer, it would've been a perfect fire for hot dogs and marshmallows. Instead, it was about to be a funeral pyre near the altar where Chuck had discovered Molly's body and her ashes scattered. It would definitely give the spot by the lake a whole different feel next summer when Rex, Drake, and I went walking there.

Several of us were invited to the private ceremony that Saturday night. Not one person had declined the invitation.

Bree and I flanked Joelle to make sure she was able to stand upright in short bursts after her accident. She'd begged to walk but we'd all insisted on her using a wheelchair over the rough terrain. Merilee draped one arm across Bree's shoulders while Tony stood between her and Officer Grant.

Drake sat by my feet and whimpered

occasionally, less due to the cold than the occasion since he wore a fluffy new doggy coat courtesy of Miss Lavinia and looked twice his normal size. Rex kept hold of his leash and patted his head for comfort.

Officer Grant folded his arms across his chest and looked like a bored teenager. He'd been specially sent by his buddy at the Conservation to supervise. No one, least of all the Conservation authorities, wanted to burn down the forest.

Simon and Miss Lavinia stood on the opposite side of the bonfire with a large white bin in front of them. While we watched, Miss Lavinia reached inside and pulled out two of the little white boxes. The dolls of her deceased patients. Her lips moved as she tossed each into the flames one at a time, but I couldn't hear a word she said.

She repeated the process, doll after doll, until the bin stood empty. The flames, fuelled by fabric and who knew what kinds of oils, rose until we all needed to take a couple steps back. Ashes drifted like gray snowflakes to land in the sacred space as well as our heads and shoulders. Ceremonial, but creepy.

Once Miss Lavinia had emptied the bin of dolls, she gazed around the fire before she held up one last doll. Molly's. She raised both arms and let out a howl that sent a shiver up the length of my back.

Drake, recovered from the drugs Emily had fed him, stood to howl with her. In the distance, wolves joined in the mournful cry.

I shuddered as I caught Merilee's gaze. Before I could say a word, she turned her face to the sky to joined in. I clutched my dad's doll in both hands and whispered, "I love you." After kissing its musty head, I tossed it into the flames and gazed at the stars to howl with the others. One by one, our voices filled the air sending up a heartfelt good-bye to the ones we'd loved and lost.

Feeling a sense of calm and release, I turned to Joelle. The stitches on her lip and across her cheek made her look like a living voodoo doll. Her right eye was black and purple. She removed Dave's doll from her pink sling.

"Are you sure you want to do this?" I asked.

Despite the immense pain she had to be in, she nodded. "He didn't earn any of this. He deserves a proper good-bye."

Bree hugged her mom, and they bowed their heads in silence. Joelle's hair fell across her battered face hiding the yellowing bruises. When she raised her gaze to the fire once more, tears dampened her cheeks.

"You were a bit of a brute, but you were always a good, honest man, Dave," Joelle said. "I'm sorry for how things ended. For both of us. I'll always love you."

"I love you, Daddy," Bree echoed.

With that, they tossed Dave's doll into the flames together before Joelle sat in the wheelchair. For someone who'd fought so hard against it, she smiled gratefully when Bree wrapped a pink blanket around her and kissed her forehead.

There was a long moment of silence before Officer Grant cleared his throat and asked, "Are we done here? I can't feel my toes."

Simon held up a hand. "Leave if you must but let us close the ceremony first. For the sake of the living."

Miss Lavinia still hadn't opened her eyes.

Officer Grant grunted and stared at the fire. He didn't look around, nor did he leave.

Taking over for his auntie, Simon sprinkled herbs into the flames and chanted. I wished I knew what he was saying, but the words were all Creole French and didn't jive with the few French words I knew. I gave up trying to translate and closed my eyes to listen to his rich voice.

The next thing I knew, the men were throwing snow on the bonfire. I must've dozed off while we stood there. Merilee herded the others toward the parking lot. Drake and I followed them to wait near her SUV for Rex.

"Hey," my husband called after me.

"Take the keys. I'll be there in a minute."

* * *

Back at our house a half hour later, Tony dunked a sugar cookie in his coffee. "So when all was said and done, why exactly did Emily kill Dave and Molly?"

Merilee sat across the kitchen table with a hot chocolate. Extra whipped cream. "Her husband was former Mayor Roger Trent who went to see Miss Lavinia and Molly about migraines and died a week later. When they did an autopsy, they discovered he'd overdosed on pain meds. Emily insisted the witches gave him bad medicine. She ranted about how they killed Roger, but admitted later she gave him the overdose. She was also upset they blocked the development of the forest since Roger stood to get a healthy kickback."

Drake's breath alternately warmed and cooled my right foot in perfect rhythm while he dozed on the floor within a paw's reach. "So when Miss Lavinia told Roger there was nothing the doctors could do, he was right."

"But what about Dave and Molly?" Rex asked.

"Molly was Miss Lavinia's business partner and Roger's number one nemesis thanks to One Healthy Green Earth. Dave and Roger had a business arrangement for

years until Dave wanted to expand his
business, but Roger was too sick to help. It
led to a beef between them that Emily took
advantage of."

"I see what you did there." Tony smirked.
"Dave the Butcher had a beef."

"Oh brother." Merilee winced.

He kissed her cheek. "Oh, come on. You
love my sense of humour."

Rex sipped his coffee. "I told you Alister
Trent had no business conducting that
investigation. He was too close."

"Yeah, slight conflict of interest,
especially since his mom committed the
crime," Merilee said. "So when did you start
seeing Miss Lavinia?"

His face reddened. "When I started
having chest pains and couldn't sleep. All I
wanted to do was come home and relax all
weekend. This was the only place I could
get any sleep."

"Drake smelled something different about
Rex and started avoiding him." I reached for
a cookie. "When he smelled the same scent
on Officer Trent, he reacted the same way.
I don't get why I didn't recognize the same
smell."

Merilee handed me a sheet of paper. "I
snooped in Miss Lavinia's file cabinet when
I stopped by to see Simon about the plans
for the ceremony. Rex and Alister Trent had
similar prescriptions, but in different ratios.
Rex's had more myrrh than Trent's, whose

had a hint of peppermint and lavender to make the smell more tolerable to the public. He used the same medication years ago before his father died and gave it another try. More than likely to get inside the shop and map it out.”

The back of my neck prickled. “Since before Roger died?”

“Apparently, the Trent’s have always had issues.” Tony grinned.

“Frankincense and myrrh.” Merilee mused. “Who would’ve thought? The interesting part is Emily’s old prescription was in Alister’s file. It was exactly the same as Rex’s. If she hadn’t drugged Drake, he would’ve attacked her.”

Rex raised his coffee mug. “Case closed, ladies. I think we did a pretty good job on this one.”

“We?” Merilee and I exchanged glances while Drake emerged from beneath the table and tilted his head.

My husband got up and reached into the cupboard for a dog treat. “Fine. Good job, Drake. You saved me from rotting in prison when your mom was ready to throw away the key.”

The dog sneezed then reached for the treat before he trotted into the living room. Within seconds, there was a loud crash. I didn’t have to look to know he’d knocked the tree to the floor again.

Rex sighed as he met my gaze. “Your

turn to pick up the pieces."

I rolled my eyes. Picking up pieces was all I ever seemed to do.

The End

Diane Bator is the author of several mystery novels—and series. She's on the Board of Directors of Crime Writers of Canada and a member of Sisters in Crime Toronto, International Thriller Writers, and the Writers Union of Canada. When she's not writing, she works for a professional theatre and is a budding playwright.

## Diane Bator books published by BWL Publishing Inc.

Wild Blue Mysteries – Books 1, 2, 3, 4 & 5:
The Bookstore Lady
The Mystery Lady
The Bakery Lady
The Painted Lady
The Conned Lady

Gilda Wright Mysteries – Books 1, 2, 3, 4 & 5:
Dead Without Honor
Dead Without Glory
Dead Without Pride
Dead Without Shame
Dead Without Remorse

Glitter Bay Mysteries – Books 1 & 2:
All that Sparkles
All that Shines

Sugarwood Mysteries – Book 1 & 2:
Drop Dead Cowboy
Dead Man's Doll

BWL Publishing

bwlpublishing.ca